CW00741663

Zulfikar Ghose was born in ~~~~ ~~~
1935, grew up in British India, and came
to England in 1952. Finishing his
education at Keele University, he worked
as cricket and hockey correspondent of
the *Observer* for five years and wrote
occasional reviews for the *TLS,
Guardian, New Statesman* and the
*Spectator*. In 1969, he left England for
America on being invited to teach at the
University of Texas at Austin where he
continues to work as Professor of
English. He is married to the Brazilian
artist, Helena de la Fontaine.

Of his previous nine novels, the most
popular have been *The Murder of Aziz
Khan* and *The Incredible Brazilian* which
have been translated into several
languages. He is also the author of short
stories (with B.S. Johnson), an
autobiography, three volumes of poetry
and a work of literary criticism.

He has travelled extensively in South
America in the region between the
northern Andes to the mouth of the
Amazon and south to Rio de Janeiro.

Also by Zulfikar Ghose

A NEW HISTORY OF TORMENTS

and published by Black Swan

# Don Bueno

## Zulfikar Ghose

**BLACK SWAN**

# DON BUENO

## A BLACK SWAN BOOK 0 552 99111 2

Originally published in Great Britain by
Hutchinson & Co. (Publishers) Ltd.

PRINTING HISTORY
Hutchinson edition published 1983
Black Swan edition published 1984

Copyright © Zulfikar Ghose 1983

*Conditions of sale*
1. This book is sold subject to the condition
that it shall not, by way of trade *or otherwise*,
be lent, re-sold, hired out or otherwise
*circulated* without the publisher's prior
consent in any form of binding or cover other
than that in which it is published *and without
a similar condition including this condition
being imposed on the subsequent purchaser.*
2. This book is sold subject to the Standard
Conditions of Sale of Net Books and may not
be re-sold in the UK below the net price fixed
by the publishers for the book.

This book is set in 11/12 pt California

Black Swan Books are published by
Transworld Publishers Ltd.,
Century House, 61–63 Uxbridge Road,
Ealing, London W5 5SA

Made and printed in Great Britain by the
Guernsey Press Co. Ltd., Guernsey, Channel Islands.

# Don Bueno

# 1

Ferns covered the banks of the river that flowed in a dark, narrow channel, with the arching limbs of the tall trees forming a canopy above it. Light filtered in diagonal streaks through the thick dark green leaves and fell on the water in spots of different sizes; the progress of the boat, with its diesel engine sending a ceaseless vibration across the deck, caused the river's surface to ripple, creating the impression that the spots of light on the water were twinkling. Dragonflies, caught by the light here and there, darted from point to point on the water or on a fern, several of them in couples, attached one to the other. Creepers and vines hung from the higher branches, enmeshed with the diagonal streaks of light, the tips of their extremities curling in the air, sucking from it a substantiality on which to advance their growth. Cries from unseen animals filled the air from time to time, piercing the wilderness with an agony of passion; or flocks of parrots went shrieking past overhead, louder than the monotonous clatter of the diesel, hurrying to another sky of less or more moisture. Even below the surface of the water there was occasionally a sudden flickering, as if of an eel's tail.

Weighted with his body, the hammock scarcely moved, for there was no other motion than the boat's laborious progress, and he lay there, across the narrow deck, staring at the nothingness that, in its fragments of particularity, was teeming with life. The woman squatting on the deck, her fat little body hunched over some busy work which had kept her preoccupied for the last ten minutes, turned

7

her face toward him when he looked at her; just before she glanced up, he observed how the two little plaits of her grey-black hair stuck out above the bent head. Her round, wrinkled face beamed at him. She thrust out a hand, and said sharply, 'Want some?'

She sat a little too far for him to put out his hand and accept her offer of shelled peanuts. 'No, thank you, Doña Carla,' he said in a soft voice.

'You are a sad one, Señor Calderón. You don't eat enough. Look at Marcos, he eats peanuts like a monkey all day and when it comes to any meal time he's the first at the table.'

A thin, wiry man, wearing only a pair of dirty shorts, sat near her, picking up fistfuls of peanuts and munching them rapidly.

'A man without an appetite has sorrow in his heart,' the woman added, looking away from Calderón.

Marcos threw a glance at him, his large sunken eyes making his thin face appear emaciated, and, his mouth partly filled with unswallowed peanuts, said, 'And a man with a full belly has love in his heart. What, eh, Carla?' he added, swallowing the peanuts and grinning at her. 'Is that why you feed me so much? It's like the captain in there –' he gestured to the glass window of the cabin through which a man was then seen to be letting go of the wheel and picking up an oil can ' – always greasing the pistons so that they go in and out all day long.'

He laughed uproariously at his own smutty allusion, showing two conspicuous gaps in his teeth, and his wife, in a tone of amorous chiding, said, 'That's all you think of! And I've given him five sons.' She turned a grave face to Calderón with her last remark as if asking him to excuse her husband's words. His dark brown eyes were staring at her just then. She saw his black hair toss up as he quickly turned his face away.

'But you want to keep trying for a daughter,' Marcos complained good-humouredly.

'You are shameless,' she said in a lowered voice. 'What will Señor Calderón think?'

'What do you think, Señor Calderón? Here's the mother of my five sons and she's ashamed of her desire to make a daughter. What is life for, eh? I don't mind saying so, the five sons are the glory of my life, thanks be to God.'

'Marcos!' his wife scolded under her breath, rapidly shelling more peanuts.

But Calderón appeared to have fallen asleep. Marcos saw him shift in his hammock so that his head disappeared within it.

'Strange man,' Marcos whispered to his wife, who stood up just then with a cloth in which she had gathered all the shells, and flapped it away from her so that the shells fell in the water, hitting some spots of light. In two or three places, the mouths of fish appeared and vanished. She walked slowly toward the bow where crates of canned food, the boat's cargo, were piled in neat lines. She was a short, fat woman, weighted by folds of coarse white cotton that covered her from her shoulders to her feet without revealing where the blouse ended and the heavy skirt began. Marcos stood up, softly clapping his hands clean, and followed her on his slightly bowed legs.

'Carla, Carla,' he said, coming up to her. 'I meant that. All jokes aside, I meant that. The glory of my life, thanks be to God. And to you,' he added, seeing that she kept her face deliberately turned away from him.

She saw two waterfowl come flapping down to land in the river near the bank where six or seven smaller creatures of the same species came eagerly out of the protection of some reeds, and, turning to look at Marcos, she said, 'It was a good wedding.'

'Ah, Miguel is a lucky man,' Marcos said, his eyes glittering. 'I only wish he had stayed with me and not gone into business in Santa Rosa. But that's life. You bring up a son and he goes away.'

'We have four more,' Carla said. 'All good boys. They won't all go away. You couldn't even get them to go to the wedding.'

'It's an expensive journey, Carla. And there's too much work on the farm, we couldn't all go away.'

9

'But what does it matter? We are happy. Miguel is happy.'

'A lucky man, a lucky man,' Marcos repeated. 'What is the betting, Carla, he makes us happy grandparents in nine months?'

The thought filled her with pleasure and, watching past Marcos's shoulder the man come out of the cabin and walk toward Calderón, she said in a low voice, 'What a long way to go for a son's wedding, but what a beautiful wedding it was!'

Calderón raised himself in the hammock on hearing footsteps on the deck and saw the man, whom Marcos referred to as the captain, come up to him.

'Well, Señor Zuazo, when will we arrive in Palmira?'

Zuazo looked vaguely at the river bank in the distance, his long, pointed nose sticking out of his thin face. 'We'll have to stop for the night,' he said. 'I know the river like the palm of my hand but at night I can't even see the palm of my hand. This ocean liner is without radar,' he joked.

His teeth were small and yellow, Calderón saw, smiling with him. 'It's a good boat,' he said to reassure its owner.

'She's old,' Zuazo said. 'With a good, steady heartbeat. But old. I named her *Princess Isabella* twenty years ago when I bought her from a Peruvian. She's an aristocratic old lady who won't be hurried but who won't do anything wrong either.'

'So we must stop for the night?'

'Yes, and resume with the first light. We should arrive around noon.'

Zuazo lit a cigarette and looked dreamily at the passing jungle. 'What will you do when we arrive?'

'Oh, look around, I expect.'

Zuazo saw him through the smoke he had just exhaled. Calderón's large dark brown eyes seemed to be watching him closely as if he knew that Zuazo had wanted to ask him some other question.

'There are telephones nowadays, you know, even in the remote interior,' Zuazo remarked casually, attempting another oblique approach to see if Calderón would not talk about the previous night.

'Sure.'

Zuazo puffed at his cigarette and peered at Calderón's face. Quite young – thirty-two, thirty-four perhaps – but closed like a fist, he thought. 'There's a good hotel in Palmira. Or you could stay on the boat until dark,' he offered to win Calderón's confidence. 'In case there's any problem.'

But Calderón only said, 'If it's necessary. Thank you.'

'You paid good money. I owe you the service.'

Calderón did not answer. Zuazo threw away the cigarette into the river and looked over his shoulder toward the bow. 'We seem to have drifted slightly,' he remarked. 'I should return to the wheel.'

'I could give you a hand, if you showed me how,' Calderón volunteered.

'No, no, there's no problem. I can handle it. Unless you wanted to come and talk. If there's any thing you want to talk about.'

'There's plenty of time for that.'

Zuazo went away to the cabin which had a bunk and a wooden chest as well as some of the boat's equipment. He steered the boat back to its proper course, and, glancing at the compass, picked up a chart. Immediately, he threw the chart back, for he knew the river deeply in his own mind. He swore at himself for feeling so fidgety. Maybe Calderón would talk in the morning, he thought, when he'd put more distance between Santa Rosa and himself.

Marcos came up to the door, and said, 'How's it going, captain?'

Zuazo smiled at him, and shrugged his shoulders. 'Just fine.'

'The wife brought some hard-boiled eggs and cold meat and some bread, too. Enough for everyone.' Marcos looked in the direction of the hammock, and added, 'Maybe we could eat?'

'That'll be better than my supply of canned food,' Zuazo said. 'We'll eat at sunset, when we stop for the night.'

'Canned food? That's your cargo, too. You know something funny? My son Miguel is in the canned goods business. Imagine that, a cargo of canned food!'

'That's all I could pick up this trip,' Zuazo said. 'And the three of you. Not much business in these parts. Only five years ago, Santa Rosa was getting to be a big town. Too bad the talk about finding manganese came to nothing.'

Marcos put his face close to Zuazo's and said in a lowered voice, 'I heard a man got killed in a bar in Santa Rosa. Happened last night. There could be money in that for someone.'

'I never heard of it,' Zuazo said, his hand involuntarily pressing the pocket that contained his wallet. 'But it happens all the time in these frontier towns. The interior is wild. People go mad for no reason.'

Marcos saw Calderón come out of the hammock and stretch his arms. 'I was at my son Miguel's wedding,' he said to Zuazo. 'It was some feast! I never saw so much meat on one table. And Chilean wine. I must have drunk ten litres of it. Couldn't do a thing afterward but snore.'

Calderón walked seven or eight paces up and down the narrow deck. Marcos said to him cheerfully, 'The captain says we'll eat at nightfall. Carla brought some hard-boiled eggs and some cold meat.'

Calderón smiled and nodded his head several times to convey his pleasure at the thought. 'What work do you do?' he asked.

'Breeding,' Marcos answered. 'I breed cattle. You should see the calves when they're born. The finest animals in all of South America.'

His eyes brightened as he spoke of his animals. 'Ah, it's a good life!' he added. 'And what about you, Señor Calderón?'

Calderón looked away from him and stared for a few moments at the river, his attention caught by a hummingbird that had just shot down from a tree and had its long beak in the centre of the pink flower of a water lily, its rapidly beating green wings radiating tiny lines of light. He looked back at Marcos, and said, 'I was in chemicals.'

12

'Chemicals,' Marcos repeated gravely, looking greatly impressed.

'Pesticides,' Calderón elaborated. 'You probably use them. To get rid of ants, mice, bats. Everyone needs them.'

The boat had been going round a wide curve in the river, and suddenly they were flooded with light, for the river was now straight and broad and the sun hung low above it. The light was momentarily blinding and Calderón turned his face toward the dark jungle. There, too, the sun's rays seemed to be penetrating in long lines and looked as if they were interwoven with the flat mass of the dense foliage.

A large tree grew out of the water, some five metres away from the bank, as if it stood on a submerged island. Zuazo turned off the engine and let the boat drift toward the tree. The river was a flaming red with the sun more than half sunk across the line of water on the horizon. Carla, squatting at the bow, rose and turned away from the light which seemed to her to be pouring like blood. Calderón saw her take quick short steps toward where he stood talking with Marcos, and for a moment she looked like a shadow that quickly passed over the intensifying red. Her body dissolved in the light, vanished from his perception, before she reappeared near him, one side of her clothing tinged with an orangish golden light from her shoulder to the hemline. Zuazo came out to the deck and stood at the bow, positioning himself to catch a branch of the tree in order to secure his boat. The sun set behind him and, in the few minutes it took him to perform his task, darkness set in. While Carla brought her basket and prepared to lay out the food, Zuazo lit a hurricane lamp in his cabin from where it cast sufficient light on the deck.

The silence that fell when the engine was switched off was brief, for the darkness seemed to awaken the beasts in the jungle; their shrieking and howling now filled the air. There were long, piercing cries.

'Listen to that,' Zuazo said, swallowing some cold meat. 'The great nightly hunt. How much blood drains into the jungle each night!'

'And how much new life gets created!' Marcos remarked.

13

Another sharp cry reached their ears, and he added, 'That is the cry of jaguars mating. Just listen to that roar! Lord, what desires you've given us poor creatures that we scream in the night!'

'Have another egg, Señor Calderón,' Carla said.

'No, thank you. I've eaten plenty.'

'If I'd only thought of bringing some of that Chilean wine,' Marcos said.

'There was nothing left,' his wife said to him. 'You drank it all.'

Zuazo turned down the hurricane lamp when he retired to the cabin, so that only a very dim light fell across the deck where Marcos and his wife stretched out some bedding they had brought with them. From his hammock, Calderón saw the couple cover themselves with a sheet and seem to fall instantly to sleep, their heads showing just above the top of the sheet, facing each other. Calderón rocked himself but was unable to find rest, and continued to listen to the animal cries.

A cry identical to the one Marcos had distinguished as that of jaguars mating pierced the air again. Calderón drew the hammock around his ears, seeing in his mind the brutal, terrifying moment of overwhelming lust. He saw the jungle being torn by rushing, leaping bodies, and the crash of the enraged male in the madness brought on by mindless desire. His face contorted as if with a sharp internal pain.

In spite of the shrieking and howling, he must have fallen asleep, for the silence awoke him. He put his head out of the hammock. It was still dark but the animals' night of blood and fury seemed to be over. He was about to sit up in order to relieve his strained back when the awareness of a new, muffled noise arrested him. It was a mixture of whispering, gasping, and suppressed little screams coming from the deck where Marcos lay with his wife. In the dim light that fell from the lamp in the cabin, Calderón could see Marcos's head above Carla's. The sheet that covered the couple had slipped about them, so that it lay only across Marcos's back, showing her feet pressed behind

14

his knees and her arms across his shoulders. Their motion was rapid, urgent.

Calderón withdrew his head and murmured, 'No, no!'

But light soon filtered into the hammock, and there were noises on deck. Marcos and Carla had risen and were folding up their bedding. Zuazo was walking out of his cabin, and Marcos said to him brightly, 'I bet you didn't think you were going to get coffee this morning.' He saw Calderón and, nodding at him, added, 'My miracle woman thinks of everything. She brought a thermos full of coffee.'

'One has to think of everything,' Carla said modestly.

'Let's get going first,' Zuazo said. 'We need to make up time. The coffee's a great idea,' he remarked when he saw that Carla was looking at him.

Calderón did not want any breakfast when the other three sat down to it, and he stood by the wheel, having received brief instructions from Zuazo as to what to do. The river had widened and the jungle on its banks seemed to have lost the menace it possessed the previous day. He imagined that the sated beasts must be asleep in the jungle's darkness, or lurking in corners, their eyes scanning obscure spaces in the ceaseless attempt to pacify some hunger.

Zuazo joined him and said, 'That woman is really capable of miracles, you missed a great breakfast.'

'I hope I've kept on course,' Calderón said, watching Carla put away the leftovers in her basket.

'We'll be in Palmira in three hours,' Zuazo said. 'What will you do?'

'Look at the town, see what I can do.'

'I can help you. If you'll square with me.'

Calderón stared at him, and Zuazo, not meeting his eyes, asked, 'How long can you hide?'

'It had not occurred to me that I needed to hide,' Calderón said quietly, deliberately emphasizing his words.

'Run, then. What's the difference?'

'You don't know me,' Calderón said in a resigned voice.

15

'Perhaps it's better that I don't,' Zuazo said, turning to look at him and offering a smile. 'It doesn't matter to me who you are. A passenger I picked up in Santa Rosa, that's all. Just cargo to deliver from one port to another. I don't have to mention it to anyone.'

'How does one get to the coast?' Calderón asked.

'You surprise me,' Zuazo said. 'You paid me more money to get you out of Santa Rosa than you'd need to fly first-class to Brazil, and it doesn't cross your mind that I might have suspicions. Like I said, you got to square with me. Suppose there's a reward for you?'

'You have a lonely life on the river,' Calderón said. 'It gives you too many ideas.'

Zuazo chuckled, and said, 'You want to go to the coast? I could help. I know a man who flies a small plane to a field south of Guayaquil. He won't ask you who you are.'

'Provided I pay.'

'No,' Zuazo said. 'You pay me for the introduction. All he'll want will be help with his cargo.'

'Which I suppose is drugs.'

'You know something funny?' Zuazo said, laughing, 'I never asked him! Just like I never asked you what you'd done in Santa Rosa that you needed to run away so fast.'

'Let me tell you why,' Calderón said, his voice still calm and resigned. 'A man there wanted to kill me. I'd done nothing to him; but he suddenly claimed that I owed him my life.'

Zuazo looked at the compass and then raised his eyes to the river.

His voice quieter than before, Calderón said: 'You will find there can be no reward for me.'

16

# 2

The fine lines of a spider's web just inside the high window shimmered in the early morning light that came in patches through the tall trees in the garden. Don Bueno rose out of bed, some unfailing mechanism in his body waking him, as it had done on each morning of the five years he had lived in Santa Rosa, at six o'clock. He stood naked on the tile floor and stretched his arms, yawning, his round head, with its close-cropped grey hair, thrown back. Straightening himself and bringing his feet together, he stood erect for a moment, not listening to the familiar sounds of that hour – a cock crowing, some birds singing in the trees and, from a kilometre away on the waterfront, the shouts of the fishermen just returned from the pre-dawn catch. He put his hands on his hips and breathed in; the muscles on his chest stood out. He raised himself on his toes a few times, taking a deep breath each time he did so, his swollen penis rising and falling gently with the exercise. He raised his arms and slowly arched his body forward to reach for his toes with his fingertips, repeating the action ten times. The muscles of his arms and legs were firm, the biceps were especially well developed. At fifty-four, Don Bueno carried no superfluous weight.

He went to the bathroom and presently returned from it in a pair of white shorts. Putting on white socks and a pair of tennis shoes, he walked down a hall and went out to the front verandah. Hanging baskets of ferns and begonias were suspended from a rafter below the eaves the length of the verandah, and just when he was about to walk down the four steps to the garden he saw the glinting thread of a

17

spider's web spanning the two hanging ferns above each end of the top step. He had to duck below it to prevent the nearly invisible web from breaking across his face. But he did not give himself enough room and some of the web caught in his hair. Combing it out with his fingers, he came out to the garden.

A butterfly with dark blue underwings floated past in front of him and alighted on a white geranium, slowly unfolding its wings, showing them to be nearly black. Pools of light fell on the flower beds, coming through the trees in diagonal beams and reflecting in little dots where drops of dew trembled on the edges of leaves.

Closing the front door behind him, Don Bueno began to jog along the narrow dirt road bordered by thick vegetation, going past the wooden hut at the corner of his property where his housekeeper, the widow Juanita, lived with her two teenage boys. The smell of burnt coffee came from the hut as Don Bueno, taking short strides, jogged past, his eyes on the ground. An object on the road some ten metres ahead of him caught his eye and he slowed his pace, coming nearly to a stop when he reached it. A snake with brown diamond-shaped markings, its mouth half open, lay dead, a large swelling just below its head suggesting that it had tried to swallow some creature, perhaps a toad, with a fatal haste.

Don Bueno jogged on, his naked shoulders and chest already glistening with sweat, but his breath came evenly, without being laboured. The dirt road narrowed to a track and entered a forested area. Paths overgrown with vegetation diverged from the track. Every now and then he went past a wooden bench with two or three slats missing. It was dark under the tall trees until he came to a clearing. At the centre was a bandstand; its tiled roof had collapsed, creepers climbed up its wooden posts, and crows nested there. A little past the bandstand was a pond, all of it choked with weeds and with tangled bushes crowding along its edge; incongruously stuck among the weeds was a plastic toy tanker that had turned dark green, almost black, with slime.

18

The track came out into the open light and ran along a high bank of the river. The sun had risen above the jungle across the river and its brightness at that angle made the vegetation on the east bank appear black. Don Bueno saw two fishing boats gliding toward the distant bend and, hearing a diesel engine, he looked back up the river and observed a small launch. He immediately recognized it as the one belonging to the mission sixty kilometres upriver; two brothers from the mission came every week to Santa Rosa for supplies. But he noticed there was a third person in the launch, a black-haired man in civilian clothes, his shirt a dark colour. It was unusual for the brothers to ferry a passenger to town, and Don Bueno wondered who he might be.

Curving along the bend of the river, the track led to a dirt road that sloped gently toward the town, cutting across several streets that proceeded from the town to the riverfront. As he ran across the street corners, Don Bueno saw some of the shopkeepers pushing up the shutters and bringing out their wares onto the sidewalk. It was the busy commercial part of the town that would be thronged with people all day long but now only had stray dogs sticking their noses into the previous night's trash that would soon be collected. He jogged past the corner where the Café y Bar Santa Cruz had already opened for the day's first customers; its owner, heavy-eyed Rufino with his huge pot belly and thin legs, waved at Don Bueno, and shouted, 'Come by tonight, there'll be music.' Don Bueno waved back, nodding his head. 'Remember, you're invited,' Rufino shouted after him.

It was a seedy, somewhat filthy bar, but perhaps that very quality made it more attractive than the cleaner places in the town, and Don Bueno enjoyed an occasional evening there, hearing the river gossip from the small-craft owners who frequented it. The bar was only a block away from the river which, at that point, had a beach of sandy loam where one could stroll for a hundred metres under the stars and enjoy the illusion of being on a larger beach beside the ocean; Don Bueno would go and pace there whenever he went to the Café y Bar Santa Cruz for a beer, or sometimes a couple of shots of rum, and the thought came to his mind, when he nodded his head at Rufino, that tonight he would go to the beach; the association of the dark water lapping the sandy loam stayed with him for a few moments as he ran on, becoming briefly an astonishingly vivid image of the stars and giving him the impression that he was floating among them.

The road went past the waterfront where a crowd of fishermen were unloading the early morning catch, the air filled with shouting voices. The wide sidewalk of the street across the waterfront was already turning into a market with Indians heaping tomatoes and limes and the season's vegetables and fruits on the ground in front of the shops selling hardware goods and, at a street corner, a butcher's with two emaciated dogs staring hopefully from the sidewalk at the man busy at a chopping block. Don Bueno turned up a street that went to the town centre, leaving the road which continued to the older, crowded part of the town where the poorer people lived. His breath considerably laboured now and sweat on his face, he jogged into the main square, going past the white stucco church with its two towers, one with a bell and one with a clock on its face, and was reminded of the wedding that had taken place there on the previous day.

The beautiful young Alegría, a shopkeeper's daughter, had been given away to a petty businessman with an oily skin, the son of some vulgar dairy farmer from a small town on the river called Palmira that had nothing more special than a brothel to make it known in the region. The sweet Alegría! Her body was the colour of honey, and it was easy for Don Bueno to believe, since memory could convert the abstract sensation of making love into a distinct taste, that the sweetness of her body had been like the taste of lavender honey. Her fragrance floated before him, and his tiring body was momentarily rejuvenated by the memory of her loveliness. He spurted forward, going round the square, past the Café Madrid where a couple of men having coffee at a sidewalk table called good morning to him. He gave them a slight nod and a wave of the hand and ran up the street that led back, threequarters of a kilometre away, to his house, completing his seven kilometre run with a determined dash.

One of the two men in the Café Madrid said when he had disappeared round a corner, 'Don Bueno, who knows who he really is?'

His companion, who was a visitor to the town, having come for Alegría's wedding, and who had met Don Bueno at the church, said, 'A man of substance, that's for sure.'

'Sure,' the first man said, 'but no one even knows his real name.'

'No! How can that be?'

'I heard that when he first came here he was called Don Napoleon. Some people – either respectfully or ironically – addressed him as Señor Bonaparte. And then when the big flood four years ago destroyed the huts of the poor people on the river, he headed the list of donations to help them out, and "Bonaparte" got changed to "Bueno". Next thing, everyone was calling him "Don Bueno".'

On returning home, Don Bueno stood for five minutes under a warm shower, turning the water to cold for the final rinse after he had soaped himself a second time; the lather ran down his body in grey-white streams, leaving a pleasant fragrance on his skin. By the time he had shaved and dressed, his housekeeper Juanita had his breakfast waiting on the front verandah. Wearing comfortably loose white linen trousers and a green shirt, he sat down in a wicker chair, his eyes darting at the new hibiscus blooms that had opened with the sun, and drank the tall glass of orange juice without pausing between gulps. He placed the empty glass next to the bowl of shelled almonds and walnuts, picked up a handful of nuts and began to chew them slowly, one at a time. The nearly black butterfly he had seen earlier fluttered above the hibiscus bush and floated away from it in a wide arc that made it swing across the verandah, hovering briefly over his head, and then out into the garden again toward a bed of variegated flowers. For Don Bueno, his breakfast was a time of serenity, of great contentment with the perfect little world he had created for himself.

He had an obscure memory of growing up by the sea on the Caribbean coast of Venezuela, stumbling on the sandy soil of a walled garden with the sound of the ocean always in the background. Some catastrophe had overtaken his family when he was six years old; he had no idea what it had been, only that the childhood garden had suddenly been replaced by a dirty street in a noisy city. All he knew for certain of that early time was that in the house by the ocean he had had a father, and that in the city there was only his mother. By the time he was twelve, the street had taught him that the world offered him nothing that he did not take the trouble to grab for himself. The more he saw his mother's eternally mournful face, watching her age prematurely, the greater the anger that he took with him to the street. She never spoke a word about his father, never told him why he had deserted the two of them. The mother was obliged to take menial jobs at which she worked long hours. He hated the world for putting her in that position.

Juanita brought him a fried egg and buttered toast and when he had begun to eat, he called to her, saying, 'Make me some more toast, Juanita, I'm very hungry today.'

He had always eaten heartily ever since the earliest years in the city when his mother had often not been able to provide him with more than one meal a day. His memories of the street were associated with smells of frying foods; and also with a knife that had a handle of carved rosewood, the only thing he still possessed from that time. At thirteen, he was one of a gang that raided the affluent neighbourhoods of the city, snatching the purses of old ladies or watches from middle-aged men, and sometimes spilling blood in the dim light of some square or in the darkness of a park. It was the year, too, when he had his first woman – a stout black woman nearly three times his age who worked as a maid in a banker's luxurious apartment and who, at weekends when the banker and his family went to their seaside cottage, enticed scruffy youths

22

who hung around the square looking for mischief, and pulled them to her on her master's bed or on the oriental rugs among the imported furniture that she spent the rest of the week dusting and polishing. He was a thin boy at the time, and she appeared enormous in his memory. He remembered how she once got him to climb up on her chest, with his knees on the rug on either side of her, and to place his penis between her huge, sweating breasts; and then she showed him how to knead her breasts so that they were gathered and crushed against his penis, making for it a hot, moist passage that became wetter with his own oozing discharge, until with a thrilling pain his semen shot out in a jet and hit her neck with a plop. She laughed aloud, screaming with delight, and said, 'Now lick it all up and hold it in your mouth.' He looked at her in wild amazement but, having just been initiated into perversity, was prepared for more. He heard her moan ecstatically as he licked the semen and the sweat from her neck and top of her chest. Then she brought her large lips to his, holding his head, and he knew at once what he had to do: he transmitted the semen into her mouth, and saw from the glint in her eyes that he had done the correct thing. She then pushed him on his back and, sitting up herself, brought her head over his penis and spilled the wet contents of her mouth upon it. She looked up at him for a moment and he knew from her wildly merry eyes what she was going to do next, and a shudder of intense pleasure went through his body.

Juanita brought him more toast and a mug of hot milk sweetened with honey that he drank instead of coffee for his breakfast. The steam rising out of the milk had a whiff of the honey's fragrance in it, reminding him of Alegría when he took a swallow from the mug. He smiled, wondering in what slobbering, uncouth manner the man she had married yesterday had made love to her. He thought with repugnance of the man's oily skin pressed against Alegría's smooth, golden body. The poor girl must have been shocked, he flattered himself into thinking, imagining a vivid contrast between the young man's urgent and primitive ardour and his own style of gentle encroachment on a young girl's body. He was a master of dissimulation when his own lust was the strongest, feigning a tender solicitude, as if a finger softly tracing the girl's breast were the extent of his desire and that he would be content if she permitted him to go no farther, but in the very gesture of transmitting the idea to her of his great regard for her virtue and the purity of his own desire, he lowered his lips to her breast, exciting in her a liberality such that in the end it was the girl, at each stage wishing to give him a little more than what he declared was her highest gift to him, who drew him on to possess her completely.

Another week, or month, and Alegría's husband would need to go to the city 400 kilometres to the north, for he had a business in canned goods, bringing down supplies from the capital to Santa Rosa whose position on the river made it a convenient distribution point to the smaller towns scattered along the river and in the interior. Alegría would be free to receive him, he thought, finishing the milk and honey. He was amused to reflect that she might enjoy the novelty of an illicit affair. He had no wish to see her again, however; he felt no love for her, nor for any woman, and besides, she had told Don Bueno four days before the wedding that she was pregnant with his child.

He heard a scraping noise from the sitting room, and shouted, 'Juanita!'

She had a scarf over her head and carried a broom.

'What do you think you are doing?' he asked in an angry voice. 'How many times have I told you not to start cleaning while I'm still sitting here?'

'My younger boy,' she said, 'he has a fever. I must go to him soon.'

'A fever, has he?' Don Bueno used a sarcastic tone of voice. 'I don't pay you for the delightful pleasure of hearing you push my furniture around and go scraping away with your broom. I've told you a thousand times I don't want to hear the sound of you carrying on like the public health department when I'm having breakfast.'

'But my poor boy,' she said. 'He –'

'I don't want to hear a word about that lazy good-for-nothing little puppy of yours. He's a whining idiot. He should be out working, but he knows he has a fool for a mother who's eager to pamper his every idle wish.'

'You don't know what you're saying, sir,' she said, her face agitated with emotion. 'My little boy was shivering all night with the fever, and . . .' She stopped, noticing that her master was glaring scornfully at her.

'I don't want to hear another word about him,' he shouted. 'Nor do I want to hear another sound in my house. Now, go back to the kitchen!'

'But I *need* to go to my boy,' she pleaded.

'Did you hear me? I said go back to the kitchen! Your pampered idiot is not going to *die*!'

'You don't know what you're saying,' she murmured, as if speaking to herself, going away. She sat at the kitchen table, the edge of her apron raised to her eyes. Don Bueno would remain in his wicker chair in the verandah for at least another half an hour, she knew, for that is what he did each morning, staring at the garden without looking at anything, and she must make no sound until he rose, while her boy needed her.

It took Don Bueno a few minutes to expunge from his mind the irritation of having had to scold Juanita and to sink again into the meditative mood which entertained no ideas but simply permitted the mind to be invaded by random images and their associations. He had known another Alegría thirty years earlier, a dark-haired Colombian beauty from a family so rich that the only excitement she could find in life was to associate herself with criminals. She became Don Bueno's partner in a gang that stole cars and then took them apart to sell everything from the engine to the hubcaps to dealers in spare parts. The first time they worked together was in a parking area in the city's business district – a hot, dusty square with three huge eucalyptus trees growing in it, the ground covered with gravel, and the cars left there in packed rows. They broke into a maroon Buick with windows tinted nearly black. Don Bueno smiled at his recollection of the

Colombian Alegría who always seemed to want to increase the risk of any enterprise in order to heighten her sense of excitement; she had brazenly suggested they make love in the back seat of the Buick before they drove it away, saying, 'No one can see us through that tinted glass.'

Don Bueno thought of his precocious Alegría with fondness; in those years it was still considered scandalous for a woman to be seen smoking a cigarette, and there was Alegría anticipating the sexual freedom of a later age. But at the time Don Bueno had said, 'You're crazy. What if the owner returned? He could, at any moment.'

'Don't be a coward,' she had said, already beginning to remove her skirt in the back seat. 'I'll take care of him if he comes.' He had never so much as kissed her cheek before, and was aroused by the nonchalance with which she raised and parted her legs, her buttocks pressed into the tan leather upholstery.

He remembered how she had shrieked with delight as they made love in the car. It had been no use pleading with her to be quiet or to make haste, for she had wanted him to attend to each of the preliminaries of a passionate lovemaking. Twice they had heard footsteps on the gravel ground coming in the direction of the car; each time he had gone still and come out in a sweat while she giggled and pushed her thighs against him. The first person had driven away from the opposite row of cars, but the second one, his measured footsteps becoming louder on the gravel, had come right up to the car and had almost stopped in front of it; after a tense moment, Don Bueno was relieved to see that the man's look was only of admiration for the car, for he soon entered his own rusted old Renault and drove away.

Alegría had possessed an astonishing knack for inventing unnecessary risks. Their last theft together was a white De Soto. She had taken out her lipstick and written JUST MARRIED all over it in large letters, and then insisted on driving up and down the streets in the city's fashionable shopping area with the horn blowing almost all the time. Of course, hundreds of people on the sidewalks and in cars and buses saw them and smiled and waved at them; a policeman gave them precedence at a congested crossing; a good many spectators probably thought it odd that the newly married couple should be dressed in ordinary clothes and that the car should be driven by the woman who, moreover, had a gleeful look on her face. Someone even took a photograph that happened to show the driver's side of the car. The man with the cheap box camera had come from the interior with his family and was touring the city's famous attractions, and had snapped, on the moment's impulse, a sight that he could show to the folks back home of the crazy things that went on in the city. But the next week the picture appeared on the front pages of all the newspapers. Seeing a news item about the stolen De Soto and reading about the reward offered by the police, the tourist speculated if he might not have an important clue, and took the picture to the police station. Don Bueno never saw Alegría after that; she could have reduced the term of her prison sentence considerably had she cooperated with the police and given the names of the rest of the car-stealing gang, but, much to her credit, she did not, finding a thrill in the heroism of her act; nor did she reveal the name of the man whose child she carried, to be born in prison.

Don Bueno called Juanita and said to her, 'Go and be with your son, you can finish your work later.'

She thanked him and hurried away across the garden and through the front gate. Mothers had a craving to be with their sons, he thought, while a father's fondest wish was to be with a young mistress. At least that had always been true of himself. He must have fathered a dozen or more children whom he had never seen and had no wish to see. He was amused to think that there must be men and women in their thirties living on the coast of Venezuela or in the cities of Colombia and Peru, in luxury apartments or in slums, whose father he was, and younger children in smaller cities and in the remote interior, as here in Santa Rosa which was so far from any national centre that, except for football, its patriotic attachments were only to

27

parochial matters; he would have recognized none of his children, and he was thankful that nature had given him no pleasure in fatherhood. Only once had he tried to be a father; for two years, in a house by the sea where he lived in seclusion on the money accumulated from car thefts, he had watched his son take his first steps and begin to utter words. Don Bueno had been filled with a profound loathing for the boy. He could not account for the total absence of fatherly affection within himself. Tiring of his family life by the sea, he had returned to the city and become involved with some of his former friends who had begun a seemingly respectable brokerage firm. At the end of a year, nearly thirty thousand people, mainly from the middle classes in provincial towns who dream of a sudden and spectacular fortune to escape from the drudgery of their existence, had lost their life's savings, and Don Bueno and his partners had dispersed and vanished into the interior. If he had thought of his son during that year, it had only been a momentary image in his mind that induced an extreme revulsion. He never saw him again.

For over thirty years since that time, Don Bueno's life had followed the cycle of pursuing some criminal business in the city succeeded by two to six years in some obscure town in the interior where he lived in quiet splendour as long as his money lasted and he could have affairs without being discovered. He could have, as some of his partners did, moved to different cities, and found some new way of swindling the public – the criminal mind, he had discovered early, was wonderfully fertile; as with perverse ways of enjoying sex, after doing it once you became remarkably inventive – but he had never been interested in money for itself. His ideal was to have nothing to do: he cultivated an elegant idleness, was impeccably courteous in society, and sought his diversion in seducing young women. The life of small towns in the interior suited him best. The natives invariably found him vastly charming, a likeable eccentric who had spurned the dazzle of the city for the simpler pleasures of the country.

Only once had his past appeared to threaten the tranquillity of his forced retirement to the country. He was living then in a town in a remote valley in the northern Andes. The event occurred in a bar one evening. He was buying drinks for some young men, and was himself not quite sober, when a man of about fifty-five rode up the street and dismounted in front of the bar. He wore a brown leather hat below the wide, stiff brim of which long grey hair, matted and begrimed, fell to his shoulders; he had a broad face, with a week's beard covering his large cheeks. A charcoal-grey poncho fell from his shoulders to halfway down his thighs, covering his stout trunk. His knee-high boots were spattered with mud.

'Can one get some food here and a bed for the night?' he shouted in a bass voice, standing in the doorway of the bar.

'Sure,' one of the young men sitting with Don Bueno shouted back, 'and you can piss through your arse and fart through your cock, too.'

The group at the table laughed uproariously. Over a dozen empty beer bottles in front of the men rattled as one of them slapped the table while he laughed.

Heavy footsteps sounded on the wooden floor as the man came into the bar. He saw the laughing group and walked toward it, his arms scarcely swinging. He stopped, and there was a moment's silence as he glared at the young men. Then another of Don Bueno's companions said, 'Where you come from, gaucho? Looking for a lost cow?'

'You'll find her in your mother's bed,' a third young man added, and the group pounded at the table, laughing loudly. A beer bottle fell to its side, rolled to the edge of the table and crashed to the floor.

Don Bueno was the first to stop laughing when he saw the old man staring at each member of the group in turn, shifting his dark brown eyes from one to the other without blinking. Don Bueno could not tell why he felt threatened by the old man's stare.

'Boy, look at that hungry stare,' one of the young men said. 'What would you like, gaucho? This fancy restaurant is famous for its fried dogs' balls. How'd you like them – tender and juicy?'

29

There were guffaws of laughter from the table, and another chanted, 'Barbecued balls are good for your brain – you don't have to be young to fuck again.'

But this time Don Bueno did not join the coarse merry-making of his friends. His eyes were fixed on the old man who, though he looked to him to be nearly sixty, nevertheless possessed a breadth of shoulder and an erect bearing that indicated exceptional physical strength, the sort that belonged normally to a man who worked on the land. He walked closer to the table and, having stared at each of the men who sat round it, looked now only at Don Bueno. He stood within a metre of the table, his hands held away from his body and raised to a level above his waist. Suddenly, he dropped his right hand to where, concealed by the poncho, a dagger hung from his belt; he pulled out the dagger and, taking a step forward, threw it on the table. The beer bottles clinked where it fell.

'You.' He pointed a finger at Don Bueno, his voice booming. 'You degenerate motherfucker, get up!'

Don Bueno leaned back in his chair, his eyes still fixed on the man. The palpitation of his heart increased; a cold fear ran through his body for a moment. Who was this person provoking him to some desperate challenge? The way in which this old man looked only at him seemed to suggest that he had found the person he had been looking for, and the thought sent the blood racing to Don Bueno's brain. He was about to rise when the old man's voice boomed out again: 'You are old enough to know better than to let these titsuckers dishonour their race.'

Two of the young men sprang up and had their hands on either side of the old man's neck and were shouting names at him when Don Bueno, also rising, pulled at the back of their collars, saying, 'Take it easy, boys.'

For a moment, Don Bueno was in the posture of not having stood up fully, so that he appeared to be crouching with his arms lifted up and pulling back the two young men, and in that moment, when the other two were resuming their seats, he found himself looking into the old man's dark brown eyes, returning his stare. The two young men sat down, muttering oaths. Don Bueno remained fixed in the crouching posture, like a wrestler about to make a move. His eye fell on the dagger that glinted from the table. A beer bottle rolled back and forth next to it. He picked up the dagger by the blade and held the handle toward the old man.

The old man looked down at the dagger and then stared at Don Bueno. He slowly lowered his head and spat in the direction of Don Bueno's hand. The white arc of spittle plunged through the space between the two men, missing Don Bueno's hand but falling partly on the blade. The old man turned round, his shoulders lifted and neck erect, and began to walk toward the counter behind which the owner of the bar stood nervously passing a cloth around a glass. For a couple of moments, his heavy footsteps on the wooden floor were the only sound in the room. Don Bueno ran up behind him and, throwing his left arm over his shoulder from behind, clasped his head in a choking grip; holding the dagger out in front of the old man's nose, Don Bueno said into his right ear: 'You don't insult anyone in this town, you hear?'

There were cries of agreement from others in the bar.

The old man put his hand up to the dagger.

'Take it and get out of here,' Don Bueno said, releasing the dagger and his grip round the old man's neck and taking a step back.

Three of the young men had come up and stood behind Don Bueno. The old man turned round and faced the four of them. His face grim, the dagger held tightly in his hand, he looked only at Don Bueno. 'You miserable little cuntlicker,' he said.

'You take that back!' Don Bueno shouted at him, tightening his fists.

'You ocean of vomit!'

One of the young men behind Don Bueno tapped quickly, softly on his back; Don Bueno instinctively threw his hand behind his back and the young man slipped a knife into it.

'You're not worth a flea on a bitch's back.' The old man's

31

voice boomed aloud as if in some dark vaulted chamber, the deep bass taking possession of the air. He raised his hand with the dagger, pulled his poncho off and threw it to the ground. He took a step toward Don Bueno, his hand still raised.

'You breed among vermin, that is all you can do in this life, fuck and fuck and fuck.' He flung down his hand, stabbing at the air with each repetition, more, it seemed, for provocative emphasis and theatrical effect than to attack his adversary. 'You turn the world into a sewer and wallow in slime. You masturbate with shadows. You sucked no milk from your mother – how could you, being born with that cunt on your face instead of lips? – you drew no love but were bloated with yellow mucus. You were born so that I should curse you and damn you and damn you and damn you!'

Again the hand flung itself repeatedly toward Don Bueno but remained short of striking distance. Don Bueno was now in a rage, not knowing why he should be chosen for such vile and entirely arbitrary abuse, and he stood tensed, his hand with the knife behind his back, watching the glinting dagger come repeatedly at him.

Suddenly, Don Bueno threw his hand out and up, simultaneously taking a step forward and throwing his left hand up to hold the old man's arm which at that moment was raised with the dagger above his head. The knife entered just below the old man's ribcage. Don Bueno tore the knife out sideways and stabbed him again.

The old man fell forward, the dagger dropping from his hand; he held himself for a moment, and staggered, his eyes glowering at Don Bueno. 'You . . . you . . .' He weakly pointed a finger, and fell to the ground, crying in a loud, raging voice, '*You!*'

Don Bueno leaped upon him and turned him over, holding him by the shoulders. Blood trickled from the old man's mouth and there was blood on the ground where Don Bueno crouched beside the dying man.

'Who are you, why did you come here?' Don Bueno shouted at him.

The other men had crowded round the two figures on the ground in a semicircle. Several voices filled the room with agitated tones.

'Breeder of killers, a race of murderers . . .' Don Bueno heard the dying man mutter.

There was a clamour from the men standing behind Don Bueno, for the old man's head had fallen and he appeared to die. But he spoke one word more, which was heard only by Don Bueno. It was his real name.

He stood up slowly, having gone pale. But the men around him were all talking loudly together. The old man had been insane, they were saying. A complete loony, a nutcase. Don Bueno had only done what he had to do. It wasn't his fault. It was a clear act of provocation and self-defence. No doubt about it. Why, Don Bueno had even returned the old man's dagger to him! He had acted with honour, perfectly like a gentleman, no question about it.

Don Bueno rose from his wicker chair and strolled about the verandah, feeling an agitation within him evoked by the memory. He had never understood the events of that evening. The town had talked of him as a hero for weeks following the killing, but Don Bueno himself remained uneasy; it seemed to him that the old man had deliberately driven him into a rage, almost as if he had *wanted* to be killed; and the memory of hearing his real name from the dying man's lips still sent an icy chill through his body.

At ten o'clock, a car drew up outside his house. He was standing beside a flowering bush in his garden, plucking out yellowed leaves, and walked up to the gate.

'Elvira!' He expressed a genuine pleasure at seeing the young woman in a pink satin blouse and dark green wide skirt. It soothed a mind beginning to be troubled by memories to see a beautifully shaped woman; the lips smiling, showing the tips of white teeth, the curve of the bosom behind the closely fitting blouse, with little pleats created by the uplifted breasts, were enough to distract one from the torment of one's past.

'I never turn down an invitation to see a garden,' she

said, dimples appearing on her light brown cheeks.

'You are most welcome,' he said, taking her hand and raising it to his lips while bowing gracefully.

He had met her socially with her husband several times in the past but it had only been yesterday, at the reception following the wedding, that he had talked to her alone. It flattered him to think how well his persuasive charm worked that she should not waste a day in taking up his invitation.

'I happened to need to visit my dressmaker this morning,' she said with a bright smile, 'and I thought why not go and see Don Bueno's garden before he forgets he ever invited me?'

Dissimulation came naturally to some women, he thought, looking at the carefully arranged curls of her black hair and the provocative brightness of her dark eyes. In this mind, he immediately cast her into the category of provincial women so driven to despair by boredom that they were easy conquests.

'This is the best time of the day for a visit,' he said, walking with her down a path beside which grew several varieties of begonias, some with long white stalks coming out of the mass of kidney-shaped leaves, tiny discs of pink flowers clustered at the ends of the stalks.

'I love begonias,' Elvira commented, clasping her hands and looking at him, the dimples again pronounced on her cheeks. 'They're so delicate. Don Bueno, you must tell me your secret, how you get your begonias to be so beautiful.'

'Some of these were growing wild in a nearby forest,' he remarked. 'They flower better here. Probably because they get more light.'

'It must be your magic touch,' she said, laughing, the glossy black curls behind her ears quivering. Making a gesture with her hands and throwing a look that seemed to take in all the garden, she added, 'How everything is blooming!'

He looked at her complacently, understanding her to mean that she did not need a longer botanical tour, and as if to confirm the impression that the excuse of visiting his

34

garden had served its purpose, she said, 'Everything, everything is lovely. Promise me you'll tell me your secret.' And looking at the house as if she had only just seen it, she added, 'And you have such a wonderful house!'

'Let us go in and have some coffee,' he said, touching her bare arm just below the sleeve with the tips of his fingers, and leading her to the steps to the verandah.

They went to the sitting room which was plainly furnished with the rattan sofa that had flowery cushions on it, a low rattan table with a glass top, and a couple of old bentwood chairs.

'Why, this is so charming!' she remarked, sitting down on the sofa and leaning back. 'Don Bueno, you are really a man of many secrets.'

'My housekeeper's taken the morning off to look after a sick son,' he said, standing by the door, 'so please excuse me for a minute while I make coffee.'

'Oh, you don't need to bother in that case,' she said. 'Besides, I don't want to take up too much of your time.'

'I have all the time in the world.' He went and sat down next to her, positioning himself a little sideways on the edge of the sofa.

She was leaning back and had flung her arm across the top of the cushion. She laughed and said, 'I wish I could say that!'

'What keeps you so busy?' he asked. 'You don't have any children, you said so yesterday.'

She withdrew her arm from the top of the sofa and with a quick movement patted his leg just above the knee, stood up and walked to a window, saying, 'Felipe comes home for lunch at one, and there's always a million things to do.' She turned round to face him, standing with the window behind her. He saw her in silhouette against the light and imagined that a strong passion emanated from her eyes. He rose and took a step toward her. She turned her head and for a moment her profile was framed in the window. 'There's never any time for anything real,' he heard her say softly as though it were the expression of some profound sadness.

35

He stood near her and said, 'Ah, the happiness that we all desire!'

She looked at him and laughed. 'You're a mysterious man, Don Bueno. And now you talk like a poet!'

He moved his hand to touch her arm but changed his mind. She noticed the aborted gesture, and took a deep breath, her bosom heaving. 'What curse brought you to Santa Rosa?' she suddenly asked, and walked quickly away from him and sat down again in her former place. He saw her stare at him and observed that though her eyes shone brightly, her look was one of serious concern.

'Curse?' He walked slowly toward her.

'Well, no one can *choose* to live in hell.'

He stood a few paces from her and watched her with a growing sense of satisfaction. He could easily write her biography, he thought. She suffered from the common affliction that young women in the interior could never escape – a too early marriage to a petty businessman, too many children at too young an age or no children at all, nothing but local gossip for diversion, an infinite longing for romance, and the eternal despair that the real world was too far away for them ever to reach even its suburbs.

'Where would you choose to live?' he asked, sitting down next to her.

'Oh, I don't know what I *want*! It's hell everywhere, only Santa Rosa is the lowest part of it. If it were only a question of wanting!' She slapped her hands on her knees as if to emphasize the acuteness of her feeling.

He traced with an index finger the veins on the back of the hand nearest to him and said, 'You are so restless, my dear.'

She turned her head away and, as if speaking to herself, said in a quiet voice, 'We are cursed . . . cursed . . . If I only knew!'

He believed himself experienced enough to be convinced that she was putting on an hysterical act that would soon require to be calmed by his comforting arms; and believing, too, that the mention of children worked as a catalyst in such situations, he said, 'You should have children, my dear Elvira.'

36

'What *for*?' Her voice was suddenly loud. 'To *die*?'

Now he was puzzled. There seemed something more to this woman than he had thought, a larger torment than the boredom of life in the interior, but he could not precisely say what troubled her. The lover in him, however, still not seeing the individual but only a type belonging to a category of his own invention, felt certain that it was the right sort of symptom for him to exploit for his own ends.

'You have a troubled heart,' he said in a sympathetic voice, holding her hand. She pulled it away but immediately raised it to touch his cheek and, stroking it gently, said, 'You're so understanding, but I must go.' She stood up suddenly and, patting her skirt, walked to the door.

'I wish you wouldn't go so soon,' he said, rising from the sofa. Walking to where she stood by the door, looking at him, he added, 'We were beginning to have such a nice conversation.'

'Believe me, I would like to learn more of life,' she said, smiling. 'You must know so much!'

He thought her remarkably bold in what she said, and was convinced that the entire visit had been one calculated performance with the transparent aim of arousing his interest in her.

'With a heart like yours, perhaps I can bring you comfort,' he said and smiled at her, believing his words to be subtly ambiguous and, for a provincial woman, the very essence of poetry. He was certain that it was a matter of two more visits from her and she herself would invite the conquest.

She stared at him with eyes so bright that he had no doubt that they were overflowing with passion. She jerked her head away and quickly walked out of the room. He took a step after her onto the verandah but stopped, noticing the determined manner of her departure.

'I shall hope to see you soon,' he said after her. 'The morning is the best time, the air is not so humid in the morning.'

She did not turn round till she had reached the gate. He followed her out to the garden. She looked back briefly

37

from the gate, giving him a wave, before going out to her car. No, she thought, unlocking the car and getting into it, she had made a mistake in thinking that an older man could understand her affliction; it was clear he had only one calculation in his head – how soon he could get her into his bed. She had feared that that would happen, but had desperately hoped that it would not, that Don Bueno would have some special power to help her. The consolation of wisdom, or a hint that human beings had access to some revelation, however remote and difficult to witness: she longed for some formula, or charm, that had to come in a combination of words, to soothe her troubled spirit. Driving away, her despair was greater than before: all that dissimulation – 'I happened to need to visit my dressmaker' – only to be thought of as a woman available for an affair. There were no saints in this world, only men with carnal thoughts.

The image of her beautiful figure, waving at him from the gate, the wide, flaring green skirt swirling as she turned her hips to walk out, stayed with Don Bueno for several minutes after he had heard her car go away. He congratulated himself on his gift for attracting young women, his natural possession of an instinctive charm that made them fall for him so easily. He had no doubt that what he had seen in Elvira's eyes was a longing to be loved by him; it was only her provincial timidity that restrained her. The prospect before him, he thought, sitting down in the wicker chair with a smile on his face, was altogether one especially cultivated for his sensuous delight.

For the third time that morning, he saw the same nearly black butterfly float past across his line of vision, make a loop over some bushes and descend again on the white geranium.

Feeling extremely satisfied with himself, he went down, some half an hour later, to the Café Madrid on the square. He passed the rest of the morning at a table on the sidewalk over a couple of bottles of beer, exchanging small talk with the usual acquaintances he met there every day. Just before one o'clock, before the businessmen in the area began to come for lunch, he went to the table inside the café where he sat every afternoon, facing almost all the tables inside the room and able to see in a large mirror a good portion of the tables on the sidewalk as well as part of the square across the road.

A clean white cloth covered the table and placed on it was an aluminium bowl containing rolls and next to it a small glass dish with little balls of butter. His place had already been set, and he had the satisfaction of reflecting that were he ever late, the restaurant full, and people waiting to be seated, his place would be kept reserved for him. He began to eat a roll with a lot of butter, and studied the menu. When he lifted his eyes, the waiter who had quietly positioned himself four paces away and was discreetly watching him, immediately came up to him with his pad and pencil ready.

'I'll have the baked fish, followed by chicken with garlic, creamed spinach, with rice, not potatoes, no salad, and probably papaya for dessert but we'll see about that later. And a bottle of white Marqués de Riscal.'

One reason for Don Bueno's regimen of morning exercise and a breakfast that excluded coffee was that from noon to midnight he could eat and drink what he enjoyed best. The alternating twelve hours of restraint and excess seemed to him to balance each other out, leaving him healthy without making him the kind of bore a person on a diet invariably was.

The waiter brought the bottle of wine and held it out for him to see the label. Don Bueno nodded his head when he read the familiar name; minute areas of the label had been eaten away by roaches, and moisture ran down the side of the bottle in tiny rivulets through the fine dust that coated it. Don Bueno leaned back in his chair and looked away from the waiter's performance of uncorking the bottle, and just when he heard the cork pop out he saw in the mirror a man in a dark brown shirt standing among the tables on the sidewalk as if pondering at which one to sit. The man looked vaguely familiar, as if he had once seen him from a distance, though, even as that thought occurred to Don Bueno, he was certain that he had never seen him before in Santa Rosa. The waiter served some wine into the glass for Don Bueno to taste. He picked up the glass and swirled it and raised it to his lips; but he stopped before his lips could touch the glass and, putting the glass down, looked sternly at the waiter and said, 'Are you blind?'

The waiter, confused for a moment, looked nervously at him and then at the glass. There were bits of cork in the glass. He hurriedly picked up the glass while rapidly muttering some words asking to be excused his error, and placed it on the unoccupied table behind him from where he picked up a clean glass. He looked into the bottle and carefully poured a small measure from it into the new glass. Satisfied that there was no mistake this time, he placed the glass in front of Don Bueno who, immediately picking it up, held it up to the light. As he did so, he could not help seeing in the mirror the man in the dark brown shirt take a seat at a table so that his back and the outline of his black-haired head now seemed fixed in the mirror. Don Bueno concentrated his attention on the glass and said to the waiter, 'It's the wrong colour. I don't need to taste it to tell that it's bad.' He placed the glass down disdainfully, saying, 'Use it for vinegar.'

The waiter apologized and took away the glass and the bottle, returning presently with a new bottle and commencing the ceremony all over again. In the meanwhile, Don Bueno had looked with curiosity at the man in the brown shirt, and wondered whether he had been some acquaintance in the past. He could not tell, for the man's face remained turned away. Don Bueno had no desire to meet a stranger in case the man happened to be someone he had victimized in the past. There was always the possibility that someone, angered at losing money in a swindle perpetrated by Don Bueno, would form the obsession of hunting out the criminal. Don Bueno knew that that was what he would do himself had he been the victim, for his temperament would not permit the dishonour of a crime committed against him to go unavenged, and therefore, during his sojourns in the interior, he was particularly cautious whenever he saw a stranger. Inevitably, there was a measure of paranoia involved, and it was easy for him to convince himself that a perfectly innocent stranger whom he had never met before might indeed be hunting for him.

'It's not sufficiently chilled,' he said to the waiter after tasting from the new bottle. 'Otherwise, it's splendid. Put it in the ice and don't serve it until after you've brought the fish and I've begun to eat.'

The businessmen had been arriving for their lunch and by the time the waiter brought Don Bueno's first course most of the tables had been taken. Several smiled and nodded their heads when they caught Don Bueno's eye. He found himself staring at the black-haired stranger outside every time he glanced at the mirror, but by the time he had drunk his third glass of wine, which seemed to be improving with each sip, a contentment began to fill his body – a physical state that induced the mind to believe that it could know no pain, for only a serene bliss pervaded the universe of which the body was a contented particle. The feeling intensified as he neared the conclusion of his meal and drank the last glass from the bottle; and instead of seeing the black-haired man in the mirror, he now saw images of Alegría and the wonderful source of joy that her body had been, images that began to be superseded by the teasing forms of Elvira's body – her green skirt swirling before his mind until it flew in a stiff circle high above her waist, the pink satin blouse being thrown open in some wildly ecstatic dance – imbuing his mind with pleasures he anticipated from her and arousing his desire for the violence of the bed.

He saw in the mirror the man in the dark brown shirt rise from his table and go away when he himself was counting some money to leave as a tip. By the time Don Bueno left the restaurant, pausing briefly by two or three tables to exchange a few remarks with acquaintances whom he saw there every day, the stranger had disappeared.

Don Bueno walked across the square where a few old

41

people sat on stone benches under the shade of flowering mimosa trees, some of them stretched out with an untidy bundle under their heads, and proceeded in the direction of the waterfront. It was his habit to stroll there under the shade of the trees, in the cool breeze coming from the river, for fifteen minutes before returning to his house for a siesta. But he stopped in the middle of the square and, feeling the desire that had been aroused in him when he finished the wine clamouring more insistently for gratification, he changed his course and walked toward a street that ran parallel to the river, a few blocks away from it.

Some ten minutes later, he was standing outside a small house with pink bougainvillaea climbing up its light blue stucco front. A sign on the wooden gate indicated that it was the residence of Dr Enrico Gonzalez. Don Bueno looked at his watch. It was 2.40. Enrico should be having his siesta, he thought, and he might be able to persuade his twenty-eight-year-old wife Norma to slip out and come to Don Bueno's house for an hour, just as he had done two months before. 'Daylight robbery,' he had called it when she came, kissing her urgently and saying, 'Stolen kisses are the sweetest.' She had been very sporting, mirthfully chiding him for raiding her treasure, and crying with laughter in her voice, 'Oh, you terrible, terrible man!'

He opened the gate and walked past the red-flowering oleander bush to the front door, remembering a fusion of several meetings with Norma that went back to his first year in Santa Rosa and her disclosure that she believed her second child, a boy, to be his – associations that made his immediate desire more potent and gave him the conviction, at the same time, that the affairs of other people were conveniently arranged to offer no impediment to the successful completion of his most selfish whims.

He had just raised his hand to knock on the door when it suddenly opened and Dr Enrico Gonzalez himself stood there, seeing off a visitor.

'Don Bueno!' He expressed his surprise, and turned to speak to the departing visitor. 'Come back in two days if you're not better, and *please* come in my office hours,' he said and, smiling at Don Bueno when the visitor was walking away, added, 'This is what happens when you begin to be successful. You don't even get time to eat lunch. It says quite clearly on the gate, 9–1, 4.30–8, but everyone has an emergency and can't wait until after siesta. I want a quiet practice, not an ambulance service! Well, I hope *you* don't have an emergency, too!'

Enrico's volubility had given Don Bueno time to reconsider his situation. 'I wouldn't have come otherwise,' he said. 'I'm sorry, Enrico. I would never disturb a man's lunch or siesta, but this pain . . . maybe it's something I ate. If it's any consolation, at least I came here instead of *sending* for you.'

'Well, come in and let me check you over,' the doctor said. 'But mind, don't go around telling everyone that I'm available at all hours. This is only for special clients.'

The phone was ringing in the sitting room at the end of the hall and Don Bueno heard Norma's voice answer it. Hearing it, he felt a real pain within himself at the collapse of his plan. The doctor led him to the consulting room and closed the door behind him. Don Bueno thought that it was just as well that the telephone had prevented Norma from putting her head into the hall; seeing her in the flesh would only have added to his present torment in which he was now obliged to undress himself before her husband and lie down to be examined by him.

Because his illness was an imaginary one, he realized that Enrico was an incompetent doctor, for after prodding his chest and pressing down on his stomach, turning him over and tapping him on his back, turning him on his back again and pressing his thumb into his groin, all rather cursorily, Enrico looked grimly at him and said, 'Your liver is in a serious state, you really want to cut down on alcohol.'

Don Bueno knew that no doctor could make so definitive a pronouncement about the condition of anyone's liver after so hasty and superficial an examination, but since he was going through the motions of an illness as much as the doctor was of arriving at a diagnosis, and both desired to be free of one another as quickly as possible, one to recover from his blunder and the other at last to get to his lunch, he looked seriously at Enrico and half mockingly said, 'It must be the end of my days.'

Enrico was quickly scribbling out a prescription and, looking up, said, 'You need to be careful. Everyone's sins catch up with them.' He gave him the piece of paper, with instructions on how frequently to take the pills and a word of caution about his diet, and the two took each other's leave.

Don Bueno walked toward the waterfront, deciding to make a circuitous way to his house. He was annoyed at the frustration he had just experienced, and realized that instead of his desire being dampened it was all the more aflame; the disappointment of not having Norma to embrace did not mean, he thought, that the world of women was closed to him. Had he been resigned to an afternoon of futile longings, he would have gone straight back to his house, but without thinking he had chosen another direction and was walking quite rapidly; realizing where his feet were taking him, he observed with amusement that his body was racing ahead of his mind.

He came to the house of María de Lurdes, a three-storey stone house without a garden at the front on a sloping street two blocks from the river. The only living thing in the street at that hour was a black horse standing in front of a cart that contained a disorderly heap of empty milk cans, swishing its tail at flies; it turned its head, hearing Don Bueno on the opposite sidewalk, and stared at him. Don Bueno looked at the horse's large eyes and felt slightly uncomfortable.

María de Lurdes kept the front door unlocked during the afternoon when most other businesses were closed – and precisely for that reason. Invariably there would be some small businessman or shopkeeper so overcome with a sense of wellbeing after a good lunch and a couple of bottles of beer that he would find a pressure build up in his body for which there was only one form of release. The knowledge that María de Lurdes maintained an establishment so conveniently close at hand where the sought-for release could be obtained was perhaps partly responsible for some men experiencing an urgent need in the first place – María de Lurdes having cunningly exploited the business principle that what is conspicuously available is the most often purchased. From soon after one o'clock to three, she had quite a steady flow of clients.

Don Bueno quietly entered the house and stood for a moment in the dark hall before taking the few steps to the door on the left. A very fat woman lay slumped in an armchair, her body appearing in that position as two great bulges, one at the chest and the other at the stomach, covered by a purple cotton dress with blue flowers, and two fat little legs spread out below the hemline that had been lifted up to the knees. Her bare arms, white and pudgy with two remarkably small hands, hung limply outside the armrests. Her head with fine orange-tinted hair was thrown back and rested on the top of the sagging cushion behind her; the dark red, lipsticked mouth was open, showing what apeared in that light to be a toothless hollow, and let out a whistling sound as she breathed.

She shook her head suddenly and jerked it forward, and peered at him through her tiny black eyes that appeared like two coffee beans pressed inside the fleshy cavities above the bulging cheeks. Her face was covered with a chalky make-up that seemed to give a bluish tinge to her white skin.

'Oh, it's Don Bueno,' she said, quickly coming back to life. 'I must have dozed off. Thought we were through with the afternoon's business.' Her voice came in a series of highpitched squeaks.

'How are you, María?' he said, smiling at her. 'Do you mind if I sit down?' he added, and took a seat in a cane sofa before she could answer. He leaned an elbow against the armrest and propped his head by holding a hand to his temple.

'This is a surprise,' she said, a sharp chirpiness in her

voice. 'You must be between mistresses to need to come to me.'

'You're shrewd! You can see into the secrets of a man's soul.'

She was about to joke back but, seeing him suddenly wrinkle his face in a grimace, said, 'What's the matter? You don't look too well.'

'Nothing. Just felt dizzy, that's all. Can I have a glass of water?'

She picked up a silver bell from a small table near her and rang it. He watched the white flabby flesh of her arm shaking loosely.

'I've been walking in the sun after lunch. I've been walking rather too briskly. Stupid of me.' He shook his head slightly and again felt the surge of dizziness, accompanied this time by a throbbing pain at his forehead.

A young girl with black hair parted at the centre, drawn back and hanging to her waist in a thick plait, and wearing a white dress, came in, and María de Lurdes said to her, 'Bring the gentleman an ice-cold beer.'

'No, no,' Don Bueno said. 'Just a glass of water, just water.'

He looked at the girl as she walked away and saw a blurred outline of what he believed must be a beautiful body, but the fact that he had not been able to see clearly caused him no concern. He turned his eyes to where María de Lurdes sat. She seemed to be floating in her armchair and he could not find her eyes.

'She's nice,' he said.

María de Lurdes laughed – a sound that appeared to be more like a short, sharp shriek – and said, 'She's sixteen. But that's the advantage of being a man, you can have a girl of sixteen to your dying day.'

'I'll have her,' he said, just before the girl came back and handed him a glass of water.

He took it without looking at her face and he thought it odd, while he sipped from the glass, that he should not want to meet the eyes of the girl for whose body he was presently going to pay money to María de Lurdes. He had

46

never done that before, committed himself to a purchase without a thorough appraisal.

The girl went away after he had taken the glass from her, and it seemed as though she had been a phantom that had appeared and then vanished, leaving a vague anxiety lurking beneath the complex mystery of feelings within him – all of which, however, were obscure because he had, for the last hour or so, recognized nothing but the feeling of sexual desire within himself and therefore transformed in his mind any other feeling into no more than a subtle manifestation of that one. The phantom that lured him was, he thought, just a lovely body and the dizziness with its sensation that he was sinking was only his own over-excited blood that would soon burst in a delirium of plea-sure; he was convinced that if he was falling it was into that delicious depth where flesh melted and all conscious-ness was nothing but an ecstasy so intense it came with the violence of sharp steel.

He took out some bank notes from his wallet but found that he could not distinguish them one from the other. María de Lurdes, standing up in front of him and appearing even fatter than when she was seated, flicked her tiny fingers through the notes, jerked her face and made a sound to indicate her pleasure but which he heard as the sharp squeaking of a bat.

Then he heard her say clearly, 'You've got generous in your old age.'

'What is money?' he joked, testing his own voice. 'You can't take it with you.' He was relieved that he could speak rationally, and when he looked at María Lurdes's hands twisting the bank notes he saw that he could make out the figure inscribed in the corner of the outer note. The dizziness had gone.

'Well, get along, then, and get your money's worth,' she said. 'The second door on the right, the best room in the house, with a view of the garden.'

He walked down the hall toward the room, feeling per-fectly composed and wondering what had come over him a few minutes ago that he had not been able to see things clearly. He entered the room which contained a bed covered with a white sheet and two overstuffed pillows on it. Bright light flooded through the window and he went and stood by it, waiting for the girl to come. The garden was adazzle in the brilliant afternoon sun, clusters of flowers covering the entire width of the house and going back some thirty metres, with a narrow path winding about the bushes. For a few moments, Don Bueno lost consciousness of himself and felt as though his body had become an enormous eye and all his being a huge screen on which the sharply focused details of the garden appeared as an overwhelming perception. The smallest petal of the most distant marigold in the garden appeared in vivid detail. The veins of a leaf, the sharp point of a thorn, the particles of earth below the stem of a plant – the entire world of matter in all its minute particularity appeared before him in precise definition of its form and substance. He closed his eyes. But the world in his perception remained the same, the light intense, and the feeling persisted of his having lost his own being.

He heard the door open and be closed again, and there was the rustle of someone walking in. Quickly opening his eyes, he looked in the direction of the door, and saw what seemed for a moment to be an apparition. It must be the effect, he thought, of turning from the brilliantly lit garden in his mind's eye to the comparative darkness of the room that made the girl, wearing a white dress, appear like a ghost that had flitted past his vision. Not seeing her, he walked toward the bed and sat down on its edge in order to remove his shoes. She came and stood in front of him, her bare feet two paces away from his own where he had just bent down and had his hands at the shoelaces. Letting his hands dangle there, he looked up slowly. She had unplaited her hair, for its long black tresses now fell from either side of her face across her bosom and down to her waist over the white dress. He raised himself to put a hand out to touch her hair – to commence what all the throbbing sensations within his body and the swelling pressure at his temples seemed, he thought dimly, to have been demanding. A strange mood had come over him, one he had never experienced before when about to make love to a young girl, and he had the obscure notion that he was going to enjoy sexual pleasure at a pitch of ecstasy that he had never before imagined was possible. It was in that moment when he put his hand out to touch her hair, just before he could do so, that he lifted his face to look at hers.

The window was directly behind her so that she was framed in the dazzling rectangle of light. The white dress took on a transparency in that light, without, however, revealing the outline of her body to his eyes but showing only a diaphanous form. He could see nothing of her face, only a glowing line of light across the curve of her head.

His own head swayed as he looked. The pressure at his temples was now intense. Light, darkness; darkness, light. The minute particularity of his earlier vision had been succeeded by a perception that was essentially abstract – blocks of colourless antitheses that he painfully witnessed without knowing what he was looking at. The rectangle of white seemed to be turning grey; involuntarily, he fell back to the bed, and when his head hit the mattress, the grey turned to black. He felt a hand touch his bosom, fingers quickly open a couple of buttons and a cold hand press itself against his breast.

'No, no,' he whispered, as from some great depth. 'Don't touch me . . . don't . . . don't. I will . . . go . . . myself . . . soon . . . soon.'

María de Lurdes was standing beside the bed when he opened his eyes, and she said, 'I just came by to see you. To check if you were still alive. You gave us such a fright, almost like the time a Franciscan father had a heart attack and had to be smuggled out, but he, poor soul, at least had some pleasure before he died.'

While she talked, her voice coming to his ears in short high-pitched squeaks, Don Bueno raised his head and saw that he was lying straight in bed, his body covered with a sheet. The light was less intense at the window, he noticed, and he looked at his watch. It was nearly six o'clock. 'You came out in a terrible sweat,' María de Lurdes was saying.

'I'm sorry to have caused you so much trouble,' he said,

49

rising out of bed. 'I don't know what came over me, but I feel fine now.'

He tested himself by walking to the window and looking out and walking back to where María de Lurdes stood. 'Yes, I feel quite all right.' He pulled out his wallet and, taking some money out of it, held it to her, saying, 'For the inconvenience.'

She hesitated for a moment, remembering the generous amount he had paid her earlier, but then quickly snatched the notes from his hand. The wallet was still in his hand and he looked into it. He took out all the notes that it contained and extended his hand to María de Lurdes, saying, 'Please give this to the girl.'

María de Lurdes looked with astonishment at what she could see without having to inspect closely was a large sum of money. 'Do you know what you're doing?' she asked, not wishing to take advantage of a man who appeared to her to have lost his mind.

'Yes, yes, take it,' he said, 'give it to the girl.'

'Let me go and call her. The least she can do is to thank you. With a little kiss perhaps?'

'No, no, I don't want to see her! Just do me one favour. Get me a car to take me home.'

Fifteen minutes later, he was back at his own house. He went to his bedroom and took off his clothes with the intention of going to bed. But when he did so, he felt no need to stay there. There was nothing wrong with him, he thought. It must have been a mild sunstroke. He had got over it. But the terrible invasion of his body by darkness that he had experienced came back as a frightening memory. He quickly rose out of bed, not wanting to lie there pondering a mystery to which there was no solution, and went to the bathroom to take a long warm shower. Drying himself, he sprinkled eau de Cologne on his chest, rubbing some of it on his forehead, and dressed himself in clean white trousers and a black shirt.

He went to the kitchen where Juanita had just arrived to make his dinner. She stood at the sink, cleaning up the things from his breakfast, and turned round when she heard him enter.

'How's your boy?' he asked.

'A little better,' she said, 'but I'm still worried about him.'

'Listen, why don't you take the evening off? I can do without dinner tonight. I really have no appetite. You should be with your boy, it's more important.'

She could smell the perfume from his body across the room, and thought that he planned to entertain some woman.

'I'll go if you don't want me,' she said.

'What were you planning to make for my dinner?'

'Bean soup, some meat and fried potatoes, and a flan. And a salad if you wanted one.'

'Why don't you take with you all that you were going to use for my dinner, and take some extra beans and potatoes, and make a nice little meal for your family?'

She looked at him with surprise and wondered what had come over him – he wasn't his normal self. Perhaps he had some really pretty mistress coming tonight and he was in a specially generous mood.

When she had gone, he poured himself a little Scotch, diluting it with a lot of water. He hesitated about drinking, but then convinced himself that he was perfectly well and that the sun had disappeared behind the house and would soon be setting. At least he did not need to fear the heat of the sun, or its light. He went and sat on the verandah with his drink.

The garden was in a general shadow but filled with an indirect light that showed the plants in all their details. It was, he thought, a soothing prospect. There was nothing startling or menacing in his vision. But he began to feel a vague resentment with life, for the unfamiliar events of the day had seemed to be threatening in a way that he could not understand; the world about him was serene, he himself was composed and without a sense of pain. But the suddenness with which his body had collapsed in the afternoon made him wonder whether the present calm was not a subtle disguise of some overwhelming affliction that had taken possession of him. He tried to think of Elvira and the

51

diverting prospect of having her as a mistress. He imagined the most rapturous conjoinings with her lovely body, and lingered over thrilling caresses. But the vivid imagery of pleasure, he realized with astonishment, did not excite him; instead of filling him with joyous anticipation and an expectation of greater fulfilment, the imagery left him indifferent and cold. He swallowed the contents of his glass hurriedly and went and made himself a stronger drink. Returning to his chair, and taking a sip, he put the glass aside, finding the drink insipid even though the burning sensation trickled down his throat. Suddenly he resolved that he had to leave Santa Rosa. Yes, he thought excitedly, *that* was it, he needed to return to the city. He had been in the wilderness long enough. The boredom that came from repetition, he began to feel convinced, was what was afflicting him, and that is why, he concluded, even the opportunity of an affair with the beautiful Elvira left him cold. He would take a trip first of all. He would go to Valparaíso and take a ship. Cross the vast ocean. Be cradled by the swelling water. Other images of the world – all mountains and great expanses of water – rushed to his mind and he already saw himself, passport in hand, crossing frontiers. This life was no more for him.

The excitement of the imaginary travels lasted some twenty minutes, and then his mood changed. It had grown dark, but Don Bueno was no longer seeing the world in front of him. The image of the boat in the river during his morning jog came to his mind. *That* was where he had seen the man in the dark brown shirt whose presence during lunch at the Café Madrid had made him wonder why he appeared vaguely familiar. He must have been worrying about it at the back of his mind all day long, even when he had passed out at María de Lurdes's. Funny how the mind worked, digging away at useless information and presenting it to you when you had no need for it.

Frogs and cicadas had begun to make a din in the garden. The question came to Don Bueno: *What have I done*?

'A life of crime and lechery,' he heard himself say. And now a new reason suggested itself to his mind as to why the imagery of making love to Elvira had not excited him. Could it be that his soul sought repentance? He chuckled, dismissing the question. What a ridiculous idea! But he found his own mirth quickly stifled when another question occurred to him. Could it be that he was sickened by his degenerate body? If he had been the instrument of God, it had only been to commit evil.

The thought horrified him. He tried to drive it out of his mind by saying to himself that he did not believe in God, that the world was nothing but a meaningless heap of matter, but realized that that was like trying to tell a man dying of cancer that the world was only an illusion. The reality of pain was too strong for any philosophy to comfort.

He swallowed his drink and stood up, and became conscious of the darkness that had fallen. A life of crime and lechery! The phrase repeated itself in his mind. The cicadas had grown louder. From a distant street, he heard the sound of drums. He remembered what Rufino, the owner of the Café y Bar Santa Cruz, had said, that there would be music. The sound of the drums was coming from another direction, though. A life of crime and lechery! A rage had built up within Don Bueno. He wished he could hurl his whole body at the world.

He switched on the lights in the verandah and walked to his bedroom where he drew the curtains across the window after turning on the light, seeing, just as he brought his hands together with the two ends of the heavy dark grey material of the curtains, a dead fly on the windowsill. He took out his wallet from the back pocket of the trousers he had worn earlier in the day and, remembering that it contained no money, he put it down on a table next to the bed. There was a safe built into the wall and he opened it after working the combination lock. It contained stacks of bank notes in the currencies of three different countries. Don Bueno took the money he needed and then, out of habit, opened one of the drawers of the safe that contained gold coins, for he had a compulsion, every time he opened the safe, to hold the coins in his hand. The gesture being an automatic one, he pulled out the wrong drawer – or perhaps he was driven to do so by some unconscious motive. He found himself looking at a revolver and a knife with a rosewood handle, both placed upon some certificates of securities that he held in foreign banks. He picked up the knife.

Its weight in his hand evoked several memories that went back to the time when he was a teenager. It was a small, thick knife, and needed a deft movement of both hands to get the blade to swing out of the handle. Don Bueno's hands instinctively carried out the movement, and the blade shone back at him. He passed a finger over its edge and found it was still keen. He held the point against the flesh of his index finger, felt a curious thrill, and then flicked the blade back into the safety of the handle.

The knife in one hand, he closed the safe, and went through the kitchen to the back of the house, taking a flashlight with him. A tree grew there which bore bitter berries. Holding the flashlight in his left hand, he made several long scratches with the blade of the knife on a lower branch of the tree until the bark was torn away. Then, in a slow, deliberate movement, he rubbed the blade up and down on both sides for two or three minutes until a milky greenish liquid appeared. He had learned many years earlier that the juice of this particular tree, when drawn by a steel blade in the manner that he had just done, had the effect of tipping the blade with poison that caused instant death when it entered human flesh.

He carefully turned the blade until it was safe inside the handle, put the knife into his pocket, and wondered, though only for a moment, why he felt the compulsion on this night to have the knife with him.

Before leaving the house, he put on a lightweight tan-coloured jacket and as he walked out of the front garden, he pulled out the knife from his trousers pocket and placed it in the right outside pocket of his jacket. The noise of drumming and the constant honking of car horns was coming from the direction of the square, and he went

54

there. When he reached it, he found the streets leading to the square, together with the streets around the square, were full of cars with people packed in them, arms hanging out of windows and palms thumping on the sides of the cars while the driver of each car had his hand pressed to the horn. Some people waved bottles of beer from the windows of cars, and everyone was shouting and repeatedly breaking out into a chant. The sound of the drums was coming from the centre of the square which was filled with people, some in grotesque masks and all of them joining the chant whenever it began from some part of the square or from the back of some pickup truck where beer-drinking men swung their arms and shouted together.

Don Bueno soon realized that the town was celebrating the national football team's victory over a neighbouring country, an event that seemed to have the effect of bringing out the devil in everyone. Not wishing to be part of that sort of crowd, he went into the Café Madrid, but found that there was not a seat to be had. He began to work his way out of the square, regretting having come there in the first place. The movement of the crowd made it difficult for him to choose a direction and the wild current of the mass of humanity carried him across the square, so that when he finally succeedèd in extricating himself from the crowd he found himself, with an enormous sense of relief, in a street that led to the Café y Bar Santa Cruz.

The bar was more crowded than usual, every table being already taken and a group of men crowding by the long counter where Rufino stood in front of an old calendar photograph of a nude blonde with blue eyes wearing a pearl necklace and high heels, trying to serve his clamouring clients as fast as he could. Don Bueno walked up to the crowd of men at the counter and said aloud, 'Hey, Rufino, I thought you'd keep a table for me – remember you said this morning that I should come?'

Rufino was deftly measuring out rum into three glasses. He filled the glasses with one swift movement of his right hand, quickly pushed the glasses with his left hand in the direction of the customers, looked above the head of the crowd in front of him and, while taking the money and counting out the change, said, 'Oh, hello, Don Bueno! It was a great victory.'

He jerked his face to stare at another customer and while hearing his order, he also heard Don Bueno say, 'Never mind the victory, I consider myself your guest since you invited me especially. What about a table?'

'In a minute, in a minute,' Rufino shouted at Don Bueno while the customer he was listening to completed his order.

'Where did all these devils come from?' Don Bueno said aloud with disgust.

Rufino pulled a glass from under the counter, turned his back quickly and in an instant flung himself round again, holding an iced bottle of beer which he opened with the rapid movement of a magician, simply by flicking the bottle top against an opener screwed into the side of the counter, and pushed both the glass and the bottle to the customer while at the same time producing before him a packet of potato chips. 'I'll make a table for you, Don Bueno, just give me a minute.' As he spoke those words, he took the customer's money and gave him his change and turned his head to the person he thought should be served next.

The man who had just bought the beer moved out of the crowd to go back to a table, and Don Bueno, exploiting the gap created for his retreat by others in the crowd, took the opportunity to push himself forward. A couple of men on either side of him pushed their shoulders against him to indicate their displeasure at his attempt to be served before them. For a moment, he thought that he should go home, for it was tiresome to be in this crowd; but the thought passed quickly out of his mind when he felt the man on his left dig his elbow into his ribs. Anger surged within him, and it became a question of honour with him that he, Don Bueno, a valued resident of Santa Rosa, a friend of Rufino who had himself said he should come tonight to the bar, should have to put up with a vulgar crowd. He dug his elbow back into the man who had offended him and, pushing still farther until there was only one man standing between him and Rufino, he shouted, 'Make mine a straight whiskey, Rufino.'

Rufino had just finished serving a rum to another customer a little to the left and seeing that it was the turn of the man who stood in front of Don Bueno, turned his face to him with an enquiring look. Before the man could order, however, Don Bueno shouted over his shoulder, 'You heard me, Rufino, I'll have a whiskey.'

Rufino still stared at the other man and again before the latter could state his order, Don Bueno shouted, 'God damn it, Rufino, I gave you my order! I said a whiskey.'

The man in front of Don Bueno turned round and stared at him. Don Bueno was momentarily startled, almost confused. But then he recognized the black hair, the dark brown shirt – the stranger he had seen in the morning in the boat from the mission and later at the Café Madrid.

'A little patience, old sir,' the man said. 'Everyone will have his turn.'

The anger that had been building up in Don Bueno now turned to a rage, and he cried aloud, 'Old, am I? *Old*! How dare you come to my world and take precedence over me? It's *you* who owe me your life! I'll show you who is *old*!' He flung out his hand and slapped the man hard across the face. There were gasps, the crowd parted, men at the tables went suddenly quiet and looked up. But the man did not flinch, only stared back incomprehensibly at Don Bueno, as if petrified by the sudden shock.

'Who knows this man's name?' Don Bueno shouted, swinging his head in a gesture that suggested the question was being put to everyone present in the bar. In the complete silence, a chair scraped the floor while someone tried to get a better view of the drama. '*I'll* tell you his name,' Don Bueno continued to shout. 'We have them from time to time, these motherfuckers who come from nowhere. They come and stand in front of you, and you can be wanting to fall into your grave but you have to ask these motherfuckers their permission. I'll tell you his name!'

Don Bueno took a step forward and threw his right fist at the man. The latter had been watching him intently and he quickly moved to the side to avoid the blow. His fist punching empty air threw Don Bueno off balance, but the position he fell into was one from which he could quickly spring up, which he did in an instant, simultaneously flinging up his left fist which caught the man beneath his jaw, making him stagger back. One or two in the crowd whistled on seeing the perfectly executed left hook. But the man, recovering his balance and apparently not hurt, stood still, staring at Don Bueno.

'Coward!' Don Bueno shouted, seeing that the man took punishment but did not fight back.

Suddenly, Don Bueno pulled out his knife, flicked it open and held it up in the air. The crowd gave a gasp and Rufino said, 'Now that's enough, Don Bueno. You've gone far enough.'

But Don Bueno stood glowering at the man, the knife held firmly in his hand, the blade pointed toward the man. One or two men sitting at the tables stood up and made to move toward Don Bueno. He swung around, brandishing the knife and shouting, 'Any other cowards here? Any other cuntlickers who want to crawl right back where they came from?' The men who had risen returned to their seats.

'You're my guest, Don Bueno,' Rufino said. 'Please drop that knife.'

Don Bueno took a step toward the man in the dark brown shirt and dropped the knife in front of his feet. 'Pick it up!' he shouted to the man.

The man stood staring at Don Bueno for a while and then stooped and picked up the knife. He held it in front of him, the blade pointing away from his stomach.

'Here's your whiskey, Don Bueno,' Rufino said, forcing a laugh from his throat. 'A double. It's on the house.'

His laughter and voice died away quickly. The crowd sat or stood without making the slightest movement.

At that moment, Don Bueno held his two fists together

in front of himself, and gave out a loud roar. In the middle of his roar, he flung himself at the man who was standing as before, the knife in front of him. Don Bueno seemed to leap through the air, his jacket front flying open, his fists up at the level of the man's head. The man stood passively, though tensed in every muscle; he jerked back instinctively when he saw the crazed older man take the flying leap at him, so that his hand moved up from where it had rested against the stomach and consequently the angle of the knife's blade tilted upward. Don Bueno crashed against him, his fists going over the man's shoulders, so that he seemed to have flung himself for the sole purpose of embracing the man. And indeed, for a couple of moments it appeared that he was tightly clutching the man to his bosom, as an overemotional person does with a long-lost relative. Then, in a slow backward movement, he became disengaged and leaned away from the man, and then suddenly fell, his body hitting the floor with a thud. The knife was stuck in just below his ribs.

The man in the dark brown shirt immediately fell on his knees and leaned next to him with his hands on the floor just above Don Bueno's shoulders. There was a cry from the crowd and several people rushed up to stand round the two men on the ground.

Several voices were shouting simultaneously; glasses and bottles resumed clinking. What a crazy thing to have happened! they were all exclaiming. Had Don Bueno gone mad, or what? How terrible! It was all his own doing; the other, poor man, had only stood there, shitting in his pants. Lord, how life turns ugly!

A fierce and terrified look in his eyes, Don Bueno stared at the man leaning above him. His mouth slightly open, Don Bueno's face shook slowly from side to side as if in disbelief that such a horror had to occur, that this was the death destined for him. He wanted to scream but his throat felt constricted, and his voice, a choked whisper, could only express one word. He was looking fiercely at the man when he spoke it.

'César!'

The look of horror in his eyes stayed with Don Bueno when he died. The man in the dark brown shirt, now stained with blood, stood up, trembling. No one else had heard the dying man call him by his name.

# 3

Holding the bars of the iron gate, the little boy stared out at the world, his dark brown eyes fixed at the ocean across the road and the sandy expanse. It was the first time he had made it to the gate on his own, dragging himself across the lawn in his blue shorts, standing up and spurting forward on his wobbly legs, falling, pushing himself along the grass with his hands and feet, standing up again and making for the gate, determined to reach it without another fall.

A woman, sitting in a wicker chair under the shade of a wide-spreading flamboyant tree, had been encouraging him, and seeing him at last clutch the bars of the gate and look back at her in glee, she clapped her hands and said aloud, 'Well done, César!'

Cars went past on the road just outside the gate, but the two-year-old boy, tightly holding the bars, stared at the ocean, fascinated. A ship with a black hull was sailing across the horizon, and he looked with amazement at the great silent object slowly gliding over the blue water.

The woman's brown eyes shone with pleasure as she watched the boy. A bead of perspiration ran down her narrow nose. She sipped from a glass of orange juice and put it down on a table beside her. Picking up her sunglasses and a straw hat with a wide brim and a pink band that trailed over the brim, she put them on. She rose from her chair to go to the boy. Her white bikini seemed to highlight her smooth tanned skin, especially when she came out of the shade into the bright sunlight. A little broad at the hips, and thighs beginning to be

61

somewhat heavy, she was well proportioned with full, rounded breasts and a flat stomach that, on longish legs, made her figure quite striking. Her skin appeared flawless, even at the neck and on the face, and where her wavy auburn hair fell on her shoulders, the tanned flesh appeared firm. She went and stood beside the boy, passing her hand over his head with its soft black hair, and said, 'What do you see, César?'

The boy lifted his face to her and she saw a look of incomprehension in his eyes. He unclutched one of his fists and raised his arm to point a finger at the ship.

'That's an oil tanker,' she said, and then repeated the word slowly, deliberately shaping her lips to pronounce the word. 'Oil . . . tank . . . er.'

The boy watched her lips remain parted at the end of the word, and, turning to look at the ship, he raised his hand again to point to it while he said, 'Papa.'

'No, darling, papa's not in it,' she said, her hand now at the boy's cheek. 'Papa's gone to the city. He'll be back soon.'

She wished she knew how soon. He had gone away so suddenly, without telling her anything.

'Pa-pa,' the boy repeated.

'Yes, darling, he'll be back soon. Let's go in now. It's time for our nap. Nappy-nap for poopsy-pooh.'

She went to pick him up, but he made an expression of disagreement, shaking his head and pulling away his hand when she held it. She saw that he wanted to walk by himself. 'Come on, then, my sweet,' she said, indulging him.

His red pedal car stood on the path and the boy stumbled toward it and, holding its rear end, began to push it around the garden, his little steps accelerating, his mouth open, a continuous loud sound emanating from it in imitation of a high-revving engine. He ran round in wide loops, coming perilously close to the flower beds, and it seemed to his mother that at any moment the car would go ahead of him, leaving him with grazed knees and a bruised forehead. But each time he swung in her direction, his eyes looked up quickly at her and she saw there his delight at being watched by her, and she stood feeling both an apprehension that he might soon be injured and a thrill that he was managing so well.

He had been slow to develop, taking far longer than other children she had observed to say his first words and begin to walk, causing her months of anxiety from the fear that he might be retarded or be afflicted with some obscure disease. She had seen signs in him of lethargy and had been made miserable by his apparently stubborn refusal to be coaxed into repeating words after her. But then suddenly he had begun to grow in a rush as if he had to make up lost time, and now he was bursting with energy all day long and picking up new words every day.

'Come on now, César,' she called as he went dashing past, 'you can play later. We'll go to the beach after your nap.'

'Beach, beach, beach!' he shouted, continuing to push his car across the lawn.

She decided to wait a few minutes to see if he would exhaust himself. His father should be here now, she thought, to see his son growing strong and healthy. He had been too critical of César's slowness to develop and had spoken of the boy with unnecessary severity. It was terrible, the way he had scorned the child. As though he were not of his own flesh, or not a human baby but bred by some monster. Once, she had seen him cringe when the child crawled on all fours to where he was sitting and tapped his foot, trying to clutch the toe that stuck out of the sandal. For a second, the horrible thought had passed her mind that he was about to kick the child away, but he'd only withdrawn his leg. César had looked up at the huge man in the chair, his distant eyes glowering at him, and begun to cry. Watching him now pushing his car around, it suddenly struck her that it had been during the last fortnight, when his father had been away, that César had entered this new phase of being so energetic.

She saw that he had tired of his game and quickly went and picked him up. He made a whining sound, and she threw him up in the air, saying, 'There, who is going to reach up to the sky? Who is going to be big and who is going to be strong? And who is going to fall right where he belongs?'

He shrieked with pleasure, enjoying the sensation of flying up and landing safely in her arms. 'More, more!' he cried, obliging her to repeat the action several times.

'César, you don't know how heavy you've grown,' she said, putting him on the ground.

'Beach, beach, beach,' he piped, walking with her to the house.

'Yes, we'll go to the beach later.'

The memory of the first five years of his life in the house by the ocean had lain buried in César Calderón's mind until one day about twenty-five years later, when Leticia, the woman he was living with, called him to the kitchen and said, 'César, cut that pomegranate and empty it into this bowl, will you, please?' She passed him a porcelain bowl from where she stood by the sink washing spinach. 'Then put a cup of red wine into it, there's enough left in yesterday's bottle.'

He placed the pomegranate on a cutting board and, taking a knife from a drawer, sliced the fruit in half. The two halves fell apart and the faint fragrance of the pomegranate rose to his nostrils; at the same time, he saw the white seeds in the smooth, glistening red flesh of the fruit, and a little juice oozing across the cut surface, a few drops appearing there like drops of blood. The sight of the trickling juice and the pomegranate's particular aroma suddenly took him back a quarter of a century to the house by the ocean. There, in the large garden, was a pomegranate tree whose arching branches were covered all spring with red flowers and then little deep-orange berries which gradually grew into large, round russet-colored pomegranates, streaked with vermilion. His mother must have given him the fruit to eat as soon as he had teeth with which to chew, but he did not remember that; his memory was of a particular afternoon when he himself plucked a pomegranate and sat down in the shade with a knife and cut it open, and proceeded to chew the fruit rapidly, spitting out the seeds into a flower bed where they would not be seen by his mother. He must have been nearly five years old then, for he remembered that they left the house soon after to go and live in the city.

The iron gate was kept locked, and he would stand for long periods of time looking through its bars at the ocean. Every morning, from ten until noon, and sometimes in the evening, his mother took him to the beach where there were other children to play with, but he lost interest in the ocean when he was on the edge of the water. He retained no vivid memory of playing on the sand, except for a vague blur of being with kids who emptied pails of sandy water on one another's heads, made sand pies or even ambitious architectural structures with the wet sand, and yelled at being dragged into the water by their mothers. The ocean had mystery only when he saw it through the iron bars, especially in the late afternoon when the beach was deserted and few cars passed on the road.

Then, heat rising from the white sand created a haze that had the effect of making the ocean appear distant and, as it were, trapped behind glass on which condensation had collected. The garden, in which he spent hours by himself, seemed to grow smaller and more confined as he grew taller; all that orange of the marigolds and white and purple of the periwinkles and the cascading magenta of the climbing bougainvillaea flooded his vision with such intensity that he felt a pain in his eyes, and he turned away to look at the soothing ocean and sometimes had the thrilling sensation that the great body of blue had drawn him into its dark depth.

'César,' he heard his mother's voice call from a window of the house, 'come in for your nap, it's too hot out in the sun.'

He hastily spat out the pomegranate seeds and wiped his mouth with the back of his hand, but continued to lurk in the garden. She did not call a second time or come out to carry him in as she used to do. Except for the daily visit to the beach, she rarely came out of the house now, but remained in her room, frowning and complaining of a headache. Sometimes the maid would tell César not to make a noise because his mother had just taken an aspirin and was lying down. He was too young to understand ideas of sadness and despair, but her absence from the garden, like a gap left by the chopping down of a tree, made an impression on him.

By calling him once, and then abandoning him in the garden, she was weakly going through the motions of her life instead of existing with any purpose. The happiness she had found in her son had been diminished by his father abandoning them, and it seemed to her that the son's birth had been the cause of the father's rejection. For they had lived in perfect contentment before, kissing each other even on the beach when they were not alone. She could not understand the brutal change in the man and his unnatural loathing of his son. When a few months had passed after his disappearance and her anxiety had turned into a desperate worry, she had gone to the city for three days, leaving César with the maid. None of the friends they had in common knew anything. She discovered at the bank, however, that he had left a good quantity of money in her name. He had closed his own account, the bank manager revealed to her when she persisted with her questions. That was all he could tell her. While it was some comfort that he had not abandoned her penniless, the transfer of the money indicated some irrevocable decision on his part, and she returned to the house by the ocean, convinced that César would henceforth remain fatherless and she in a most lamentable condition – cast aside without a word by the man who had loved her so dearly. Her misery was the greater because he had shown no concern at all for her feelings; had he left after a quarrel, or after disclosing why he preferred to live separately, or in any manner that gave her an understanding of his reasons, she would not have felt so insulted and despised as she now did. By transferring the money to her name, he gave the impression of paying off a whore he no longer wished to see. The passing of the months, and then the years – it was three years now since he had disappeared – first brought on moods of depression in which she could not eat and was irritated by César's demands on her, then a prolonged period of indifference to the world around her, and finally a profound inertia in which she did not have the will to do anything. She did the things that had to be done, but perfunctorily and without any interest. The skin on her face had gone slack; tiny wrinkles had appeared at the corners of her mouth and her eyes; her narrow nose that had been so admired by everyone now seemed to stick out prominently, for her cheeks had become sunken; and although she was only thirty-one, streaks of grey had begun to appear in her hair. She kept the shutters of the house closed, finding the light insufferable, and the ocean's blue, which could be glimpsed from most of the rooms, too blinding.

One afternoon, César realized he could climb up a tree that grew on the side of the house and sit cradled among some branches and gaze out at the ocean. From there, he could look down on the neighbour's garden, and he saw that one limb of the tree hung low over some bushes there. There was a stone wall at front of the garden but the gate there was a wooden one, held only by a latch as he observed when a maid came out of the house, went to the gate, and opened it simply by flicking up the latch and pulling at a handle. He came out in a sweat, suddenly terrified by the thought that he could easily, by jumping into the neighbour's garden, sneak out. What he had longed for in his own garden, to turn to the ocean when he was trapped behind the locked gate, could easily be achieved, and the idea frightened him so much that he hurriedly climbed down the tree and went running into the house where his mother lay in a darkened room.

'What's the matter?' she asked, sitting up in bed and holding him when he flung himself toward her. 'You gave me such a fright, what happened?'

But he could only cry and press himself to her where she rocked him gently, passing her hand over his head. Assuming that he must have been asleep in his own room, she thought that he must have had a bad dream. The confusion of feelings within him prompted him to say something, even if it was only one word, and through his sobs he found himself repeating, 'Papa, papa.'

She held him close, saying, 'My poor boy, my poor darling César!' And she herself began to cry with him. He clung to her tightly, his cheek against hers, and finding the stream of tears on his cheek came from his mother's eyes, he fastened his arms around her even more tightly.

'You're hurting me,' she cried but did not ask him to release her.

'That's easily explicable,' Leticia said when he had described his memory to her. 'You longed for freedom when you knew you could not have it but, seeing an opportunity to be free, you ran from it.'

He looked at her with a slight sneer on his face. She always came up with glib explanations, reducing situations that to him had no meaning or a meaning too mysterious to be understood to some banal psychological perception. She loved to hear people's dreams and give them complicated interpretations, and could not see a movie without wanting to have a long discussion at the end concerning its real meaning. 'Leticia, I was five years old then!'

'The memory is more complex than that,' she said in the complacent manner of one to whom everything is subtle, but perfectly comprehensible. 'You were afraid that if you took the way open to you and went out into the world, that you would find your father. That is why you ran to your mother, and why you clung to her so fiercely: you wished to return to a prenatal state.'

He wished that he had not mentioned the memory to her, for he hated it when she insisted on analysing every detail. 'But, Leticia, don't you see I was afraid of drowning myself? It's as simple as that. Besides, I missed my

68

father. Why should I have been afraid of finding him?'

He realized as he asked the question that he was invit-ing a deeper analysis from her whereas his intention had been to stop the discussion before it became an argument.

'Because,' she said calmly, 'you really hated him.'

'That's ridiculous! There's nothing a five-year-old can do if he hates his father.'

'That is precisely the point,' she said. 'You are five years old, you hate your father for his desertion. You don't want to go into the world where you might find him. Not because you might do something to him but because you are too small to do anything. Your rage is against yourself, at your own impotence. You have a huge fear inside you that you will always remain small, always be in the same situation of terror. You should know, César, that at the age of five we are closer to the truth of our being: we haven't begun to wear masks, and everyone knows us by our first name.'

He could see that she was warming up to a long lecture and tried to stop her by agreeing with her and praising the astuteness of her perception. She smiled, savouring the flattery that she had no reason to believe was not sincere, and he took the opportunity to talk of a new subject.

Night had fallen but it was still too early for his mother to return from work. The small apartment on the second floor picked up every sound from the narrow street and reproduced it as a continuous roaring noise. César stood at the window, his bare arms hanging over the sill. At eight years, he was slightly taller than the urchins who played in the street and whose company his mother for-bade him in order to save him from becoming like them. There was not much flesh on his cheeks; that, together with the absence of any peculiarity in the shape of his nose, made his dark brown eyes appear large and, perhaps therefore, melancholy. He looked down on the conges-tion of dilapidated old buses, with black clouds of smoke from their exhausts; rickety trucks that rattled when they moved and whose engines made a loud, clattering noise when they idled; little yellow taxis honking their horns; and innumerable hand-drawn carts, both on the road and on the sidewalks. The wares of the shops flowed out to the sidewalks, and clusters of people stood in front of them, gesticulating and talking loudly. Barefooted boys ran in and out of the traffic and the crowds of people, the tails of their dirty shirts flying behind them out of their shorts, chasing one another in some wild game of chance or trickery.

César hated the hour when it became dark and it was still too early for his mother to return. Until this night, however, it was only her absence that he dreaded, and the fear that she might not return; but now he noticed two men standing in front of a shop across the street, looking up at him while they talked. The gestures of their hands and the way they jerked their heads in his direction made him think they were talking of him. Their grins appeared to him to be malicious and full of evil intent. He wanted to move away from the window but found himself frozen there, and was terrified. He had begun to feel a new kind of fear that had nothing to do with the absence of his mother. The men suddenly shook hands and walked away in opposite directions. César breathed a little more easily, but the idea of fear had become lodged within him, and he wished his mother would come at once so that he could pretend that nothing had changed.

The dinner hour approached and the congestion in the street gave way to a steady flow of traffic with the buses grinding past in second gear. César felt hungry, but knew he must wait. He had looked into the kitchen. There were a couple of pots and a pan, all scrubbed clean; of the jars on a shelf, one had half a kilo of rice in it, another some flour, and three others were empty. He put a pinch of rice grains into his mouth and chewed them, but found the taste revolting.

Seeing that the street was less crowded, he had an idea. He slipped out of the apartment, closing the door behind him, and raced down the dark staircase where a naked bulb, long dead, had remained unreplaced. He walked rapidly down the sidewalk, dodging past the cluster of people outside some shops. He was glad that the urchins had gone home by now. But he was mistaken and his sense of having the freedom of the street was short-lived.

'Hey, Mr Good Guy!' a voice shrieked behind him.

'Hey, mama's little backscratcher!' shouted another.

'Hey, motherfucker!' yelled a third.

César saw over his shoulder the three kids running after him. Earlier in the year, one of them, seeing César for the first time, had invited him to some game in the street, but César, too naïve at the time to know better, had truthfully answered, 'My mother does not want me to play with you.' Screaming 'Fuck you, snotnose!' the boy had aimed a fist at him, but César had escaped unharmed. Since then, it was an agony for him to venture alone into the street. He knew from their taunts that if they ever caught him they would not leave him until they had scratched his eyes out. He had even found himself hoping one day that one of the boys would get run over and be killed so that the parents of the others would then forbid them to play in the street.

And now, there they were, running after him, a dozen paces behind. He bolted like a rabbit, making a wild dash for the street corner where the traffic light was changing. If he could get across just before the traffic began to move, his pursuers would be blocked by it. He could hear some of the drivers already revving up and others honking their horns. He flew over the sidewalk and onto the cross street where there was a roar of engines to his right. He was in the middle of the street when the light turned green and the entire block of traffic seemed to take off like a great steaming monster let loose from hell. He saw nothing but heard the loud screeching of brakes and felt the hot mouth of a radiator grill close to his right arm and leg, but it did not swallow him up, and he reached the opposite sidewalk, hearing, in the same confused moment, a thud and then a crash behind him, but he went on running without looking back.

71

He did not stop for breath until he had reached the square where he made straight for the corner where two policemen stood outside a supermarket. He felt safe by the door near which they stood, watching the customers come and go. His heart still beating fast, he stepped inside the open door, and stood beside the row of empty carts with their green handles branded in white with the supermarket's name. There was quite a crowd in that corner, with people coming in constantly, pulling out a cart and wheeling it away, and others who had just checked out, walking away with their full sacks. He had to look hard to find her through all those people who obscured his sight. But there she was! At a checkout counter, pushing aside the items she had already punched on the cash register. He thought she looked important as she counted out great sums of money and then deftly rang up the next customer's shopping. He stood there, watching her for several minutes.

Suddenly, she dashed out of her counter, and he saw her run down an aisle. He slipped through the crowd to see where she had gone. She was already coming back, holding a boy of eight or ten by the collar. The boy wore a buttoned-up shirt over blue shorts and from the bulge at his stomach, César could see that he had hidden something there. He watched his mother in amazement as she dragged the boy to a glass booth where a man sat with piles of paper in front of him. He could hear her voice without hearing the words, and from the tone and the gestures of her hands he could tell that the boy was in trouble. Soon she was back at the counter, and the man in the glass booth disappeared with the boy to the rear of the supermarket. Afraid that he would meet a similar fate, César quietly walked out of the supermarket and went and stood on the sidewalk. He decided not to stand too near the policemen, but not too far from them either in case the urchins discovered him there. The twenty minutes before the supermarkets closed and another ten before his mother came out seemed to him a long wait. He practised arithmetic by adding up the numbers on the licence plates of cars that went by: 315 was 9; 244 was 10. He diverted himself by giving himself an imaginary prize each time the numbers added up to 10. It happened thrice and each time he stood to attention and, imagining that his hand belonged to someone else, some principal of a school, he pinned an unseen medal of distinction on his own breast.

But there she was at last! Walking out with a sack in her arms. She looked serious. He restrained the impulse to run up to her. She might scold him. He was supposed to be at home. So, he walked behind her, trying to step with his little feet exactly on the same spots on the sidewalk where her feet had trod before him.

They came to the crossroads where he had had to run for his life. There was a huge congestion there. A bus had run into the back of a car. A police car stood behind the bus. A red light beamed from its roof. The traffic there was squeezed into a single line. Many people stood near the bus, talking loudly. There were several policemen in the crowd. His mother did not stop but crossed the road as soon as she could. He trotted behind her while looking anxiously around him to see if any of the urchins were about.

At another time, Leticia said, 'You're full of fears, César. In all your memories someone is out to get you.' She was standing at the kitchen sink, cleaning mushrooms, too preoccupied to enter into a discussion. He enjoyed sitting at the kitchen table with a beer when she worked on the dinner. She moved busily about between the sink and the range, now washing the peeled potatoes and slicing them on a chopping board; turning to stir something already being cooked; mixing some ingredients in the blender; taking spices out of a cupboard and banging it shut – she made a continuous din while cooking and scattered a lot of pans, plates and knives on the working surface next to the sink. Later, after they had eaten, she would sit with the remains of her glass of wine while he quietly did the washing-up. When she was not talking, she liked to hear him speak, and when he was not there she switched on a small transistor radio.

When he returned from the school one afternoon – he was twelve at the time – he was surprised to see that his mother was at home. She called to him from her bedroom when she heard him enter the apartment, and he found her sitting up in bed with her glasses on, mending one of his shirts. He looked at her but avoided her eyes, knowing they looked funny behind the thick lenses: larger and slightly cross-eyed.

'I've sent for my mother to help us out,' she said.

He stared at her stupidly, not knowing what had happened. She said something about not being well, but could not explain to him that the grinding misery of her existence was slowly crushing her. The money César's father had left her nearly ten years ago had seemed an enormous sum at the time, and indeed would have served her handsomely had someone advised her that she ought to invest a good portion of it to secure a future income. But the shock induced by the abandonment had made her sink into a profound lethargy, almost a total inertia, during the years that she still lived on in the house by the ocean, where what little she did, like taking César to the beach, seemed to be prompted by habit and not by an immediate will. Only the persistent headaches informed her of a present that had to be endured, and she lay, dosing herself with pills, hoping for that very present to turn into oblivion.

What had rescued her from that state of inertia had been another shock – a bank statement that showed her that she had practically nothing left. She could not believe it, especially as she had not engaged in any form of extravagance. She recovered her will, and her drive to live, and wrote to her bank demanding an explanation of the loss of her fortune. The manager replied: did she not know that there had been an inflation of over 100 per cent during the last several years?

Now thirty-eight, her face seemed to be drawn back by wrinkles, the skin sagging at the corners of her mouth;

during the last three years her eyesight had deteriorated, and the spectacles, which made her eyes appear so frightening to César, seemed to enlarge the wrinkles around her eyes and make her nose look conspicuously pointed.

The grandmother arrived, and entered into César's memories as an unceasing monologue. Into the background cacophony of street noises was introduced the shrill voice of the bent little woman with her stooping shoulders and grey hair pulled back and stuck into a rubber band. She talked even when she was alone in the kitchen and César, doing his homework by the window to the street, found that even when the street was a crush of traffic, with every vehicle filling the air with the clatter of its engine and the honking of its horn, and people in front of the shops shouted and the kids yelled as they flew about the sidewalks, he still heard the grandmother's voice, sometimes as a drone and sometimes as sharp little phrases that pierced his ears.

'Going away with the first man who comes along in a fancy car, if you please! No religion, no fear of God; who was born for such a life? I always told you, keep your skirt on, wear blouses with high collars, buttoned up. You can't trust any man who's not decent enough to stand with you at the altar. It's God's judgement. A little romance, if you please! Running away from home to live among pimps and whores.'

'Mother!'

'What's the difference? A life of idleness and sin. Who was born for such a life? We had a nice patch of land, strong god-fearing young men in the town to whom the land was a good dowry. But we have a modern daughter who wants a modern life, if you please! Now look at you, a fine home you've made for yourself and your boy! And where are all those friends with cars and houses by the sea? Who wants to know you now? Who wants the burnt scrapings from the bottom of the pan? Oh, it's modern living this and modern living that. And money falls from the sky, if you please! A life of pimps and whores. Who was born for such a life?'

'Mother, please! You don't want César to hear.'

But the grandmother never stopped, and César believed that she must talk even when he was at school and his mother at the supermarket.

One day he was sitting at the window, struggling with algebra, when the grandmother came shuffling up to him. Some of her hair had fallen out of the rubber band and stuck out over her ears. Her hollow, wrinkled face, with the front teeth missing, and her black beady eyes that caught some light from the street, the entire face coming close to his with a scowling look, frightened him. She stood less than a metre away from him and, jabbing the air with a pointed finger that seemed intent on poking his right eye, she said, 'And you, nice airs you take on! She is going to make a good man out of you, a gentleman, if you please! As if a boy can become a man without having a father, as if you can ever hope to spend a day without looking for him!'

His mother had earlier withdrawn to her room, but she called from there, 'Mother, please!'

But the grandmother took a step closer to him. Her small figure appeared to him to become monstrously large. 'Go, go and find him, if you please! Run from the woman, and go and find your father, hug him, embrace him, but stick a knife into his chest and let him fall at your feet. Is this why he gave you life? Ha!'

She waved her arms around and swung her head, and César saw the dingy apartment, heard the ferocious noise of the street, and behind the shrieking fury in front of him he caught a glimpse of his mother's shadow in the doorway. In the light, the grandmother's mouth opened like a black hole, her beady eyes were again close to him, the finger once more threatened to poke his eye. 'Who was born for such life, ha! How can you call yourself a man until you have killed the monster that created you? The fruit of a sinner, you must sin too. Go, go and find him, go hug the man who did the foul deed. You will never be free until he falls at your feet and with his dying breath claims you as his son!'

Sweat had begun to fall from César's brow; he was

trembling. He saw that his mother had fallen in the doorway. But his grandmother was spread above him like an enormous spider, the wrinkles of her face stretching out, it seemed, to create a vast canopy above him. He threw himself up, as in a dark entangled forest there is nothing to do but make a dash for it, tearing through the web, and crying, 'Mother, mother!' ran to the heap that lay in the doorway and fell beside her, holding her, attaching himself tightly to her, crying.

'César, you're hurting me,' he heard her say. 'Please, darling, it is all right, you will be all right, it will pass, see, you are all right already.' And she kissed him on the mouth.

César realized he was in bed with Leticia. Their conversation earlier in the evening had remained alive in his unconscious mind when they went to sleep, stirring memories, awakening the past as a living dream, turning people into demons, and converting the scattered rantings of an old woman into terrifying commandments that shaped themselves as the demands of some tormented ghost.

Leticia would have insisted on knowing the details of his dream had she not perceived that he needed the comfort of her physical presence more than he did the understanding that her analysis might give him. A woman's breasts consoled a man, she knew, when he found himself fallen into some unspeakable grief, and she stroked his cheek and hair, encouraging him to draw new strength from her breast.

He refrained from talking about himself for the next few weeks, but one evening when he sensed that Leticia would switch on the radio if he did not find something to talk about soon, he began to tell her about a boy named Xavier Urquiaga, his closest friend at school when he was thirteen.

At that age, Xavier Urquiaga cultivated a melancholy manner, with a lock of his black hair always falling in the shape of a crescent across his forehead. One day, Xavier, sighing significantly and raising his hand with great effort, gave César a brown envelope.

'What is it?' César asked when he saw 'To X' inscribed on the envelope.

Xavier turned his face away as if overcome by a vast sadness that no words could measure. 'Open it, and you shall see,' he said weakly, almost despondently.

César quickly tore open the envelope and withdrew from it a piece of paper and unfolded it. The ruled paper with a jagged edge had obviously been taken from a school exercise book. On it were four lines of writing:

I come closed in an envelope of silk.
Honey my words, my intentions pure as milk.
What can I be in this secret disguise
Who come to you at night and leave at sunrise?

Xavier remained turned away while César muttered the words to himself, then frowned and read the words again. Xavier cast a furtive glance at his friend, but stayed resolutely patient while César puzzled over the words. At last, César said, 'I don't get it.'

Xavier looked at him in despair, and César said, 'I can't identify the poet, I've a terrible memory, you know that.'

'Oh,' Xavier moaned and sighed. 'The poet is . . . the poet . . . is Xavier Urquiaga.'

He brought out his own name quickly and turned his face away. César ran his eyes over the lines again and said, 'Shit, Xavier, this is fantastic, it's real poetry.'

Xavier turned to look at him, and now his eyes were shining. 'You really think so?'

'Shit, yes!'

'Please, César, don't use that word,' he pleaded, wanting his self and his work to be surrounded only by a pure fragrance.

'Well, it's just great,' César said enthusiastically, going over the lines once again. He quoted the last line, saying ' "Who come to you at night and leave at sunrise" – hey, Xavier, what have you been up to?'

'Nothing.' Xavier shrugged his shoulders.

78

'Come on, you can tell me. Here you are confessing about a secret disguise and spending nights with someone.'

César's admiration for the verse was giving way to envy, and he refused to accept Xavier's explanation, 'It's only a poem!'

'But you had to write it with someone in mind,' César insisted, and then looked suspiciously at Xavier. 'Why did you give it to me?'

'To see what you'd think.'

César thought the answer somewhat ambiguous and said, 'What do you mean by that?'

'You know.'

'You mean what I'd think about it as literature, or what I'd think?'

Xavier turned his face away and César walked round him and thrust his hand beneath Xavier's chin, raising his face. His eyes were moist. 'Shit, Xavier, why don't you say something? Is it a poem to a girl or is it some kind of shit?'

Xavier suddenly burst out with, 'Why do you have to spoil it with your shit, shit, shit?'

'What the hell am I spoiling?'

'Oh, nothing!' Xavier went to snatch his poem back but César held it away from him.

'This envelope,' César said, now becoming critical, 'this is a cheap brown paper envelope. Your poem says "an envelope of silk".'

'It's a metaphor, can't you see?'

César did not wish to lose his tone of critical triumph and looked again at the lines, shaking his head to suggest that he was having doubts. 'This language,' he said, 'why say "an envelope of silk" when "a silk envelope" would be more economical and neater?' And seeing his friend's lips begin to quiver, he added, 'By the way, Xavier, what does a silk envelope look like? I've never seen one. Where do they make them, in China?'

Xavier groaned, and César pressed the point with, 'I don't know about words being "honey", it's a bit trite, and do you really want the cliché of "pure as milk"? Is pasteurized milk pure?'

He stopped, seeing that his friend had tears in his eyes. 'Come on, Xavier, don't be so serious about it! I was only fooling, playing at being Señor Gonzalez – remember how he tore up that poem by Gabriela Mistral? And then showed how it was still a good poem? That's the way yours is.'

'All I wanted to know,' Xavier said, dabbing a handkerchief at his face, 'was what effect it would have on the reader. I mean, suppose you were the girl and received it?'

'But I am not, am I?' César said with some exasperation. 'Why didn't you show it to a girl?'

'I don't know any whom I really like.'

'Xavier, how can you write a poem to a woman about your passion and not have any woman that you're passionate about? I don't get it.'

'I *felt* like writing it, see?'

'But it's a bunch of lies.'

'No, it's true,' Xavier maintained. 'The words are true.'

César repeated that he did not comprehend Xavier's logic, and the latter began to sulk and remained very cold toward César during the following fortnight. Irritated by Xavier's attitude, César cultivated the friendship of two of the school's soccer players and deliberately tried to be seen in their company when he was certain to be noticed by Xavier.

'César,' Leticia said when he paused in his story, 'do you know what all that really means?'

'Yes, that we're fools when we're kids.'

'No, you have to look at it seriously,' Leticia insisted. 'Did you ever have a homosexual relationship?'

'I find that question offensive,' he said.

'But it's quite clear that Xavier wanted to be loved physically by you. And you surely suspected that and even wanted him that way. That is why you made friends with the soccer players – you resented that Xavier was being cold toward you, and you wanted to make him jealous.'

'All that is nonsense, Leticia.'

It was indeed nonsense as far as he was concerned, but he was astonished that Leticia had hit upon the truth about Xavier. Nothing in his behavior during their remaining years at school indicated anything other than the development of a sensitive young man given to adopting various poses of which the melancholic one continued to predominate. He had written more poems, but one day made the declaration that he had abandoned poetry for fiction and announced that he had begun to write a novel. He had decided to concern himself exclusively with reality. He carried a little notebook in his pocket which he took out from time to time and, looking dreamily up at a distant wall, would close his eyes as he pondered a thought, and then quickly scribbled something in his notebook. And if asked what it was that he had jotted down, he would shake his head and say, 'Nothing, it's nothing.' Thus the impression would be enhanced that some great idea had occurred to him in one's presence and one marvelled at one's good fortune. Or sometimes, he would ask a friend to repeat a phrase he had just uttered, and taking out his notebook, would say, 'That's priceless!' He would copy down the phrase, smiling to himself and looking up at the friend as though to congratulate him on having him, Xavier, as a friend, for his words would now be immortal. But during his last year at school, César noticed that Xavier had abandoned the habit of scribbling in his notebook, and asked him how the novel was going. Xavier scowled, affecting a manner indicative of profound contempt, and said, 'The novel is dead. Ours is the age of the image. The cinema, alas, is vulgar, and television cheap. The only respectable art form is painting.' César had the impression that Xavier had rehearsed this little speech several times and had been waiting for an opportunity to pronounce it. César's ironical tone when he remarked, 'Is that so?' was lost on the young aesthete, who went on to declare solemnly that he had begun work on an abstract canvas.

Deciding to give Leticia credit for some of her perception, César said to her, 'But you do have a point about Xavier. I did not see him after we finished school but ran into him some years later. I asked him what had become of his art. He looked at me disdainfully. Didn't I know? he asked. Didn't I read anything? I had only to see the arts supplement to the Sunday paper and find his name on the third page devoted entirely to the plastic arts.'

César, by then a businessman, did not confess to Xavier that he normally threw away the arts supplement without looking at it. On future Sundays, however, he did look at it scrupulously, and discovered that his old friend was now an art critic. He read Xavier's reviews for several weeks. Each one seemed to be a vitriolic attack on some new exhibition; the only artist he praised was one he claimed he himself had discovered in a village, an illiterate carpenter whose primitive paintings, asserted Xavier, revealed the very soul of South America.

'But the story about him that I wanted to tell you is this,' César said to Leticia.

Not having heard of Xavier for many years, no sooner had he accidentally met him again and begun to read his reviews than he ran into two people who knew him. One of them, a woman artist, had said, 'He gives bad reviews to just about everyone, especially to women. He hates women artists. But you should see the reviews he gives to handsome young men, you know the ones?' And she fluttered her eyelashes and shook her shoulders to suggest her meaning.

Leticia laughed aloud. 'César,' she said, 'you could have saved mankind if you'd let Xavier kiss you when he gave you that poem. He'd have got over his crush. Your rejection has made him a queer, and what's worse, *you* harbour a deep guilt about it.'

'Oh, nonsense!' César said, laughing with her. But she proceeded to elaborate her analysis. He interrupted her with an occasional ironical remark, but let her enjoy the pleasure of talking, for that was precisely why he had told her the Xavier story. It was amusing to tell and possessed the potential for Leticia to find all sorts of significance in it. Given the burden of memories, it was easier to cope with the lighter ones. But the intention to keep to a subject that both would laugh at, one moreover that appeared irrelevant to their immediate life, was confounded by the subject becoming a basis of confrontation; a silly story, told to pass the time, led to a trivial remark that generated contention and bitterness.

For later, when they were in bed, Leticia said, 'What's the matter, César? You're not thinking of your pretty boy Xavier, are you?'

He leaned back from her body. 'Why did you have to say that, Leticia?' He fell back on his pillow and stared at the ceiling.

She turned over and resting on her shoulder brought her face close to his. 'What *can* I think when you can't make yourself love me?'

'I was trying, god damn it!' he said with irritation but without raising his voice. 'Why do you have to *talk* so much?'

'That's typical, of course,' she said in the voice of one whose reason understands everything. 'Instead of looking clearly at the problem and trying to find out how you can overcome it, you prefer to blame me.'

'There isn't any *problem*!'

'*There* is your problem,' she said, pointing to his penis which lay limp next to his left thigh, and turned to her side of the bed.

It was not the first time that each pretended to have gone to sleep when neither could do so for another hour. She could leave him, she thought, if his capacity for physical love showed signs of continuing to diminish. But then sex wasn't everything. He was the third man she had lived with for any length of time and, at the age of twenty-eight, she felt comfortable with him. It was not that often that he could not arouse himself, and normally he made a good lover. He respected her as a woman to whom her profession was important. When she enumerated his positive qualities, she could not think of leaving him. Only his refusal to listen seriously to her interpretation of events infuriated her; it was as if he despised her intellect.

In spite of her confidence that she understood everything with a coldly objective rationality, Leticia had a blind spot. The thing closest to her, her own self, that she took for granted and that she believed she had a complete comprehension of was obscurely striving after effects that she would have been shocked by if she were to be told that that was what she was really after. She had offended her parents by ostentatiously discarding the traditional ways of her society. For their daughter to live in open sin with a succession of men was a horror and a tragedy, filling them with shame. Leticia knew of the great unhappiness she had caused her parents, but, believing that to be a necessary sacrifice, she tried not to think of it. What she did not know, however, was that unconsciously she thought of it a good deal of the time and that many of her actions were motivated by an obscure force within herself to prove to her parents that her way could be an acceptable one. During recent weeks, she had thrice forgotten to take her contraceptive pill. On each occasion, she convinced herself that her forgetfulness had been caused by the fact that she had been extraordinarily busy and that there had been too many things on her mind. But had she subjected herself to the same sort of analysis with which she interpreted the actions of other people, she would have come to the conclusion that she had deliberately been forgetting the pill in order to invite that accident which would make her pregnant. For a child would reconcile her to her parents: they would accept her way of living when they saw that family happiness could be obtained even when the old traditions had collapsed.

César Calderón, whose mental energies were largely consumed by his business, and who preferred not to have to think why anything happened, had recently startled himself into having a psychological perception into himself that, had it come from Leticia, he would have dismissed with an ironical laugh. The odd thing was that he was not thinking of anything and suddenly a truth flashed across his mind. There had been a number of occasions when he had not been able to make love after having begun to do so; at the crucial moment, he went limp and found penetration impossible. The first time he had felt humiliated but then, when Leticia taunted him, he complained to her that it was her fault that she talked so much when she ought to be performing her part of the foreplay with greater attention. For some time he remained convinced that there was no other cause for his impotence. After another failure, she mocked him by calling him Señor Softy. That so infuriated him that he shocked her into two days of silence by the uncouth remark that instead of applying her mouth to so many empty words she ought to apply it to his cock.

Then the terrible thought occurred to him that *he did not want sex*. Penetration brought with it a painful awareness of procreation. He had nothing to fear, of course, for Leticia was on the pill, but on each future occasion that he succeeded in satisfying her, he himself did not experience the blind, overwhelming pleasure of the act but instead found himself staring at the interior of an enormous womb. He came out in a cold sweat, which Leticia assumed was the result of his strenuous performance, and collapsed on his side in despair, which appeared no different from natural exhaustion. The thought that he should ever be a father horrified him.

And that was what he fled from when Leticia unconsciously contrived her pregnancy. She announced it quite blithely to him one day. He turned away so that she could not see the look of pain and disgust that had risen to his face, and poured himself a strong drink. She thought he was celebrating, and said, 'You can pour me one, too, but add some water to it. I'll need to be careful from now on.'

He brought her an undiluted Scotch and, taking a gulp of his own said, 'Better see about an abortion, Leticia.'

'*What? César*, I *love* the idea of a baby. And no, I'm *not* going to drink that Scotch. I'm not a murderer.'

He saw that argument would be futile and sat down with the bottle of Scotch next to him. Her voice came at him in tormenting waves, but he was not listening to her; there was another, even more tormenting voice inside his head.

\*     \*     \*

85

When her time came, Leticia had already been abandoned by him for six months. She had her baby in an expensive nursing home, and when the baby's mouth first fastened itself to her breast, the young nurse who attended her asked, 'What are you going to call him?'

Leticia looked at the window where the curtains had been drawn.

'Let me see the light,' she said.

The nurse pulled back the curtains. It was a bright morning, a section of blue sky could be seen.

'Where are we?' Leticia asked. 'What's that street called?'

'Avenida Simón Bolívar,' the nurse said.

Leticia looked down at her son, and said, 'Simón Bolívar.'

The evening when Leticia made the announcement of her pregnancy was the only occasion on which Calderón drank himself into a near unconscious state. He remained in bed all the next day, painfully reminded by each throbbing pulse at his temples that his brain was incapable of driving out the voice that spoke within it even when his body had passed out and become an inert, helpless mass. It spoke silently in an agony of dreams when he lay benumbed by whiskey, its imagery a loud cacophony. With consciousness recovered, the voice became an incoherent muttering as though someone just out of one's hearing were expressing a vile torrent of abuse and one caught the odd dreadful word in a general flow of obscenity of which one grasped only the tone. It sent charges through his body. His skin seemed to break out in little fires, so that, lamenting his fate, he stumbled to the kitchen to fetch another jug of iced water, falling back into bed with a groan and once with a scream so loud that he was himself terrified. He heard crows cawing, a shrieking raucousness from a mass of black plumage. Whales rose out of an ocean, filled the air with piercing cries. Then again the voice that appeared to have been electronically altered to obscure its identity, so that the heard sound needed to be translated into words; or the voice from some backstage gravely speaking the lines of an invisible ghost, the distorted sounds with their hushed cadences swirling upon the darkened stage. Nothing could be discerned clearly; only a sense of menace prevailed, the feeling that when the message was distinctly heard, the pain it would bring would be worse than the horror of continuing to live with its meaningless presence.

When Leticia returned from work that evening and saw that he lay comatose in bed, she said, 'César, you are the most miserable of men.'

He did not mind the distraction of her sharp voice. 'Most men would be overjoyed at the prospect of fatherhood,' she went on. 'But look at you! One would think your business had collapsed.'

He could not bring himself to affect a joyful face and while Leticia changed from a dress into jeans and a shirt she threw reprimanding glances at him and kept up her scolding voice. 'It's the most natural thing in the world. Every man, at least every *normal* man, longs to have a son to whom he can pass on his name. This has been going on for thousands of years. But no! Our dear César seems to have dropped dead at the thought of a son as though the doctor had told him he had cancer. I give you life by recreating the gift of life out of my body, but you look as though I were preparing your *funeral*.'

She spoke in anger and almost spat out the last word. Going some distance away from him, she tucked the shirt inside the jeans and, buttoning it up, she slowly walked back to him and sat down on the edge of the bed. 'What is the matter?' she asked in a softer, more conciliatory voice. 'I thought you loved me. I believed in you, in our life together. I've always wanted to share everything with you.'

At last he spoke, though almost in a whisper. 'How did this happen, Leticia? You never told me you had stopped taking the pill.'

'Oh, let's not argue about it!' she exclaimed, her voice again loud and aggressive. 'I did what I had to.'

'I don't call that sharing,' he said bitterly. 'If you were

honest with me, you'd arrange for an abortion without delay.'

She stood up suddenly and said, 'I do not want to hear that word again! I *want* to have my baby, and I *will*. Don't make me hate you, César. You're miserable and pathetic when you act this way.'

'I'm not acting in any way.'

'You should look at yourself,' she cried. 'You're the picture of despair and fear when you should be full of joy and happiness. You're horrible for having drunk yourself into a stupid state. You've thought nothing at all of me, you don't care about my feelings. A woman in my state usually receives some kindness, a little tenderness from her man. Oh, you are the most wretched, wretched of men!'

He shrank from her raging voice and was relieved to see her leave the room. By the next day, he resumed his normal life, and avoided the subject of Leticia's pregnancy. A tension seemed to hang in the air during the hours when they were together, for each felt that the other was pretending that nothing had happened and that the outward harmony and appearance of the usual routine were not forced. She was convinced that it was only a mood he had fallen into and was certain that in due course he would not only accept the idea of fatherhood but would also begin to be thrilled by it, for that was the common experience of mankind. She could not sense that his rejection of the idea was irrevocable, absolutely final.

Why it was so, Calderón himself could not have explained. He found it difficult to sleep. His nights were a torment of noise inside his head. A perplexing language muttered its strange words, and he feared that he was unable to grasp some important message while at the same time remaining in terror of what he might hear should the words suddenly become clearly audible. The attempt to maintain outward pretences with Leticia disgusted him, and he felt himself detached from the person who carried on the world of appearances with her.

After about six weeks, he realized that that was not a world in which he could continue to live. He formed no plan, worked out no details, but found himself making arrangements to go away into the remote interior. He did not believe that some sort of pilgrimage would bring him relief; he only had a blind desire to leave, and dimly anticipated that he was possibly not seeking an escape from affliction but entering that unknown where his pain would intensify. In the clamorous confusion of his mind he desired that acute suffering which, like a bright light that blinds, would take away the sense of being and give him knowledge of the source of his pain. As if he sought to return to some primeval beginning, the image of a mountain with a waterfall creating a mist on its side somehow became associated in his mind with the abstract thoughts and seemed to give focus to the general vagueness of his inner perceptions, creating the appearance of a real destination when he knew that it was only a trick of his imagination.

Driving to his office one morning, going across the traffic that proceeded to the downtown area, he took his usual route toward the industrial zone in the suburbs from where he operated his business, but inadvertently found himself on the wrong side of two fast-moving lanes from which he could not extricate himself in time before he was on the highway going to the south of the city. It was three kilometres before the next turn-off, but after the relief of having been freed from the congested traffic the sudden opportunity to drive at a high speed on a highway free of traffic was exhilarating, and he continued on it until twelve kilometres later the dense city was behind him. At that point, the highway had climbed out of the vast valley in which the city lay. A small park had been constructed by the side of the road. Calderón drove into the park and went along slowly on its narrow winding road that, on the outer skirt of the park, afforded distant views. From the north, he could see the city. The pollution of the morning traffic had created a large floating disc of yellowish haze out of which the downtown skyscrapers rose like phantoms. He drove along the curving road and saw to the west an undulating land, variously cultivated, with scattered villages, becoming a range of hills on the horizon beyond which, but invisible from there, stood the Andes. The prospect to the south was different. There, the land was thickly forested, and revealed no hint of husbandry or habitation. Calderón stopped his car and stood outside it, staring at the great mass of green in the south as if searching for some clue; but he saw only the shape of darkness and could not think why he should find it so thrilling.

He drove back to the city and arrived at his office an hour later than usual. Two of his company's trucks, with the large symbol of a brown insect in a green circle and a red diagonal line across the circle to indicate its extinction, stood in the parking lot, and two of his men were loading them with supplies. Calderón entered the warehouse section of the building. A man with a pad and pencil was checking the inventory, two others were preparing a solution of some chemicals and filling spray guns with it. A strong smell hung in the air. Calderón walked up some stone steps, and entered through the back door of his office. From his desk, where his secretary had placed the day's mail in a neat pile, he could see the activity in the warehouse through the glass wall on his right, and look over a low partition six metres to his front into the area where two female secretaries and two male clerks worked. Everyone seemed preoccupied in the same manner that he observed them in on each working day, and he, too, almost automatically began to do what he had to do. He started to open the envelopes in front of him, and they also were no different from those on any other day: invoices for the products he had purchased, cheques for services his company had rendered, one farmer requesting an estimate for the cost of ridding his corral of bats, and another from the owner of a plantation of soya beans complaining that the aerial spraying that he had been promised for the fifth of the month had not taken place till the twelfth and that since the danger of infestation had not been eradicated in time he expected a substantial reduction in his bill.

Calderón continued throughout the business day to work as he normally did: he attended to the correspondence, dictating letters to one of the secretaries – the farmer wanting to rid himself of bats was informed that an estimate could not be given until he submitted dimensions of his corral; the complaining planter was politely told that the delay in the aerial spraying had been caused not by Calderón's company but by the firm that leased the plane, a circumstance out of his control, and therefore a reduction in the bill was out of the question.

Finishing the correspondence, Calderón called in the warehouse foreman to obtain from him a list of supplies that needed to be ordered; went to the bank before lunch to pay in the day's receipts and to draw some money; returning to his office, he spent the afternoon conferring with the salesmen assigned to different regions who had been scheduled to report to him that afternoon. They were working well: the business was prospering and growing.

When at the end of the working day, he rose to go to his car, he had a word as usual with the secretary who would close the office, and exchanged some remarks with the other workers on his way to the parking lot. He placed his briefcase on the seat next to him and switched on the ignition. Just when he was about to engage the first gear, he looked at his briefcase, and paused. What had he done? he wondered. Instead of carrying some papers to work on at home, he had filled the briefcase with the money that he had drawn at the bank. He had not thought, when drawing the money, for what purpose he did so; the salaries were not due to be paid and he had enough in his wallet and at home for his own immediate needs. He drove away, thinking that he would take the money back to the bank the next day, but after another tense and embittered evening with Leticia, he realized what he needed the money for: without thinking about it, he had begun to make the arrangements to leave her.

And so in the following weeks, he looked more closely at the state of his business and calculated what he could take away of its capital without causing it to collapse. He changed the money into bills of large denominations in the currencies of three countries and bought some dollars on the black market. A lawyer worked out the necessary papers that gave the business to Leticia. He did not care whether she sold it or decided to run it herself, for his only concern was that he should not abandon her with nothing.

One morning, after Leticia had gone to work, he filled a small canvas bag, which was once used for weekend trips to the seaside, with some clothes and the money and what papers he might need, and wearing a khaki workshirt of heavy cotton and beige twill trousers, he walked out of the apartment in which he had lived with Leticia for five years.

Taking any bus that travelled south, he proceeded in stages on his thoughtless journey, driven by a compulsion that did not permit its motives to be questioned. The third of the buses that he took reached its destination, a small town some seventy kilometres south of the city. It was evening, and Calderón was told when he inquired that there was a biweekly bus scheduled for the following day. He found a room for the night above a noisy café. When having a meal in the café, he asked the proprietor who served him – a short, pot-bellied man with thin lips and a high forehead – about the town in the south and what lay beyond it.

The town was there because of the coffee, he informed Calderón. Full of bow-legged old men who had spent their lives carrying heavy loads of coffee beans. The river there was the colour of coffee and tasted of it, too. Even the incense in the church smelled of coffee. But without coffee, the place would be savage like the rest of the interior. There were towns on junctions of rivers. Wild reputations they had. The law of the jungle everywhere. There was a strange monastery he had heard of. Curious place in the middle of nowhere. Built there two hundred years ago by some Franciscans or somebody. God alone knows who got it into his head to bring religion to savages. A mission it must have been to convert the cannibals to Christianity. But the building was only threequarters completed. Seems to have been abandoned. Maybe the Franciscans got converted into stew. You never know, the interior is full of jokes. But a bunch of funny priests still live there. You hear stories of miracles in the backlands, people going on their knees to some shrine those funny priests had constructed and living to tell of some miracles. But that was not the half of it. The interior went on beyond there. It was wild, people with crazy dreams lived there. As far as he was concerned, it was a world of parrots and monkeys.

# 4

The old bus bounced along the reddish dirt road through the jungle, an orange spiral of dust rising from its rear tyres. Calderón sat by an open window to the right of the driver, three rows behind him, the seats in front of him unoccupied, so that he could see through the windshield the undulating terrain they were driving through. Fifteen other passengers were scattered among the seats behind him, poor people in rags, two of them cripples on crutches, and one so sick that he lay passed out on the long back seat. After six hours on the road, everyone was in a state of exhaustion and longed for the miracle of arriving at their destination.

Only 130 kilometres separated the coffee town they had departed from to the village of Santa Clara where the land route in this part of the country ended; but the stretches where the bus could hit its top speed of fifty kilometres an hour were short, for the road was marked by irregular ruts and twice the slow progress had been brought to a halt because trees had fallen across the path of the bus. The slightest uphill grade was, for the old bus, a slope steeper than any in the Andes, and it laboured up in first gear, noisier than an old propeller plane at take-off, at less than ten kilometres an hour.

Two of the passengers moaned constantly, and one cried 'O God, O God!' at each bump of the road; a fourth had stood up and begun to make an incoherent speech with the repeated phrases, 'It will come to pass, believe me!' and 'That too is the unspoken prophecy, that too, that too!', bellowing with a howling sort of laughter each time he uttered one of these phrases before rattling on in a fresh outburst of rapid meaningless speech, until the driver stopped the bus, walked back to where the man stood with uplifted eyes and his hands joined in front of his chest, held him by the shoulders, shook him, and thrust him into a seat, giving him a mild slap across the face. 'Your salvation is at hand, brother,' the driver said to him, 'but let us get there first, all right?'

Calderón could discern no variety in the landscape through which they drove. It was the same mass of trees with their creepers and underbrush that had commenced not half a kilometre out of the coffee town where, after a wait of four days, he had taken the bus. Occasionally, there had been a flock of parrots rising from some trees, and once a colony of monkeys grooming themselves in the middle of the road, but otherwise the journey had offered no distraction, and had certainly shown no glimpse of a landscape in which one might wish to spend any time. For much of the laboured progress along the narrow road, they had been under a dark jungle; recent heavy rains had intensified the humidity, the air was still, and even the silence broken by the noisy bus and its crazed passengers possessed a choking quality.

'Here we are,' the driver shouted when the bus came out into the open and he brought it to a halt beside a thatched hut where coffee and snacks could be had. 'Santa Clara, the end of the lunatic road.'

He put on his peaked cap and stood with his back to the windshield, folding his arms. 'Exit here for the asylum!' he shouted, grinning. The two with the crutches had already begun to hobble out, and Calderón followed them.

'You're sure this is where you wanted to come to?' the driver asked Calderón, following him out of the bus.

'Why do you ask?'

Just then two of the passengers carried out the man who had been lying in the rear seat and placed him on the ground. He immediately threw himself on his hands and knees and, looking up at those who stood around him, his round, sunken eyes suddenly bright in his small, wrinkled face, said with remarkable clarity of voice, 'Show me the way, for love of God.' And before anyone could respond, he began to drag himself on his hands and knees as though he knew himself where he had to go.

'Take a look around you,' the driver answered Calderón, 'and see the kind of man you have to be to come here.'

At that moment, the passenger who had made the incomprehensible speech in the bus alighted from it, shouting, 'O Lord Jesus Christ! O Son of God, show me thy Father's steps, take me unto His arms, O Lord!' And his head up in the air and his arms swinging extravagantly, he marched off as if he were at the head of a military band in a parade.

'Crazy, eh?' the driver laughed, looking at Calderón who was watching the man marching after the one rapidly dragging himself on his hands and knees.

'I was told there's a monastery here,' Calderón said. 'An old mission.'

'Yeah, about twenty kilometres past that jungle.' The driver raised a pointing finger. 'But just in there, only half a kilometre from here, there's the shrine these lunatics are headed for. There's a rock with a crack in it with some underground river forcing a fountain of water through that crack. And that's all it is! But the priests made that into a shrine to stop all these loonies from pestering them at the mission. You'll find two of the brothers there by the shrine, doing their sacred duty and dying for their turn to end. Go there if you're looking for a miracle. It's crazy how much faith people have in water spitting out of a rock.'

Some old men and women in tattered clothes were coming in the direction of the bus, several of them with bent bodies and a cane in their hands, their heads shaking and eyes rolling. A one-legged man was swinging his leg flamboyantly as he pushed himself with his crutches. An old woman was hopping like a bird, jerking her head now to the right and now to the left each time she hit the ground. A middle-aged man carried a legless boy with a large head that wobbled incessantly, and when he came closer Calderón saw the face more clearly and realized he was not a boy but an old man.

'Here come the cured,' the driver said. 'Sure you don't want to join them? The journey back is faster, only five hours.'

'No thanks,' Calderón said.

'You sure must be looking for a miracle, too!'

Calderón walked away, hearing the driver's laughter behind him. He followed the direction taken by the others who had come on the bus, and passed some of them going the opposite way to make the return journey.

They came out into a wide open space from where a commotion seemed to have been coming; the space, naked orange-red earth, was like a large square and far to its right was a line of little huts. A throng of people was milling about there as at the booths of a fair and, approaching the huts, Calderón heard a mixture of loud shouts and cries. His attention was caught by a short man wearing a pink satin tunic with green embroidery on it, a yellow turban, and dark glasses with black lenses.

'This way, this way, this way!' the man shouted, holding wide his arms and bowing in a gesture of welcome when he saw that he had Calderón's attention as well as that of a few other people. 'This way, this way for a new life. Minced parrots' tongues for the dumb. Sap of the iron tree for the lame, freshly drawn in sterilized bottles. This way, this way, this way. Powder of dried python skin for the leprous. Jaguar's blood for the anaemic. Charms of alligators' teeth against bad dreams. What is your pain, what is your sorrow? Suffer no more! This way for a new life. Here, sir, here, this vial of oil drawn from monkeys' balls is the remedy if impotence is your curse. Or a jar of raw snakes' eggs beaten in palm oil, a teaspoon before going to bed and even a man of eighty may do it three times in the night and be a father again. Come back to the living, come back to the living, this way, this way, this way!'

Calderón shrank from him. Other men in front of the

huts were beseeching him and the rest of the crowd that had gathered there. A group stood at the window of a hut and Calderón, coming to it, paused and raised himself on his toes, craning his neck. A large woman in a loose white blouse and skirt, her greying straight hair falling behind her, sat cross-legged on a table as if in a trance, her dark-brown face immobile, her black eyes fixed at the window. A middle-aged man, his face smeared with ash, was lighting a home-made cheroot. He puffed at it rapidly, blowing out thick smoke toward the window, sending a vile smell there.

'What, you think you have seen wonders?' he said, blowing at the cheroot, creating more smoke. 'What, you have seen human footsteps on the face of the moon? What, you have heard the voices of the dead? You have seen nothing, you have heard nothing, you know nothing! Compared with what you are going to see! Go, cross the Pacific in the belly of a whale. Go, stand under the sky and be pelted by falling stars. Go, awake the dead from their graves! All child's play compared to what you are going to see. Look closely, friends.'

He held the cheroot up in front of the woman. Smoke hung in the air, drifting around her. She raised a hand with an automatic gesture and took the cheroot without looking at it and carried it to her lips.

'Now watch!' the man exhorted the crowd at the window. 'A mother of twenty boys she is. You think you have seen wonders, you know life? Go away, go away those of you who are not strong enough to see a miracle happen before your eyes. I beg you, go away before it is too late and you find your eyes hanging out in wonder! O mother, great mother, the soul of fertility, show them your miracle, see, they stand in awe before you, their breath comes hard, and their eyes are bright with your glory, O great mother! Show them, O sacred one, the seeds of life.'

The crowd was frozen at the window, staring at the woman holding the cheroot at her lips. The woman took a puff. A little smoke rose from the lit end which glowed as she breathed in. Her mouth closed over the smoke she had inhaled, and she held the cheroot away from her face. Then she opened her mouth. A black hole, without front teeth. No smoke was exhaled. And then suddenly a red berry fell out of her mouth, and then two more. The crowd gasped. The woman took a longer puff of the cheroot, again moving her hand automatically as if she were only a medium for the miracle and had no will of her own; the cheroot burned ferociously, sending up smoke, and this time, when she opened her mouth, a stream of red berries came tumbling out and fell with a clattering sound upon the table, like little marbles.

The man took the cheroot from her and came to the window to show the people standing there that when he puffed only smoke came from his mouth. He threw the cheroot down and picking up two of the berries from the table, put them on the palm of his hand, and brought them to the window, moving his palm across the eyes of the spectators and saying, 'This is the gift of the mother of twenty boys, the most fertile woman in the world, even her breath is made up of the seeds of life. One of these berries will make any woman fertile. You have seen yourselves it comes from the very soul of fertility. What? Some of you do not believe me? You have not seen enough to believe what you have seen? Oh, what an age, cursed with disbelievers! Mother,' he said turning to the woman, 'show them, O sacred one, so that they may believe.'

The woman still sat as before, her face immobile, her eyes fixed at the window. The crowd had again become frozen. The woman raised her hands to the top button of her blouse and undid it; there were five more buttons below that and she undid them, too, performing the action slowly. Then she held the two ends of the blouse together, and rested her fists across her chest for a moment so that the unbuttoned blouse still covered her front. The crowd stared, the eyes fixed in wild expressions, not knowing what to expect. Suddenly, she threw her hands apart and held her arms open, the two halves of the white blouse snapping out like wings. The crowd let out a cry. The woman had three pairs of breasts, one above the other, the

99

top one rather shrunken and sagging but the two lower pairs full and rounded.

Calderón drew back from the window where some of the people had began to bid for the berries and the man in the hut was saying, 'Let your woman take two with a glass of buffalo milk, and she will have twins.'

The next three huts were souvenir shops that offered plastic religious statues and rosaries. Beyond them was a hut that had two windows made to look like a pair of spectacles. A number of people stood at each window and Calderón joined one of the groups. Inside, the black wall was covered with black and white reproductions of engravings, each one containing an optical illusion. In one picture, a young woman with rounded cheeks sat in front of a mirror, but when Calderón looked at it again from a different angle, instead of seeing the rear of the woman's head and the protuberance of her cheeks, he saw a human skull. In another, two peacocks in a tree formed a pretty picture until – the eye shifting to take in other details – the peacocks seemed to disappear and the entire image transformed itself into the Crucifixion. Several of the other examples showed birds and flowers but the eye of the beholder also saw in them scenes of hilarious obscenity – two doves in one taking on the form of buttocks and a section of the iron railing of a balcony above which the doves fluttered becoming a phallic rod, the ocean in the background a blue bedcover.

A man inside the hut, wearing oversize spectacles with yellow lenses that arched to the middle of his forehead and covered all his cheeks, was saying, 'Now you can see everything, come look, look!' In each fisted hand he held three or four pairs of spectacles by their frames, so that several yellow discs threw back reflections at the people in the two windows as he gesticulated. 'Study the illusions on this wall,' he went on, speaking rapidly, 'see for yourself how everything is two things, come, look, look! Is that how you're going to go through life, not knowing what you're looking at? Here is the miracle of vision, come, look, look, and see truth for the first time, wear these spectacles and

100

see nothing but the truth, see how a person's skin turns purple when he lies, see the make-up vanish from a whore's cheeks, see behind the face of evil, come, stare at the naked world, see how it was at creation, stare fearlessly at the eclipsed sun, come, look, look, see the truth and nothing but the truth!'

Behind the line of huts, which were more like booths at a fair of grotesques, there were two rows of larger dwellings. Some offered accommodation on straw mats to the pilgrims, others proclaimed themselves as restaurants. There was one that was just an empty room with a small metal desk behind which sat a smiling bald-headed man with a black mustache. Having no front wall, the room was exposed to the street, but had a sign hung from the top: Holy Holidays. The man darted out from behind the table when he saw Calderón loiter past, his canvas bag in his hand. Calderón quickened his pace, but the man had already come out and stood in front of him, obliging him to stop.

'Sebastian Moncayo at your service, good sir,' he said, bowing. 'Sebastian Moncayo, proprietor of Holy Holidays. Planned tours offered. Air-conditioned buses chartered. Conducted excursions. All reservations made. Come in, good sir, come in, and we can talk business.'

'I'm sorry, but –'

'No, no, no,' the man interrupted Calderón, putting a hand to his arm and guiding him. 'Come, sit down, sit down, take a refreshment at least.'

He put two fingers in his mouth and whistled loudly. A boy came running from across the street, and Moncayo said to him, 'Quick, bring a beer for the gentleman.'

He offered Calderón his chair and perched himself on the table, saying, 'Yes, let's talk business. I can see you are a man of business.'

'I was about to tell you,' Calderón said calmly, 'that I can have no business to offer you. I am only passing through.'

'Passing through? In transit!' Moncayo grinned at Calderón, seeming to be overjoyed. 'No problem, no problem at all. Passing through!'

The boy came running back with a bottle of beer and a

glass. Moncayo filled the glass with beer, handed it to Calderón, and began to swig from what remained in the bottle. The boy ran off. Calderón thanked Moncayo and took a drink. The beer was tepid but still welcome.

Jumping off the table, Moncayo began to talk business, shuffling about the room, sitting on the edge of the table again, and then walking around once more. Calderón was relieved that he was not being offered anything, that Moncayo had not cornered him to sell him some bogus tour. In fact, Moncayo had nothing to sell at all. The 'business' he wanted to talk about was entirely hypothetical. What did the good señor think? he kept asking as he described his great scheme to make Santa Clara the most famous resort in South America. 'And all because of water spouting out of a rock!' he cried in amazement. So much business potential in so small a thing, imagine! His eyes blazed as the words rolled out of his mouth. Offices in all the big cities – Bogotá, Lima, São Paulo, everywhere, imagine! Secretaries in yellow blouses and blue skirts speaking into red telephones. In New York and London and Paris, too, why not? This is an international business. Holy Holidays. Would the señor like to see a copy of the letter he had written the Pope? International Holy Holidays. His eyes bulged out at the incredible thought. A twenty-storey luxury hotel right there in the middle of the square, what did the good señor think? And out there a perfect site for an airport. Avianca, Varig, Lan Chile, Pan Am, Air France, imagine! Jumbo jets. He collapsed to the ground in an agony of inner turmoil, overwhelmed by his own vision.

Calderón stood up and took out a large bank note from his wallet – enough to pay for a case of beer – and placed it under the empty glass on the table. Moncayo lay slumped on the floor, staring at the wall as at some unbelievable phenomenon, and slowly recited the figures 747 and DC10 and 727 again and again as though they had been the winning numbers of a lottery for which he possessed the wrong tickets. He did not notice Calderón quietly walk away.

A clamour of human voices filled the air, selling a new vitality to the disabled and withered bodies that hobbled or dragged themselves about the two streets behind the square. One establishment, calling itself a hotel, proclaimed that its mats were woven of a fibre from trees growing only on the highest altitudes of the Andes, none below 5000 metres, and had the proven quality of curing all back ailments. Another claimed to have a secret spring of its own and offered a glass of water to its clients, to be taken before going to bed, with a guarantee of a dreamless sleep.

A man dressed in tapering black trousers that, from the calf down, clung tightly to his legs, and a black shirt with ruffled cuffs, open at the neck, walked about the street looking distraught. He had painted his face a chalky white and his eyelids an ashen grey, with a black line above the eye lashes. He held his head a little to the side, as though it was poised there precariously and was in danger of falling off at any moment. His dry lips, with cracked red paint on them, remained open. He walked slowly, languidly, staring at every passer-by with a tragic expression. Every now and again, he stopped, twisted his shoulders sideways, and leaning his neck out and, pointing a finger at no one, said aloud in a painful stammer, 'Why woo . . . woo . . . woulds't thou be . . . be . . . be a breed . . . breed . . . breed . . . breeder of . . . uh . . . uuh . . . sin . . . sin . . . sinners?'

Calderón walked away from the street, went across the square, and found the path that led to the shrine. It went through a partially cleared forest. Two old men, coming from the shrine, hobbled past him, their eyes bright as though they had just received the assurance of recovering some long-lost treasure.

He heard the sound of water gushing just before he came to a wooden fence. Near an opening, a hut had been built. A man in a white robe sat in its porch, his head shaven clean and a black beard falling down his chest. A woman with a wrinkled face stood outside the hut, and was speaking rapidly to the man, her right arm gesticulating, now

103

pointing to the man and now to a young girl on whose shoulder she supported herself with her other arm. In the distance, a plume of water rose out of a long straight crevice in a bulging rock that was covered with moss, and fell in a continuous clatter to form a pool. A number of people were submerged in the pool, and a man in a white robe, with a shaven head and a black beard like the one in the porch, stood with raised hands in the gesture of one performing a ceremonious benediction.

'Funny priests you are,' the woman in front of the porch was saying in a complaining voice that contained intonations of anger and despair. 'She is my staff, my hope, my only treasure.'

Calderón looked at the girl as the woman went on to speak of her own illness. The girl was fourteen or fifteen years old with a thin body and a pretty face. She was staring at the priest with a mixture of fear and hatred. 'My girl and I have gone hungry during our week's journey to get here, the poor thing has made enough sacrifices already, all I'm asking you, begging you, is to let me touch the water, it is God's water, not yours, I don't have a single peso to spare, and you want to use my precious girl as your whore, you don't have any pity, any charity. . . .'

The priest leaned forward in his small wooden chair, raised his robe and scratched his left calf. He glanced wearily at Calderón and then leered at the girl.

'It is not enough for you to sin with your eyes,' the woman went on, 'and in your secret thoughts, but you ask me openly. And what will I say to my Maker when the time comes? Dear God, I was in pain and sacrificed my daughter to a priest's lust, I forced my girl to become a whore because that was the payment he demanded. What happened to your goodness,' she screamed at the priest, 'to your pity, to your charity? No, I won't give you my girl, even for a second!'

The priest yawned, looked at her with a bored expression, and said, 'Two hundred pesos, then.'

'Where can I find two *hundred* pesos?'

'Fifteen minutes with the girl.' The priest jerked his

hand over his shoulder, pointing a thumb to the room behind him.

'No, no, *no!*'

'Ten minutes, then.'

'No, O dear God!'

'Five minutes. Let her do it quickly with her mouth, and keep her virginity. You lose nothing.'

The woman stared at him, speechless, her eyes wild. She looked at her girl who had begun to sob. The woman stroked the girl's hair, tears coming to her own eyes. 'My sweet, my precious,' she said, clutching her shoulder, for in that moment the girl seemed more in need of support than the crippled woman.

The priest leaned his head back and stretched his arms. Holding his hands behind his head, he said, 'Well?'

The woman stared at him. The girl sobbed loudly. The priest, his hands still behind his head, stared back at the woman coldly. Calderón watched.

'No,' the woman whispered, shaking her head sadly.

'Two hundred pesos, then.'

The woman let out a wailing scream.

'Let me pay for her,' Calderón said, taking out a bill in excess of two hundred pesos and walking to the porch to hand the money to the priest.

'God be praised,' the woman cried, stumbling forward and falling at Calderón's feet. 'Bless you, sir,' she said, holding Calderón's legs and bowing her head to his feet, 'for saving my innocent girl. A miracle, a miracle!'

Her daughter took a couple of quick steps to hold her up. The daughter's face was turned, looking in awe at Calderón, as she helped her mother to walk in the direction of the water.

The priest laughed loudly, and said to Calderón, 'It is a way to pass the time, nothing more.'

'I will say nothing,' Calderón said. 'I don't judge other people.'

'What could you say, and to whom? You were too quick with your money. How do you know that in another minute I was not going to let the woman go, telling her that I was

105

only testing her virtue, as it is only fit that a representative of God on earth should?'

Calderón took out some more money from his pocket, and holding it to the priest, said, 'How can I get to the mission?'

The priest stood up and quickly put the money away into a pocket. 'Why do you want to go there?' he asked.

'Perhaps it is God's will.'

The priest looked at him suspiciously, and asked, 'What's your trouble?'

'All I know is I was born, that I have life.'

The priest chuckled, and looked in the direction of the pool and then up the path to see if anyone was coming. 'You understand that it's not a real mission?'

'I do not know anything,' Calderón said. 'If it is more money you want . . .' He reached for his pocket.

After some more questions, the priest concluded that there was nothing to fear from Calderón who appeared to him obviously not some government official looking for taxes to collect and certainly not a spy from the Church come to find out what was happening on its property. He took the money and gave Calderón instructions. Calderón could borrow his mule, but he must be certain to send it back with the priests whose duty it was next to work at the shrine. The path through the jungle was well trodden. It would take him three hours. He should get there before night fell.

The evening light, falling through the yellow-flowering acacias and the taller trees with their thick green foliage, reflected off the white stucco walls, casting diagonal shadows of the arches of the gallery that ran along the two sides of the courtyard. Calderón sat on a wooden bench, a decorative orange tree behind him, and saw the bare-footed moving figures in the gallery as they stepped on the black and white tiles of the sunlit floor and glided into the darkness of the shadows, a succession of ghostly bodies in their habits of white coarse cotton with a strip of black cloth serving for a sash. Having been with them for three

106

days, Calderón did not envy their life of improvised holiness and mimicry of a Christianity of which they followed a vague outline – as if the religion had long been lost to mankind and these few had an obscure memory of it but confused some of its tenets and rituals with memories of other beliefs. A confusion of ceremonies prevailed at the uncompleted and abandoned mission now occupied by self-styled priests.

A stout, short figure with an enormous belly stepped off the gallery and walked slowly toward Calderón, his brown hands held together on his paunch and his face bent forward so that his thick grey beard pressed against his chest and the clean-shaven top of his head glinted as he came into the light. Looking at him, Calderón thought that he played the part of a spiritual leader rather well, calling himself *Father* Pedro when in reality he was plain Pedro Cordero. But he had told Calderón quite candidly during their first long talk that he possessed no theological training, had never been ordained, and that the twenty-three men with him, who were known as *brothers*, were not priests either. As a young man in Santa Rosa, he had always been fascinated by the trappings of the Church, but with no learning and no family connections, he had had to reconcile himself to the prospect of spending his life as a labourer or a fisherman, like his father. Both activities were loathsome to the lofty ideals of his daydreams. Once, rowing up river with three men, he had come to this old ruin he had known about all his life. The Church had abandoned it for two hundred years, so why not create one's own church there? Yes, of course, there had been the question of money, but you'll be surprised how quickly and easily things fall into place once you make a decision. The shrine had been a godsend. When Calderón asked why they had adopted the outward appearance of monks, Fr Pedro gave him a simple answer: the place demanded it. Originally intended as a mission, the building had risen out of a Christian monastic tradition and it was unthinkable to live in it in a way contrary to its design. He and the brothers were called Franciscan monks in the region, but

107

of course everyone knew that that was not true, it was simply a convenient label. At first, Calderón had thought Fr Pedro an interesting and an intelligent man; there seemed an inescapable logic to his reasoning; but very soon Calderón perceived that the reasoning was only a glib and complacent from of rationalization, and he could not help concluding that the entire set-up at the mission was an elaborate fraud to serve only one end: Fr Pedro's love of his own body. He was like an actor who, failing in all the auditions in the city, puts on a play in a distant small town, casting himself in the principal role.

Calderón stood up from his bench when Fr Pedro, coming up to him from the gallery, raised his head and said, 'The best function the evening service performs is to make us all hungry.' His broad forehead shone and his eyes looked merrily from under the bushy grey eyebrows. His thick lips were held open, the lower one wet with a trickle of saliva at the corners, as though his mouth were already watering. He laughed gently, and added, 'Well, let's take a little stroll before dinner and improve our appetite.'

There was no wall or continuation of the building on the eastern side of the courtyard, that being the uncompleted part of the mission, and the two walked in that direction along a path that led to a vegetable garden.

'Have you been able to meditate?' Fr Pedro asked. Calderón had found himself talking to him earlier about some unidentified fears and Fr Pedro had recommended he look into his soul.

Calderón, glancing at one of the brothers picking tomatoes and putting them into a basket, said, 'My mind wanders, I'm afraid. I'm incapable of sustaining a thought.'

Fr Pedro chuckled and said, 'Then you must be healthy and sound of mind! Only lunatics with an obsession can think. Normal life is not made up of thoughts, but of tomatoes and baskets.' And calling to the man with the basket, he said, 'Brother Juan, let's also have some spring onions and basil in the salad.'

The man in the garden, stooped over a tomato plant, grinned back, nodding his head, and said, 'Just what I was planning! With olive oil and lime juice.'

'And freshly ground black pepper?' Fr Pedro asked.

'And freshly ground black pepper,' Br Juan affirmed, shaking his head vigorously.

Fr Pedro smacked his lips, walking on with Calderón, and said, 'This is a rich land, the soil is excellent. You spit out a seed without thinking, and the next thing there's a tree growing.'

They walked over a narrow bridge made of tree trunks over a stream beside which bananas and papayas grew, and entered a field with scattered mango trees and coconut palms. A dozen cows grazed on the pasture that, in the distance, reached the edge of a wide river. Fr Pedro made a high pitched sound, and two of the cows raised their heads and turned to look at him. 'That's Carmen,' he said to Calderón, pointing to a russet-coloured cow. 'Good girl!' he shouted at the cow, and addressing Calderón said, 'She had trouble with her last calf. I had to help her. It's a funny feeling, putting a hand up a cow's cunt to help her to give birth.'

He laughed, and Calderón felt uncomfortable. 'But it's got to be done,' Fr Pedro went on. 'Nature goes crooked sometimes and breeds deformed creatures.'

He proceeded to tell a smutty story about a brother caught in an indecent act with a calf. 'His punishment was to lie naked for two hours in the pen there where it's ankle-deep in cow shit, and then he was made to take a bath and given money to go and buy himself a woman in Santa Rosa.'

He laughed uproariously. Calderón felt a slight nausea and, wanting to change the subject, asked, 'Are there any Indians in this area?'

'Plenty. A hundred kilometres west of here, the jungle is full of savages. What I always say is that they can stay there!'

'It's funny to think, though, that someone built a mission two hundred years ago to try and convert them.' Calderón's voice was only mildly sarcastic.

'Debauchery is the word, my friend,' Fr Pedro said, laughing.

Calderón looked at him and said, 'I don't understand, what do you mean?'

109

'In any war, women get fucked,' Fr Pedro said, nodding his head and chuckling, his bushy eyebrows going up and down. 'The same when people move to a new continent. All you end up with is a bunch of fatherless children.'

Calderón was not sure if there was any clear reasoning behind these remarks, or indeed whether there was any sense to what he said, especially when he heard him add, '*Convert* – my arse!'

They came to the end of the field where a line of tall trees marked the top of the bank, and sat down on a stone bench between two trees, looking at the river.

'I had meant to talk to you,' Calderón said, 'about what drove me from the city.'

He looked at Fr Pedro as he spoke and noticed that he was staring dully at the river and did not appear to be paying attention to his words. He wondered as he spoke why he felt the necessity of talking about himself, especially to this absurd charlatan. It was almost as if the man's habit and the posture of a patient listener, with a demeanour that, at a certain angle, appeared wise, were eliciting the words from his mouth. 'There was a commotion inside my brain. Something unintelligible that was driving me mad. Because I couldn't understand it. It was as if a ghost spoke to me from the other world but his words reached me only as a vague sound.'

Now Fr Pedro turned his gaze at Calderón and slowly nodded his head. 'Why do you stop? Go on.'

'I found myself in the grip of some mysterious power,' Calderón said, 'driving me to actions not of my choosing. Perhaps I am still in its power.'

Fr Pedro stared at the river as if he divined a profound meaning there, and said with a serious air, 'No one can escape his destiny.'

Calderón pursed his mouth, feeling annoyed with himself. The phoney priest had nothing but clichés and banalities to offer him, why had he bothered to talk to him? It was like doing business with someone who you discovered too late was selling you stolen goods.

They heard the bell ringing in the mission tower, and Fr

Pedro said, 'The best sound in the world! The summons to dinner.'

When they began to walk back, Fr Pedro asked, 'And what about the woman?'

Calderón looked at him questioningly, and Fr Pedro added, 'There's always a woman in a situation like yours.'

'I must be the exception,' Calderón said, having decided to say nothing more to the false father.

They walked back in silence, except for the sound Fr Pedro made when he called to a cow in the field. Calderón hated the high-pitched sound that carried no human meaning, and realized that the anger he was beginning to feel against Fr Pedro and the counterfeit world that he had created at the mission was really directed at himself: not knowing what he was doing, he had become committed to actions he did not wish to perform. He wondered whether he should not make a deliberate attempt to reverse the course on which he had embarked and return to the city.

In the grey light before day broke, the jungle on the left bank was a mass of black but had little clearings on the opposite shore taken up by huts or small banana plantations, and Calderón, enjoying the exhilaration of leaving a place that had begun to oppress him, looked now at one bank and now at the other as if he were in that deep dream where the imagery is so vivid that the sleeping mind possesses an awakened consciousness and expects the next scene to be profoundly revelatory either of some unimagined happiness or of an equally unpredictable horror. He was in that ecstasy of apprehension when the mind, dead to living phenomena, is wide awake to interior perturbations, when unbelievable forms take shape and the imagination, being then involuntary, becomes an agitatedly passive receiver of the transmission of events that precede memory or have no semblance to the living self's knowledge of itself. The mist rising from a landscape lit by the morning sun becomes the transformation of a ghost from an unknown past, and the body shrinks, clinging to the bark of an ancient tree, becomes tinier than a lizard.

Calderón was in fact watching the mist rise from the western bank as he sat in the boat with the two brothers from the mission who were going to Santa Rosa for supplies. The two were in an ebullient mood, like two young men going on holiday, exchanging jokes, and talked about the things they would do while in the town.

'The best time to go to María de Lurdes is the morning,' one of them was saying. 'You get the best pick then, and the girls' bodies are still swollen from sleep. Warm and lovely.'

'Yeah,' the other said, showing his yellowed teeth, 'that way, if we have money left over, we could go again in the evening before returning.'

'You can bet your shaven head,' the first one said, 'we'll make damn sure we have money left over.'

They laughed loudly, and, paying no attention to their passenger who sat morosely with his canvas bag beside him, began to reminisce, telling coarse stories of past adventures.

Calderón had earlier ascertained from the brothers that a small plane flew twice a week to the city. As he sat in the boat, trying not to hear the smutty talk of the brothers, he made up his mind to take the first flight back. Perhaps Leticia would forgive him. He hoped so.

The western bank rose to form a bluff just when they were in the middle of a wide bend in the river. The sun appeared above the mass of trees on the left bank, lighting up the river and the opposite bank where one or two houses could be discerned in the distance. Suddenly, Calderón saw an unexpected sight: a figure appeared high on the bluff; wearing only a pair of shorts, he was running at a regular pace along the line of the river, his naked back shining with sweat. Presently, the man's path led him away from the river, and the boat, proceeding around the bend, arrived ten minutes later at a series of piers where the early morning fishermen had docked, with a crowd of people already on the waterfront arguing prices.

# 5

An outcrop of rocks had narrowed the channel, making the river's current more swift, and the *Princess Isabella* had swayed in a gentle motion, lifting up its bow in a steady rhythm for the length of nearly a kilometre, the two banks of the river nothing but glistening rock, until the rock sloped away and the river widened again where the current, carrying the momentum of the narrow passage, was even swifter. For a few minutes, the boat swung from side to side and then settled to a steady motion.

'Another hour and we'll be in Palmira,' Zuazo called from his cabin.

Marcos, who had put on a shirt, was sitting on the deck with Carla, eating a pastry that she had brought out of a tin. 'Miguel and Alegría, what a beautiful couple!' Marcos was saying, flakes of pastry stuck to his lips. 'Ah, how time passes! There we are, young and just married, making our first child, and the next thing he has grown up and is rolling with his woman. Ah, Carla, what passion we had then, eh! How you cried for more and more when we were making Miguel, what passion, eh!'

'Marcos!' Carla said under her breath, throwing a glance at the hammock. 'Why do you have to talk so plain?'

'And I'm not finished yet,' Marcos said, not heeding his wife's caution. 'God willing, I have more sons in me.'

'Do you want another pastry?' Carla asked him, showing him the open tin, her voice sharp and hurried. Her husband's words had touched off memories that made her breath come faster.

113

Without thinking, Marcos put a hand into the tin and took another pastry, and began to munch it rapidly while she quickly snapped the lid on the tin. 'I knew you'd need a snack,' she said.

'You think of everything, Carla,' he said, grinning, his teeth all covered with flaking pastry, and raising a hand to touch her cheek.

Calderón looked at the middle-aged couple, and thought of what he had seen early in the morning, finding it hard to imagine the two conjoined in anything but an animalistic coupling. There could be no thought prior to action, no love preceding desire; only a blind, eager penetration, a coercion of time that had to be killed – even when all that was achieved was a moment's distraction. One might as well be on a roller coaster, accelerating down at a terrifying speed when all one wanted was a second's sensation that the body had been left behind, that there had been, for this brief duration of time, a timelessness, when the body, in its space, was unaware of its own mass, and dispossessing itself, had a sense of nonexistence without being dead.

Suddenly, Carla screamed, but then quickly clapped a hand to her mouth, and soon began to laugh. An alligator's head seemed to have appeared out of Zuazo's cabin. When it moved out to the deck, they all saw that it was a mask made of straw that was realistically painted and covered Zuazo's head. He removed it and showed his grinning face. 'Neat, eh?' he asked. 'Had it made in Santa Rosa, for the carnival.'

'You scared me,' Carla said, standing near Marcos who was laughing.

'That was the idea,' Zuazo said. 'Nothing like being scared, what do you say, Señor Calderón?'

Calderón smiled faintly. 'Amusing,' he said, his eyes following Zuazo as he returned to the cabin.

The river widened over a flat plain where the jungle receded; there were pools of water beyond the river's banks; six or seven flamingos stood in a pool that reflected them like a mirror; from another, a swarm of insects rose

114

like a strip of black cloud and in a lightning movement disappeared into the light; the land sparkled.

Marcos stood up and stretched his arms while Carla remained squatting on the deck, tying up a sheet with some contents into a bundle. Zuazo left his wheel and came out to the deck, looking in the direction of the flamingos. Carla tightened a knot and rose to her feet, standing near Zuazo.

'All that land . . .' Marcos said.

'How bright the light is,' Carla remarked, moving next to him.

'You could put a thousand cows there,' Marcos said. 'Whose land is it?' he asked, turning to look at Zuazo.

'God knows,' Zuazo said, shrugging his shoulders, and added, 'But there are stories.'

Carla held a hand across her forehead, shading her eyes. 'The light . . . the light,' she muttered breathlessly.

'There's a story that the Indians had a village here once,' Zuazo said.

'Who drove them out?' Marcos asked.

'Themselves, it seems,' Zuazo said. 'You can never tell with Indian stories, though, they're always so unbelievable.'

He paused, but seeing that even Calderón was looking attentively at him, went on: 'You know how it is with them. Tribes taking revenge on one another in fantastic ways.'

Carla was watching him open-mouthed, and he continued: 'The tribe that lived here was ferocious and greatly feared by others. Among Indians when power fails them, they resort to magic, and the story goes that the warriors of the other tribes, having suffered many defeats, got together and summoned the power of magic. They transformed themselves into spiders and crawled into this land. And one night they crept up the legs of all the women of the tribe and wove an invisible and impenetrable web across their sex.'

Marcos laughed as though he had heard a dirty joke, but Carla clapped a hand to her mouth, whispering, 'Holy

115

Mary!' Calderón wiped the sweat trickling down his face and looked intently at Zuazo who went on with the story.

'Of course, after that, the men of the tribe received nothing but scorn from their women. What kind of men were they who couldn't make their members enter the female sex? There was no end to the taunts and the abuse the women flung at them for their strange incapacity. The men were thoroughly humiliated. And having, as it seemed to them, lost their virility, they had no more faith in their bodies and did not again take up arms. There was nothing left for them to do but die.'

'Why didn't the other tribes take this land?' Marcos asked.

'Do you jump into a pond into which you yourself have emptied poison?' Zuazo asked. 'That land,' he added, pointing a finger, 'is infested with a spider known as the black widow.'

Carla gasped and Marcos looked at the land with disgust. Calderón turned and paced to the front of the boat.

They began to pass the occasional hut in small clearings just above the banks of the river, with a person seen in a doorway or standing on a small patch of earth with a hoe in his hands. Near one hut, a man was paddling out in a canoe that was laden with corn. Clusters of settlements appeared and with them more canoes on the river. A church with a pink stucco façade stood on a hill on the right bank, two rows of palm trees in front of it. On the opposite bank, far up on the sloping ground, was a large house, painted white, with dark brown shutters, that looked like a mansion; the area between it and the river was a large lawn broken up by flower beds with winding paths, a small wooden bridge over a pond on which there were two swans and, in one corner, a rock garden. Large trees grew on the wide expanse of the lawn, obscuring parts of the garden, and it was not until they were directly in front of the house as they sailed past it that Calderón saw an attractive young woman in long white gown standing by the pond and throwing food to the swans. It seemed to him an astonishing sight in what he considered to be the

116

middle of the jungle, and he was surprised to hear Carla say, 'What a shame, what a terrible, terrible shame!'

By contrast, both Zuazo and Marco were staring in the direction of the house with dreamy expressions in their eyes. The garden remained in view for several minutes, the house seeming to float away slowly behind the succession of tree trunks, and it appeared like some charmed place, or a vision seen by travellers who have remained too long in the jungle, the glimpses of light and shadow falling on their perception now in the particularity of bright details and now in a splash of dissolving colours. Then the bank grew thick with vegetation, and they entered a long loop in the river. Carla heaved a sigh, shaking her head, and Marcos, smacking his lips suddenly, said, 'I'm going to have an ice-cold beer as soon as we disembark.'

'Another ten – fifteen minutes,' Zuazo said.

Clusters of wooden huts apeared on both banks of the river, painted green and pink and blue, with rickety piers coming into the water from their front doors. The brown faces of middle-aged or old women watched from windows. Nearly naked boys splashed in the water, jumping from the piers. Men in canoes called to one another or some woman in a hut. There was a faint putrid smell in the air, of trash decaying.

'There's Angel!' Carla said, spotting her second son in the crowd on the waterfront when Zuazo was docking the boat.

Calderón saw a look of pleasure on Marcos's face as he said, 'My boy never lets me down.' And cupping his hands round his mouth, he shouted, 'Hey, Angel, we found a bride for you. A beauty!'

'Oh, stop teasing the poor boy!' Carla said, looking severely at Marcos.

'Where did you leave her,' Angel shouted back, 'at Marie Antoinette's?'

'Shame, shame,' Carla said, hearing Marcos, and even Zuazo, laugh, and seeing the grin on Angel's face. The banter between father and son would go on all the way on the drive home; she would maintain a disapproving

117

commentary, but there was nothing in human discourse that she enjoyed more in the world.

When she and Marcos had disembarked, Calderón asked, 'What is Marie Antoinette's?'

'That house we saw just now on the river with its beautiful garden,' Zuazo answered, and when he saw that Calderón remained puzzled, added, 'You should go there if you've got money to throw away on women.'

Calderón winced, and said, 'How far are the mountains from here?'

Zuazo stared at him in amazement. The man seemed to have no interest in pleasure. 'After what you told me this morning,' Zuazo said, 'you don't have to hide. There were witnesses, the bar was full of them, No one saw you do anything. Seems like the man *wanted* to get killed. The only funny thing is, why did you have to run?'

'How far?'

'There are no roads to anywhere from here,' Zuazo said. 'There are some old silver mines to the east of the town, but the land's dead there. There's a road goes up to Marie Antoinette's and, some way past that, to Marcos's farm, but there isn't a road that goes anywhere out of this region. But as I told you, I could get you on a small plane to the coast. You'll have to wait, though.'

Two men came up to the boat and Zuazo talked to them rapidly, giving them orders to deliver the crates of canned goods to a store. Calderón stood on deck, watching the throng of people on the waterfront and looking at the houses across the street. The midday heat and the high humidity induced a feeling of suffocation in him, and he thought of Zuazo's question – why had he run? Everyone in the bar had seen him standing frozen to the ground, the knife in his hand, mesmerized by the maniacal gestures of the man; and even earlier, when the man had abused him and then slapped him, he had stood passively, unable to bring himself to respond. He had been stunned by the ugly tone of the man's voice and the arbitrary violence of his movements. Everyone had seen the man become crazed as the uncalled-for hatred flowed out of him, had witnessed

118

the bravura with which he had thrown down the knife and compelled him to pick it up. Calderón had no sense of having possessed a will at the time, and when he stood there, knife in hand, it was as if he was only there as an instrument of another's will, caught in the space for a moment, having been brought there after a progression of accidental turnings to be frozen into a statue. And when the man had leaped at him, the crash of his body had only produced a momentary shock, and during the brief duration of time after that when the man seemed locked in an embrace with him he had been overcome by a feeling of serenity that astonished him to reflect upon. And then the man falling to the ground, blood pouring out of him, and Calderón himself kneeling over him, feeling no horror, no pain, but experiencing a detachment from the event. It was not till the man spoke his name that he was jolted back into his reality, that he was indeed César Calderón who had been, through no fault of his own, except that he was there, the instrument of death. And he realized now, suddenly, the answer to the question why he had run. The dying man had seen something in his face that touched off recognition, gave Calderón his identity, and he had run, terrified of what he himself might discover of the identity of the man he had been born to kill. Not wanting to stay two more days in Santa Rosa before the next scheduled flight to the city, he had taken the immediate opportunity that had presented itself: the *Princess Isabella* was sailing early in the morning. Lying in the hammock on the deck, hearing the cries of the beasts in the jungle, he had thought of Fr Pedro's trite remark about destiny and realized that whatever the obscure force that had driven him to leave his house, its energy was not yet spent, that he was obliged to continue, and that there was no question of returning to Leticia.

The two men began to carry off the crates and Zuazo, returning to Calderón, said, 'As I said, you could stay here if you wanted to. But you'll be more comfortable in a hotel. You'll find one on the square, three blocks up that street. A nice place, run by an old Danish lady.'

'When can you find out about the plane?' Calderón asked.

'I'll bring you word soon,' Zuazo said.

There was a commotion on the waterfront and some of the people there began to run along the quay. Zuazo and Calderón looked in that direction on the river and saw that a white launch had just come into sight. Zuazo chuckled. Calderón looked at him questioningly, and Zuazo said, 'A party of explorers!'

'What's so funny?' Calderón asked.

'They're headed for Marie Antoinette's, that's what they've come to explore. You get parties of them every month. Sometimes my friend with the plane brings back a couple of businessmen looking for mineral prospects.'

'How do people know about Marie Antoinette's?'

'The underworld holds this planet together,' Zuazo said, surprising Calderón with the observation. 'Travel agents, hotel managers – there's a network of whispers in the underworld, offering the exotic and the sublime. You've only got to have your ear to the ground.'

The launch had drawn nearer and was making to dock. It was twice the length of Zuazo's boat, three portholes on the side suggesting a number of cabins.

Zuazo laughed, seeing half a dozen middle-aged, or older, men in colorful shirts and slacks standing on deck, and said, 'Look at those fuckers! A bunch of turtles! How far won't men go in search of a thrill? Just a little more into the darkness and maybe there will be light. In the eye of a sweet young whore! The promise of life, eh?'

The launch swung round, being positioned for docking, and Calderón saw its name that had been only partially visible earlier: *Simón Bolívar*.

Calderón saw Mrs Sonstroem's white head as she squatted near a flower bed, her small white hand almost transparent in the late morning light, plucking out weeds. From the second-floor window of his room, he had a full view of the terraced garden at the back of the hotel where its owner spent most of her day. She was small, with tiny blue

120

eyes set back in a deeply wrinkled white face, and he would watch her bent little figure carrying a watering can, or standing with a slight stoop of the back in her stained flowery cotton dress, her hands hanging limply, contemplating a row of flowers, or, her feet in the dirt, determinedly hacking at the earth with a hoe. Sometimes he would watch her for half an hour at a time, her hand flitting among the flowers like a butterfly, or her little beak of a nose now held over the petals of one flower and, with a quick turning of the neck, now over another, like a hummingbird. Calderón saw her stand up from where she had been weeding and walk slowly down the path toward a shed next to the house, and walk back with a broom in her hand.

He turned away from the window and walked across his room. He came out to a larger room that had two sofas and an armchair in it together with a long low table on which, in three neat piles, were yellowing old magazines, all of them German. A round table against the far wall had at its centre an arrangement of flowers. An oval sepia photograph in a rectangular gilt frame caught one's attention from its dominant position on the wall behind the flowers – the portrait of the late Mr Erik Sonstroem with his heavy mustache and his piercing eyes that seemed to follow one everywhere in the room. A man who left his native Denmark with a passion for discovery, Mrs Sonstroem had told Calderón in scattered phrases, or a man exiled from the land of his fathers, a subtle equivocation of motives had brought him into his country of rivers and a debilitating jungle. A look of horror had passed over Mrs Sonstroem's face when she turned her gaze away from the portrait and walked to open the door to the balcony, showing the new visitor the amenities of the hotel, but Calderón had heard the words she spoke almost to herself. 'What a terrible thing destiny is!' And there, showing him the view of the square from the balcony, while he looked across to his right at the white church with its green woodwork, he had heard her say, as if completing some earlier remark, 'A chaos of dreams.'

121

He sat down in an armchair and picked up a magazine. A maid came out of another room with a broom and dusting cloths in her hands, and, seeing him seated there, went into his room from where he soon heard a brushing sound as she swept the floor. The magazine bore a date of thirty years ago. The thought quickly passed Calderón's mind that he was four years old when the magazine was printed, and the image came to him of the house by the sea with its walled garden and of the huge black tanker. He did not know a word of German. The magazine looked like a learned journal, printed on thick paper that had gone moldy in the humid air and was clammy to touch, the text in double columns. Two of the articles were illustrated with drawings of archaeological sites and sketches of objects presumably found on the sites; the illustrations to one of the articles, especially with the repeated reference to Greek names in the captions, indicated that the site was in Greece, obviously, but the other was harder to identify. A full-page drawing, printed sideways, so that he had to turn the magazine to look at it, seemed to Calderón a composite illustration of all the archaeological pictures in his untrained mind. The drawing showed an excavation of the foundations of a city long buried in human history. It looked like an enormous crossword puzzle without clues; the eye followed a passage, turning with it this way and that, and then came to a dead end. Part of some temple perhaps; or perhaps only a sketch of the city's gutters that carried its scum. If he knew German, all would be clear to him, and he would know what the passages meant, understand the inevitability of directions inherent in any structure.

The maid finished cleaning his room and came out quietly and went next into the bathroom that was shared by the occupants of the three rooms on that floor. Calderón thought it fortunate that he had been the only guest at the hotel the five days he had been there; he did not have to suffer the irritations that accompany the presence of other people. And perhaps it was this sense of peace that made him feel contented and stifled the anxiety to be moving on.

During all the time that he had continued to move on, he had felt no remorse at having abandoned Leticia. When he had resolved, on leaving the mission, to go back to her, it had not been out of a desire to make reparation for the injury he had caused her; it had been out of pity for his own condition. But coming to this hotel, he had, for the first time, questioned his own action, wondering at the queer motives that must have composed the compulsion that had led him on so violent a course, a behaviour that must appear contemptible to any objective observer. Surely, Leticia must have cursed him a million times by now. On the other hand, she might have cried *Good riddance!* Since becoming pregnant she had appeared as if she lived in a world separate from his, and indeed alien to it. He had taken up paper and pen with the intention of writing her a letter, but had only stared at the blank page, not having anything to say. Finally, he had written, 'My dear Leticia,' but looking at those words, he felt absolutely indifferent. He found that he could not clearly see her face, only the shape of a female body. Somehow, that produced a revulsion within him, and he tore up the page. For the woman he saw in his mind lay naked on hot sand, her legs parted and raised, with a greenish-yellow slime flowing from her vagina. His dreams were bad enough; he did not want to encourage his waking mind to witness the same surreal imagery, he thought, throwing the torn bits of paper into the waste basket. He reminded himself that he had provided well for Leticia; she had the kind of stubborn will to make a success of the business. The real question that concerned him, however, was one he found difficult to formulate; he saw the question mark without the words that should precede it, knowing only that there was some terrible fear deep within his mind, a vague torment that must have its source in memory, but he could *see* nothing. It was as when he looked out of the balcony and observed the poor Indians outside the church, sitting along the wall with soiled cloths stretched out in front of them covered with desiccated herbs and curious little charms and candles – he could see them all in the particularity of colour and definition, as he could see the men sitting in the café across the square, some on the sidewalk and some inside, sipping coffee or beer and talking with rapid gestures; but yet at the same time, even in the very moment when he noticed some minute detail, like a missing tooth in the mouth of a man laughing in the square, the world receded, and he saw nothing there. What was present was continually vanishing as if something in his mind were forcing an emptiness in his brain to make room for some incredible, some overwhelming, vision. And his real terror lay in the thought that the revelatory moment, when the question suddenly formulated itself or the elusive image took shape with a brutal convulsion of memory, was perhaps at hand, and would seize him in the next moment with all its horror.

In the dark dining room with its high windows recessed in the thick wall and its long mahogany table, Mrs Sonstroem's voice warbled as the silver clinked against the dark brown stoneware and separated the bone from the fish's flesh. Calderón was the only guest, and a black maid glided in and out of the dining room like a shadow. Mrs Sonstroem ate slowly, chewing small mouthfuls thoughtfully, her cheeks becoming sunken as she swallowed. She had brought in a bouquet of purple flowers from her morning in the garden and placed it at the centre of the dining table, having arranged the flowers in a crystal vase. A point of light, somehow reflected from a high window, caught at the base of the vase, and she stared at it with eyes that appeared like black holes. Her voice flew out of her mouth in swift little phrases, and then held itself in the still air, sometimes in a flutter of sighs.

'But of course everyone was saying Europe is finished, Europe is finished. . . . The German fatherland was murdering its sons.'

Calderón tore at the roll and slapped butter on it hurriedly.

'The knowledge of passion in fragments of dreams, it's the same whether the man cursed to wander is driven or driven mad. . . . Erik knew, running from his fatherland like he'd seen a ghost, coming to the darkest America, finding everywhere it was too cold or too damp, too cold, too damp, for his soul. . . . He fought the first instinct, to cling to me, his woman who once had superfluous flesh on her body and golden hair. . . . But not all men can hide their despair inside a woman. . . . Sometimes there's not space enough in the womb.'

Calderón heard his own chewing, the bread and fish in his mouth.

'The papers had to be written in German or English and he knew German. But he loved best to draw, capturing the texture of stones among weeds . . . the imprints of a civilization gone silent. . . . Scratches on stones. . . . From Mexico to Guatemala and then down to Peru, he searched for stones. Pyramids overgrown with creepers, cities buried under the sand. He scraped away at the earth as if he was working toward some secret centre. But one day he suddenly said, "Anna, scholarship is useless." Like I say to the cook, "The meat is overdone." '

The maid glided in with a bowl of salad and Calderón served himself, replacing the wooden serving spoon and fork gently in the bowl. Mrs Sonstroem drank from her glass of water and stared at the fish on her plate and cut a tiny portion of it. Calderón remained silent. Mrs Sonstroem sighed.

'Only once his eyes clouded over and I thought he was going to cry and I said, *You have nothing to repent*, and he turned away and perhaps a tear did fall, I don't know, I did not look for any signs when he faced me again. . . . There are silver mines in this region that were worked out by the last century, empty caves that no one enters now, after a man's blood was shed at the mouth of one.'

Calderón felt the vinegar stinging his gums and he swallowed some beer. He did not want to ask whose blood it had been. She would reveal in her own manner if she wished him to know.

'This is where we settled at last, in the proximity of the disused mines, among mineral prospectors, among people

125

who have known life only on banks of rivers on the edge of the jungle. . . . A house anyhow, a house anywhere. . . . Why should you repent, I told him, you haven't been to a brothel? . . . He would never go into the garden and never said a word about the flowers I brought into the house. . . . A nostalgia for stones must have attracted him to the mine, but he had received a letter from his uncle, recalling his father's death, a coincidence perhaps. . . . My hair was golden then. . . . White now. All white.'

Mrs Sonstroem remained silent and seemed to be making a deliberate attempt to finish her fish. She spoke only to ask the maid to refill her glass of water. She took one section of tomato and one leaf of lettuce from the salad and cut them into thin strips before eating them. The maid brought in a plate with cut-up papaya and placed it in front of Calderón. Mrs Sonstroem had finished but waited silently while Calderón was served coffee.

An old taxi, whose engine made a whistling sound when idling, took him through the dirt streets to where the town ended along a narrow river with murky water. The small stucco houses were all coated with pink dust that rose from the streets. Barely clothed children played in groups and yelled at the taxi as it crawled behind an ox-drawn cart. Another old taxi appeared at a crossroad, and the two drivers stuck their heads out of the windows and shouted at each other, making plans for a game of cards in the evening, while several men, riding on mules, went past. The taxi proceeded along a street that had wooden huts in it with dark-skinned men, wearing only trousers, sitting in front of them, looking exhausted, their bloodshot eyes expressive of an enormous fatigue. Both the street and the town ended abruptly, and the taxi turned left along the river, on a bumpy dirt track, and halted next to a rusted old iron bridge. He would have to go on foot from there, the driver told him, standing outside the taxi and giving him directions.

Calderón walked up the bridge and looked through the diamond pattern of the ironwork on either side, wondering

126

at the human drive to construct passages into forbidding territories. The river below him was dark and thickly overhung with trees. But within a quarter of a kilometre from the bridge, the jungle suddenly ended and the land before him was rocky and desolate. It looked as though some great granite mountains had been shattered and now lay in vast heaps of broken rock, tiny points of light glittering from the dark grey boulders and smaller fragments. That, however, was only a first impression, he realized as he walked on; for, coming to the top of an incline, he saw a series of bald hills, some greyish mossy vegetation clinging to them, sweeping away to the horizon, with here and there a small valley appearing to be packed with broken rock. He could not tell what curiosity impelled him to want to continue in that empty land; perhaps it was only a desire to climb up the highest eminence in the region to see what was visible from there; or perhaps it was a detective's compulsion to go over a new piece of evidence even when he could tell after one quick glance that it was irrelevant to the mystery. But the land was not entirely dead, after all! Coming over a hill, he was surprised to see clumps of greenery in a hollow in the land. A little yellow bird flew out of a bush, followed by another. Arriving in the hollow, he saw that there were pools of water beside which the bushes grew, green and red berries on them. The larger hill rose beyond the hollow, much steeper and higher than it had seemed from a distance, and he was relieved that he did not need to climb up to its top. For he could see the mouth of the old silver mine, and walked slowly toward it, wondering whether Erik Sonstroem had been drawn to it by the same inexplicable curiosity that he felt now.

He stood outside the dark mouth and found himself trembling. The mouth of the mine seemed to have been cut with jagged blows as if with the tools of primitive man. A metre and a half high and no more than two wide, the passage narrowed – he could see in the diagonal light that fell across it – and disappeared into total blackness. He stood there, his hands tightly clasped together to control the trembling, sweat trickling down from his armpits, feeling a compulsion to enter that darkness and at the same time a terror of what might happen to him if he did. 'No!' he cried aloud involuntarily seeing his feet move into the mouth of the mine – a sharp, piercing cry. His echo came roaring back. But what stopped him was not his own will. Two or three bats came flying out and almost smashed into his head but swung past him with shrill, squeaking cries. He threw his hands up against his face and hurriedly stepped back, and fell to the ground. More bats came screaming out. He found himself crawling away on his hands and knees. The bats streaked across the sky, swooped down and disappeared back into the mine. Calderón stood up, his clothes wet with sweat, a giddiness in his head, and his legs unable immediately to support his body, so that he had to sit down. It was unimaginable that a man should have chosen to live inside that mouth as though he were no more than a parasite feeding on the gums of a beast. Even more unimaginable that he kept his woman with him in that darkness. Unthinkable their copulations.

'Too cold, too damp.' Mrs Sonstroem's phrases beeped in her bird voice in the dining room. 'It was the opposite of the icy slopes of Denmark. . . . the burning rock.' She stared for a long time at the sliced chicken breast on her plate, absently stirring the red sauce with her fork. But suddenly she looked up at Calderón, her voice sharp as a querulous wren's. 'How can you live with a sick soul?' Calderón remained calm, knowing that he was not being addressed. 'Erik was careful about his food, always got the butcher to trim away the fat. . . . With his little pointed knife.' She lifted a slice of chicken and then let it fall in the plate. 'And vegetables . . . only steamed lightly. . . . He exercised too. . . . Ran around like a fool in all weather. . . . And drank weak tea.' Calderón stared at the point of light in the crystal vase that contained freshly cut flowers every day. The voiced warbled. In the silence when she paused, a scattered phrase fell into his mind and settled next to one lodged there a long time ago. He thought of the crow in the fable; she was like the crow, dropping pebbles into his mind to raise to a level where he could reach it, whatever lay sunk there. Months began to pass. Sometimes weeks separated the phrases of a thought and he had the impression that he had already witnessed the event only now being revealed. No longer going forward, he did not need to think of time. Years began to pass. He must have heard her say ten thousand times, 'Too cold, too damp.'

There was a commotion in the square, and from the balcony Calderón saw a crowd of children yelling and laughing as they followed a man on stilts wearing a costume of shining blue, yellow and red with an enormous mask of a toucan on his head, two large yellow projections forming a beak that kept opening and shutting. The man was taking random steps in the crowd, scaring the kids by appearing to fall among them, so that they screamed with delight, knowing that the threat was only a pretence; suddenly, he would hop up and down and beat his arms and all the children would yell in chorus, 'Quack, quack, quack.' People in the sidewalk café and at the fronts of shops were looking and laughing at the man's antics, and the Indians outside the church were pointing in his direction and talking among themselves. Clop, clop, clop he hopped, and 'Quack, quack, quack,' yelled the kids.

Carrying on a grotesque act, the man reached the front of the hotel and with two long strides came to stand right in front of the balcony, his head only a metre below Calderón. The eyes on the toucan mask appeared remarkably animated and there was something pathetic about the way the beak kept opening and shutting. From Calderón's point of view, the kids who had gathered around the man's legs were tiny and distant, so high was he on his stilts. From inside the beak came laughter, and then the shout, 'How are you doing, Señor Calderón?'

Calderón laughed back at him, shaking his head.

'The girls at Marie Antoinette's keep asking about you,' the voice shouted. 'They want to know why you don't visit them.' He laughed hilariously.

'Who are you?' Calderón asked, looking slightly upset.

'Tommy Toucan, bird of the streets, it's carnival time, don't you know? Tommy Toucan sets the pace, it's carnival time like never before!'

He made a flapping gesture with his arms, took a few steps back, hopped around, scattering the children, and stood again immediately below Calderón where, holding a part of the balcony's railing, he raised his mask with the other hand, and shouted, 'Captain Zuazo of the *Princess Isabella* at your service!'

Calderón grinned at him and said, 'What on earth are you doing in that costume?'

'My dear old lady has broken her heart,' Zuazo said, 'and I've got to make a few pesos somehow.'

'What do you mean?'

'The *Princess Isabella* needs a transplant. No money, no new heart. But she'll come back to life one day. I'll get the parts one by one and fix her myself. Anyway, how are you finding life in Palmira?'

'Never a dull moment,' Calderón said.

Zuazo looked down, stooping a little, and called to the kids to stop making a row, and, turning to face Calderón again, said, 'I got news for you. The plane I told you about. The man got busted. He was forced to land in Guayaquil. He got twenty years for his services to the underground economy. So, what are you going to do?'

'Hang on, I suppose.'

'I could get you a passage on one of the launches that bring men to Marie Antoinette's, but they go back to Santa Rosa.'

'No, I don't want to go back,' Calderón said. 'Maybe some time, but not now. I'm fine here.'

The kids were getting restless and Zuazo, putting on his mask, made a swooping gesture that sent them scattering, and he strutted after them.

The next day more men dressed up in fancy costumes appeared in the square, and carnival music was heard from the streets. It happened each year that suddenly one day there was a man on stilts, made up as some bird or animal, and people would say, 'It's carnival time again!' Everyone would be surprised how soon the time had come round again, but then would abandon themselves during their leisure hours to music and dancing in the streets until the final day when the square would be packed with glittering bodies and throbbing music. And Calderón, too, found himself saying one day, 'It's carnival time again!' and was astonished to think that though it seemed only yesterday that he had seen Zuazo as Tommy Toucan come hopping across the square, already three or four years – he could not be sure how many – had compressed themselves into that one image, bursting out from it each time it came to his mind and being scattered like the children running from the make-believe demon in the square.

Very occasionally, there was another guest at the hotel; twice a year, for some reason to do with trade on the river, all the seven rooms would be taken; otherwise, Calderón occupied it alone with Mrs Sonstroem who took his presence for granted. He gave good tips to the maid and the cook at Christmas, and handed an envelope containing money to Mrs Sonstroem on New Year's day; the maid and the cook thanked him for his generosity, but Mrs Sonstroem never said whether he had paid too much or too little. In fact, when he gave her the envelope, she simply put it next to her plate, and continued to eat and talk. She usually forgot the envelope there and the maid would have to take it to her when clearing the table.

'What have you done, you feel so guilty?' Mrs Sonstroem was prodding the chopped spinach with her fork, and Calderón was eating silently while the shadow of the maid hovered in the doorway to the kitchen. 'What great error?. . . . We had left the desert a long time before. He abandoned the scholarship that had begun to make him famous in Europe. . . . His heart throbbed with remorse. He was born with the disease. . . . We are simple creatures, really. Why must we suffer? . . . He could not answer. Or would not. He talked so little. But I had made a home for him . . . where he would be safe . . . even if he

131

would not look at my flowers . . . gave him the warmth of my voice, at least . . . the comfort of words – for how else can you know? . . . It is terrible to be afflicted by hideous passions, to be touched by some sinister finger at birth.'

Calderón looked at her with apprehension. He could scarcely discern the blue in the hollows where her eyes were, but saw the two black holes staring at him. The folds of the wrinkles beneath her eyes were red from her morning in the sun. Her profoundly piteous glance still fixed on him, she went on, 'He had to cross the iron bridge. . . . Dreadfully quick, the copulation of beasts . . . ah, the destiny of animals!'

Her stare was still fixed on Calderón. He swallowed some beer, and turned his eyes to his plate.

'And the children spring on their parents, all teeth and claws. . . . A bristle of fur and the inflammation of lust. . . . I saw nothing but I know how it happened. . . . He walked to the nearest silver mine. God knows with what curiosity, what desire, what awesome expectation. . . . And who invents the extraordinary circumstances . . . that force a man to wander . . . among winding passages . . . until he must come – ah, the catastrophe of creation!'

Calderón knew then that he would have to go and see; cross the iron bridge himself into the barren landscape that she was describing. He felt as though he knew the landscape already, that he had been there, as if in some dream, or somewhere in the fictions of memory, that he had already looked through the diamond pattern of the iron bridge and seen the sluggish black water of the river below him, and gone among the broken rocks. A yellow bird had flown out, and then another, from a bush. Erik Sonstroem came to the black mouth of the silver mine in the early evening light that cast diagonal shadows across the bald hills. He stood there only for a moment, and did not hesitate, felt no fear. He entered calmly as though through the front door of his own house.

In Ecuador once, in the underground passage of an excavation, in a corner beside some broken pottery that he had himself dug up, some twenty years ago, he had forcibly held the Indian girl's slippery body and she would not stop thrashing her legs until he had penetrated her, pinning her to the ground, panting when he discharged his semen in her womb.

Mrs Sonstroem ate a little of the spinach. 'I was in Otavalo with an Indian woman, learning to weave. She had said, glancing at the pattern of the weave, "Such desire – only to make his own death!" Who? What? "The blade that springs from the ground." What are you talking about? She muttered something else and pretended she had only been talking to herself.'

In the underground passage, he had stopped her mouth with, 'My dear child!' crushing her lips, but her legs continued to thrash.

'When he returned to Otavalo, his eyes were like a drunkard's. You don't come to my bed like that. I don't want a lecher breathing down my skin. . . . The Indian woman saw him go into the other room, his face twitching. "There is nothing you can do," she said. . . . What? . . . Why? . . . There is nothing. . . . She shook her head sadly.'

Calderón closed his eyes, his head hanging over his plate, his hands beside it holding a fork and knife. The maid's shadow seemed to retreat in the doorway. The light shifted across the black mouth of the mine and just when he entered he saw the savage young man spring up from the woman who remained spread on the ground and his eyes caught a glint of the knife in the man's hand. Mrs Sonstroem had gone quiet. Calderón opened his eyes and saw that his own hand had tightened over the knife.

The man stood at the door of the hotel when Calderón went down to see him. He wore a light blue turban on his head with a large stone the colour of a ruby at its center just above his forehead. An emerald hung from his right ear. A wide black mustache curled up on either side of his nose and his eyes stood out from the shining black lines painted around them. A pinkish-brown make-up covered his face, his lips were a glossy red. Pearls hung from his neck. He wore a peacock-blue cloak and bright pink pantaloons. One hand on his hip and the other holding up a sabre, he struck the haughty pose of an oriental despot. When he saw Calderón come to the door, he raised the hand from his hip to his head, bending slowly from the waist at the same time, and said, 'Salaam, salaam. Your poor servant Ali Akbar from Basra!'

'Zuazo! Don't tell me it's carnival time again!'

'For two days already,' Zuazo said, laughing and bowing again. 'Where have you been, Señor Calderón? I heard you went to look at a silver mine. So, that's your secret, eh?'

A group of young boys had gathered behind Zuazo and had begun to chant, 'Genghiz Khan, Genghiz Khan!' Zuazo turned round and gave them a mock-imperious stare, raising his sabre; thrusting his hand into his pocket, he brought out a dozen discs that looked like gold coins and threw them up into the air. Little points of golden light fell to the ground and the boys dashed to pick up the discs.

'Come on,' Zuazo said to Calderón, 'let's go celebrate. We're getting old standing here.'

'Well, a drink, why not?' Calderón said, walking with Zuazo across the square which was beginning to be crowded with the carnival merrymakers.

One of the boys shouted, 'Watch out, the Moors are coming,' and he and several others went running ahead of the two men. Other figures in carnival costume strutted about the square, each with a following of young boys raising a boisterous din. Sounds of drums and flutes were in the air.

From their table on the sidewalk, Calderón watched the little explosions of merriment in the square and heard Zuazo's chatter. Did he know the latest? They'd found more silver in the mines east of town, but some twenty kilometres away. It was crazy. People were going mad. The earth was an unending miracle. For a hundred years bats and snakes lived in abandoned mines. And then, plop, out comes more silver. Like fish, jumping out of still, black water. Wasn't that what Calderón was up to, eh, looking for silver? No? Well, that was all right, anyone should be free to take a walk among the bald hills and have a pow-wow with the bats. It wasn't his business. But since the last week the town was going crazy. There really was more silver. The same thing was going to happen that happened a hundred years ago. A bunch of shits was going to get rich and another bunch of shits was going to find nothing.

Calderón was struck by the unreality of an oriental prince talking to him about events in the South American interior. Some of Zuazo's make-up had come off with sweat, which he absently wiped away with his sleeve, and his face when seen close was covered with splotches and streaks. Night had begun to fall and after his third drink, Calderón began to feel uncomfortable. The crowd in the square had increased, there was more music, drums every-where, as if mankind were beating its fists against the air it was obliged to breathe. Calderón no longer heard Zuazo's words though he followed the movements of his face and occasionally spoke something himself. Without thinking, he had more drinks.

Some people were running toward the waterfront and word soon came that the launch *Simón Bolívar* had arrived with clients for Marie Antoinette's.

Suddenly, Calderón clutched Zuazo's arm tightly and said, 'The ocean! Zuazo, I want to go to the ocean.'

'Why don't we go to Marie Antoinette's?' Zuazo asked, grinning. 'Got any money on you? There'll be a party there. A world of fantasy. Women in the shapes of god-desses rising out of an occean. Women swimming before your eyes.'

'Zuazo, listen to me seriously. How can I get to the ocean? Can you get me a passage on that launch?'

'It only goes back up the river, and then there's a small plane to the city from Santa Rosa. But what do you say we go to Marie Antoinette's and have some fun?'

'Here, take this money,' Calderón said, plucking notes from his wallet. 'Go enjoy yourself. But get me a passage on that launch.'

Calderón walked unsteadily down the street, having

decided not to suffer going through the crowd of noisy merry-makers in the square. He had drunk too much and thought that a walk along the three sides of the square to the hotel – which was really directly opposite the bar – would do him good. Coming to the end of the street where a group of musicians stood at a corner, beating their drums and piercing the air with their flutes, Calderón turned to walk across the front of the church. The air was still, with occasional erratic spurts of a breeze, and very humid. He felt short of breath. Old women were coming out of the church. Some Indians still sat near the entrance, selling charms and candles. The music from the square came in bursts and was counterpointed by short explosions of drums from the nearby corner.

He should not have drunk so much, he thought. His head throbbed. A whiff of breeze carried the smell of jasmine to his nostrils. He was in front of an arch in the middle of a stone wall to the right of the church. He walked through the arch. A narrow garden had been laid out along the side of the church and then spread wide at the rear. It was deserted and dark, though a diffusion of light from the neighbouring houses and the lampposts in the street produced a milky glow in the garden.

He sat down on a stone bench at the back of the church, surrounded by vegetation. The sounds from the square were muffled. The outer leaves of the trees stirred very slightly. Odours of herbs – rosemary and lavender – made the humidity bearable. Sitting in the scented air, he was breathing a little more easily now. Soon he was overcome by a pleasantness and felt dreamily that he was dissolving into the current of the still air that hung over the rosemary bushes. He sat there motionless for a long time, losing sense of himself, as if he were only the space between two tiny thorn-like needles on a sprig of rosemary.

The couple that entered the garden furtively, taking soft steps and throwing glances behind them, did not see him.

He came out of his trance when he heard the woman moan softly. The couple lay on the ground among rosemary and lavender bushes five metres away from him, to

136

his front and left. The milky light reflected from a raised white leg, making it look pearly; two gleaming points of light trembled along the thigh. Crushed rosemary released a heavy odour.

Calderón rose from his bench and tried to walk away quietly. But his breath caught in his throat. He was gasping for air. He seemed to be smashing his way blindly through the garden. His legs stumbled in their haste. He turned round the corner and could see the arch to the street. He found himself trying to run. But he fell on his hands and knees and was seized by a violent cough. His body dripped with sweat. It flowed from his forehead as he coughed into the ground. The coughing stopped. His breath seemed choked for a moment. He swallowed hard and opened his mouth to cough again. Vomit poured out of his mouth and he remained there, on his hands and knees, open-mouthed and staring wildly at the pool of slime that his body had discharged.

# 6

But he had to flee from the ocean, too. There were the resorts with their gaudy tribes of vacationers where one felt stifled on the beaches; there were the great ports with their commerce with the United States, Japan and the Persian Gulf, long seafronts of cranes and warehouses; there were the naval dockyards with their incongruous little gardens of frangipani and palm trees, with the base of their trunks painted white, in front of the barracks; but nowhere was that ocean glimpsed through the iron bars of a gate. Halfway down the Pacific coast of South America, Calderón realized his error – that there was nothing to look for: it had only been a maudlin sentimentality that had made him think that there was. The eyes that he had had when he was two years old had long been blinded, and it was the circumstance only of the dying man calling him by his name that had aroused the terrible suspicion in his mind. Of course, he could have been a madman seeking a lamentably heroic death, forcing upon a stranger a deed of some obscure and pathetic honour. No image of the ocean touched off that memory that showed what the man had looked like thirty-two years before, when Calderón was two, his hands on the iron bars of the gate, watching the black tanker sail silently across in the distance.

He turned then from the ocean to the mountains, entering the wilderness of the southern Andes where the winds came in sweeping cold gusts, his only desire to leave the chronicle of accumulated errors behind him and to enter that habitation where he could survive the solitude of his future. Where there were no more trains and buses, he took horses or mules. And riding slowly up a trail through a coniferous forest or under the great rauli trees, where the sky was not visible and it was like being in an enormous damp cathedral, the mule's legs sinking into the soft layers of humus, he knew he would recognize the place when he came to it; for there, in the icy winds, he had a sense of not where he was or where he had come from and why but an impression of a vision anterior to existence – as if he was not yet born but already foresaw the manner of his death and knew his living days must be spent in wandering the earth until he arrived where he must meet it; so that the present moment, which could not have been happening to him, had happened in the history of his being and was to occur again in a dream of an improbable past. That, and that alone, made of the living present a marvellous mystery, filling the breast with passions both exuberant and mournful.

Emerging from a forest, he descended to a wide valley in one corner of which there was a hamlet. The late afternoon sun lit the entire valley, the light reflecting back in patches from the loops of a river where it was not obscured by the vegetation. Tall trees, like poplars, and others that looked from a distance like sycamores and chestnuts, only a few hundred metres below a coniferous forest, indicated that the disposition of the walls of the mountains and their obstruction of the winds gave a milder climate to the valley than could be expected at this altitude. There were little squares of cultivation, and here and there patches of pink, purple and yellow suggested a profusion of wild flowers. The air was so dry and the light so clear that a tiny speck in a field could be seen to be a horse; above this valley, the range of snowcapped peaks and a long plateau of ice formed a wide oval skylight; and the sky seemed to be one solid sheet of brilliant blue. Calderón took deep breaths, exhilarated by the air, as with bright eyes he descended to the valley.

Coming halfway down the slope, he saw a part of a distant mountain on the opposite side, facing the hamlet about ten kilometres away, that had earlier been obscured by the forest. There, flowing from over a ridge, was a wide waterfall. From where Calderón saw it, it appeared like a massive column a couple of hundred metres long, its lower part diffused in a mist.

He felt an enormous sense of release as from some severe internal constriction. Six years after abandoning Leticia and wandering through regions that only deepened his despair with his own life, he had come to that small area of the earth which seemed to have been created for the ecstasy of his soul – as if this was where the eternal time in which the body lived was at last to end and that timelessness begin which was pure being. He had awakened from temporal terrors and entered the dream of his existence.

The valley and its hamlet were called San Clemente de los Andes. Some three hundred people lived there. The majority of the men worked as lumbermen, cutting down trees from the coniferous forests on the slopes that encircled the valley and floating the trunks down river. Women cultivated the land, growing corn and vegetables. Small herds of cows and sheep provided the valley with its meat and dairy products as well as hide and wool. The population was a mixture of Indian and Spanish blood. Everyone, except the very old, had black hair and a ruddy complexion, and seemed to be taller than is the average in the Andean countries. Calderón, with his black hair and dark brown eyes, seemed one of them, especially after he had been there for some time when his light brown face began to be tinged by an orangish-red at the cheeks. An elderly couple offered him shelter in their house while, with the help of two lumbermen, he built a small one for himself in a grove of sycamores in front of a brook that ran into the river, two weeping willows on the nearer bank of the brook neatly framing a view of the waterfall at the far end of the valley.

It was a two-room cottage made of fir logs and boards with a narrow verandah at the front where Calderón formed the habit of sitting in the morning in the pinkish light and watching the glowing land around him begin to sparkle here and there until the whole valley was saturated by the brilliance of the risen sun. Even the sycamore leaves that hung darkly a moment before appeared to be green transparencies as he looked up at them. He did not need to plant a garden. The land that sloped gently in front of his cottage was covered with bushes bearing purple and magenta flowers and, with time, he trod a path that wound round the bushes to the brook a hundred metres from the cottage. There, a rock just next to one of the weeping willows formed a comfortable seat from where one could watch the fish in the clear, cold water, or look across at the meadow on its other side where sheep and some cows grazed to the banks of the broad, swift-flowing river. Along the banks of the river, especially among rocks near its wide sweeping bends, away from its main current, there were pools where children bathed, and one where Lucila, the washerwoman, did her daily work.

She had come to see Calderón when he was still living with the old couple and spending his days measuring, sawing and nailing boards together with the help of the two lumbermen, Belisario and Olmedo. She was a stout, strong woman, with slightly sunken cheeks and very marked wrinkles. Her black eyes fixed Calderón with a serious stare. He must have washing to do, she remarked, as though it were an accusation. She did not so much offer her services as made an announcement that she had come to take his things away. In time, Calderón grew fond of her. She was a woman of few words.

When his cottage had been completed, Calderón began to join one of the parties of lumbermen, a group that included Belisario and Olmedo. They had given him more than their spare time in helping to build his cottage and he had the impulse to pay them back by doing some of their work for them. The forests were owned by a corporation in a distant city, and every three months a train of mules brought a *señor administrador* and three or four of his assistants, together with such supplies as rice, sugar and coffee, and they worked out with the appointed foremen what each lumberman was owed. The foremen kept a

141

tally of how many trees had been cut by each lumberman, and that formed the basis of payment. Calderón's idea was that he would divide the trees that he cut between Belisario and Olmedo, and thus compensate them for the time they had given him.

He watched fascinated as the men, stripped to the waist, their strong backs glistening with sweat and the muscles there forming quivering patterns as they raised their arms with the long-handled axe, rhythmically performed their work. At first he found the axe heavy and when he swung it at the base of the tree, instead of making a clean incision, with a chip of wood flying out, he merely managed to inflict upon the trunk a slight scratch. The blade glanced off the tree, the axe fell out of his hands, and he stumbled forward.

Belisario came up to him, smiling compassionately. 'You're standing too far away,' he told him. 'And don't try to strike a blow, just swing evenly. Hold your back straight, keep the legs apart and firmly on the ground, and don't strain at the wrists, let them remain loose.'

Belisario watched him attempt to follow his advice, and encouraged him. 'That's the way,' he said. 'now keep up the rhythm, keep it even, don't hurry and don't slacken, it's as easy as walking.'

Calderón became excited when his body discovered the correct posture and his arms began to swing effortlessly, and each time the blade hit the tree precisely he felt a thrill that rippled right through his whole body. Without looking at the others, he could see that his body moved exactly like theirs, and that, in fact, with each succeeding swing, he was becoming indistinguishable from the others. The sense of exhilaration was enormous within his body when he felled his first tree and heard, when its crash had died down, a spontaneous applause from his fellow men.

In another part of the forest there was a nursery from where saplings were taken to replenish the forest, and when Calderón had been with the lumbermen for a month – having continued to work for the pleasure he derived from it long after he had paid his debt – he moved to the nursery with a party of others, following a pre-established principle of rotation. Planting the young saplings was lighter work but was no less satisfying than the harder labour of cutting down trees.

In the evenings, the young men and women of San Clemente de los Andes came to the small park above the bank of the river, and the air was perfumed with jasmine and filled with the soft talk of the couples, the cries of younger children, and the ostentatious laughter of youths trying to catch the attention of girls. Sometimes Calderón would go there and sit with some of the lumbermen he knew, drinking maté brought there by a vendor from the place's only bar across the park. Inevitably, he would, when walking back to his cottage, pass a young couple under some trees, in the darkening light, standing in an embrace, and occasionally even on the ground, a shadow of two bodies pressed together, and he looked away, but not without a smile on his face. The earth was a riot of passions, and if he himself, now at the age of forty, felt that he had not as yet escaped the purgatory of a loss of desire, he was not any longer appalled by the manifestations of the desires of others. The young crushed the wild violets that covered the ground, pressing their ardour into the earth, but the little flowers sprang back the next day as vivid as before in the spots of sunlight that fell through the trees.

Lucila brought him a white robe of coarse cotton one evening, and said, 'Tomorrow, just before sunrise, wear this and wait for a knock on the door.'

'What is it?' Calderón asked. 'What should I do? Why?'

'You will know,' she said, communicating very little with words, as was usual with her. He knew it was no use persisting, and watched her depart, the stout, firm woman with the black eyes that looked so deeply.

It was still dark outside when he rose the next morning after a sound sleep. The sky was turning grey by the time he had washed himself and had some breakfast. He put on the robe. It had wide sleeves that came to just below his forearms, a round opening for the head, and fell to just above his ankles. No sooner had he put it on than there was a knock on the door. Belisario and two other men stood in the verandah, wearing identical robes. Seeing him come to the door, they turned round and began to walk away in single file. He followed them. Their bare feet scarcely made any noise as they walked over the grassy ground. Arriving at another cottage, they stood before it and one of the men knocked on the door. A man in a white robe opened it, and now the five of them walked away in single file. They went to two more cottages.

The seven men in white robes walked across a field at the corner of which an outcrop of rocks formed a jagged pyramid no more than twenty meters high. The mountain ridge over the wide oval of the valley was tipped with sunlight. In the distance, under some trees, a group of horses snorted and kicked their legs. The men came to the rocks, and one of them entered a narrow crevice. The other six stood outside silently. The man came out, wearing a mask on his head. Calderón entered the opening after two more men had done so and emerged wearing masks. He found himself in a small circle, lit up by candles. Four masks stood on a natural platform made by a jutting rock. Each was identical – a large male head made of pulped wood and brightly painted. Calderón put one on and went out. Soon the seven men rode away on the horses, trotting at an even pace. The sun showed itself over the eastern rim and flooded the valley with light.

A hundred metres from where the waterfall crashed down with its unceasing roar, past some large boulders which trapped the enormous force of the water, there was a wide circular pool of clear blue water, and next to the pool a meadow of soft green grass and little yellow flowers. Leaving their horses under a clump of trees, the seven men climbed up some rocks and came to a wide ledge overlooking the pool. They sat down on the ledge, their backs straight, their hands on their knees. The air about them was misty with the spray from the waterfall that roared behind them. A few minutes later, five figures in purple robes and wearing female masks walked across below them and climbed up the rock above the men to sit on five scattered boulders.

A wisp of smoke rose from the meadow, two or three tongues of flame flared out, and a large fire lit up. A group of some twenty girls, no more than twelve or thirteen years old, their slim narrow bodies naked, the light brown skin gleaming in the sun, formed a wide circle round the fire and, stretching out their arms, held one another by the hand. They began to move round the fire, first slowly and then with longer and more rapid strides until they were running round and round, their long black hair flying behind them. Their faces became flushed, their bodies shone. Now one saw a single girl, as if she had become isolated in one's imagination, her eyes shining brightly, her slender legs leaping, the slight ripple at her chest where two little cones formed her emerging breasts, and now as the bodies flung themselves through the air, one saw the entire group broken by the light into tiny, diagonal shimmering lines, the rapid movement appearing a form of stillness as if one looked at a swarm of insects hanging in the air.

They stopped and ran back from the fire and then, one by one, ran to the fire, plunged into it, and leaped out of it, ran on, and dived into the pool. In a few minutes, they were all in the pool, swimming in two concentric circles.

Two middle-aged women appeared. They wore simple white dresses with black shawls over their shoulders and carried between them what appeared from where Calderón sat to be a lifeless young girl, a black sheet wound round her body. Gold earrings were fixed to her ears and a gold necklace was looped round her neck. Her eyes were open, however, the pupils shining. The women in purple came down from where they had been sitting; the men rose and followed them. The girls came out of the pool and formed two lines. The lifeless figure was placed between them. Calderón saw that it was an effigy. Everyone stood still. One of the masked women stepped in front of Calderón and made a gesture with her hand. He understood what he must do.

He bent down and picked up the effigy, and stood up, holding it in his arms. In the emotion of the moment, its face seemed to him to be alive and its painted blue eyes appeared animated. The girls in the two lines sat down and, resting the backs of their hands on their raised knees, put their heads against the palms, their long black hair falling over their legs. The woman who had earlier made the gesture to Calderón now raised a hand and pointed a finger to the pool. Calderón walked through the lines of the girls and stepped into the water, the effigy in his arms. The pool was icy cold. He continued to walk until the water came up above his waist. He placed the effigy in the water and saw it begin to float away from him. He stood there, watching it beginning to sink. For a moment, it appeared to drift back to him, and he found himself taking a step toward it. The current released by his sudden movement sent it away again. It rocked slightly in the rippling water, and sank.

When he came out of the water, the girls and the women had gone and the six other men had removed their masks. He kept his mask on because there were tears in his eyes.

When Lucila visited him the next day to take away the robe, he did not ask her for meanings, believing that she would say nothing. He thought he saw a look of exceptional compassion in her eyes, but he could not be sure. When he sat with Belisario in the park that evening, he was about to ask him about the strange ritual they had both engaged in the previous day, but then remained silent. Belisario himself had said nothing, and Calderón thought he would wait to talk about it in due course. He did not, and Calderón began to feel that it would be impudent to raise a subject that his friend so scrupulously ignored.

Calderón imagined it must have been some sort of initiation ceremony, a puberty rite, for the girls. But language had been drained from the ritual, and it seemed to him, in retrospect, a pathetic mimicry of some tradition lost to the tribe but whose images, corrupted by the passage of centuries, thrust their confused presence in its

146

memory. A crude theatre of unassimilated symbols had superseded a dead reality, but who was he, who, on coming to San Clemente de los Andes, had felt that he was entering the dream of his existence after deliberately killing his past, to find comical the dream in which others existed?

Whether the ceremony took place every year, he was never to find out. Perhaps different men were chosen in succeeding years to wear the masks and observe the girls, and one of them was selected at random to bear the effigy into the water. No one talked about it and with the passing of the years, he himself forgot the strange mime he had been engaged in so long ago; and the one or two times when an image of it came to him, he wondered if it was not some curious dream that he had once had.

An unfamiliar sound awoke Calderón earlier than usual one morning. He remained in bed, staring at the grey light at the window, wondering whether he had not heard the strange sound in a dream. But there it was again, shriller and more prolonged than before. He sat up, frightened. The sound died and he remained sitting on the edge of the bed. He shook his head and rubbed his eyes, passing the index fingers over the eyelids and slowly bringing them down the sides of his nose. And there it was again, loud and clear. The cry of a baby. He hit the palms of his hands on his thighs, slapping them vigorously. The baby's cry continued. He stood up and hurried to the door which opened on to the verandah. There was a pearly light outside; soon it would be pinkish. The baby's crying was now continuous. It was coming from a basket that had been placed on the verandah, near the door. He looked down at it with horror. Kneeling to the ground, he could see clearly the little puckered-up face, the tiny open mouth through which the baby was crying with increased force – as though it were now aware that someone had come to it and were scolding him for taking so long. Calderón gently touched the face with a finger. The crying stopped for a second and then continued. He

147

lifted the baby out of the basket and stood up, starting to talk to it.

'Don't cry now, sweet. There, you are all right now. No one will harm you. My poor child, my sweet little darling.'

Calderón was astonished at his own words. But he talked on, mumbling whatever nonsense came to his head, for his words seemed to reassure the baby and it stopped crying. It held out a hand and touched his face, and made a gurgling sort of sound. *Guh-guh.* The light had turned pink and was already becoming bright. Holding the baby close to his chest, he swayed his body to and fro. The baby stared at him, its mouth open, and knocked its hand against his cheek.

From where had the baby come? he wondered. Who had chosen him as the person on whose doorstep to abandon the child? He would have to talk to some of the women and see if someone could not adopt the baby. It was out of the question for him to keep it. The person who had left the child on his verandah could not have known that a single man lived there. That must be it. A mistake in the dark. The child must have been intended for a house that had a woman in it. No one could dream of leaving it with a single man. It was too absurd. He would talk to some of the women.

He went to replace the baby in the basket with the intention of taking it indoors and finding a way of giving it some milk. The person who had committed the desperate act had placed straw in the basket to make a bed for the baby. Just when he was putting it back, Calderón saw something there. A piece of paper. He picked it up, still holding the baby in his arms, thinking that the paper must contain some heart-rending plea. He walked out into the garden to be in a brighter area.

He read:

My name is Sofía, by no man chosen.
I am the daughter of ice and fire.
Only he can love me who is frozen
On the burning lips of desire.

148

Calderón read the verse several times, but did not know what he should understand. No plea, no anonymous call for sympathy and compassion, no expression of sorrow, no prayers for the safety of the child. Only that verse. He did not understand it. The baby was making a gurgling sound. He kissed her softly. 'So Sofía is your name. Pretty name.' The brightness of the sky had intensified. He noticed that she had blue eyes and that the fuzz of hair on her head was blonde. He kissed her again, and walked from the garden to the door and, leaving the basket behind, placed her on his bed and sat down on the edge himself, and found himself talking to her.

She was dressed in only a frock of coarse cotton that was stained and dirty. Calderón took out a white cotton pillowcase that Lucila had given him. He cut a hole in its narrow, sewn side and slipped it over Sofía's head. She began to cry. The effect of her new dress was ridiculous and he took it off and cut two more holes for the arms and put it on her again. By drawing some of the material back and tying it in a knot, he created the guise of a clean frock, but, of course, there was nothing he could do about the length of the pillowcase without cutting it in half, and he did not want to take it off again. The poor thing must be starved. He had to find a way of feeding her.

Later in the morning, carrying her in his arms, he walked out of his cottage, having decided to go to Doña Hurtado's house, the older woman who had given him shelter when he first arrived in San Clemente de los Andes. She would advise him as to what to do; probably take the child herself. As he walked, he carried on a monologue addressed to Sofía. 'We are going to the good Doña Hurtado's. The kindest lady in all the Andes. She will take you in her arms. And she will give you home-made candies.' Sofía looked curiously about her and stared at Calderón with her blue eyes and occasionally uttered some baby sound. *Guh-guh.* 'How old are you, my darling Sofía? Five months, six? Oh, but you are going to be a fine lady. Oh, yes!' Then he made up jingles as he went along:

My little Sofía, how are you?
O dear sir, my eyes are blue.
My little Sofía, where do you go?
O dear sir, I do not know!

He laughed, hugging her close. 'What a funny little thing you are.' *Guh-guh*.

Coming near to Doña Hurtado's house, Calderón stopped. He looked at Sofía. She was just then staring at him. *Guh-guh*. Calderón smiled at her. She pursed her lips and pressed her breath through them. Bubbles appeared on her lower lip and saliva trickled down its sides. *Guh-guh*.

Calderón turned round, clasping the child to his breast, and walked hastily back to his cottage.

The next day Lucila came to fetch his washing. As usual, she said little, but just stood beside the door and waited for him to bring out the bundle of his dirty clothes. Her senses, however, always picked up impressions too remote for others to see or hear. When she returned some hours later with the tidy pile of clean clothes, she gave Calderón another package. She said nothing and he did not question her; nor was he surprised when he opened the package and saw that it contained a quantity of baby clothes.

In the following days, other people of the community brought more clothes and toys for Sofía. Some brought gifts of fruit for Calderón. Belisario came up one evening, carrying a crib he had made himself. And for weeks there was a train of people visiting Calderón's cottage, wanting to see the baby with the blue eyes.

While everyone entered into speculations about the mother of the baby, no one could tell who she might be; all the babies that had been born in San Clemente de los Andes during the previous six or seven months were accounted for; the nearest village was over the mountains, a couple of hundred kilometres away; it was a mystery to everyone from where Sofía could have come. But soon the people of San Clemente de los Andes stopped wondering about her origin, for they were used to gifts from nature, and did not see any portent, or menace, in a remarkable event.

It did not occur to anyone to suggest that a house with a woman in it would be more appropriate for the child's upbringing; instead, everyone admired Calderón for the love with which he devoted his time to the girl. *The good Señor Calderón*, they called him when they talked about him; and then only *The good señor*, after which it became normal for people to address Calderón as *Señor Bueno*. By the time Sofía was ten years old and Calderón had turned fifty, the community had fixed upon the name by which he was called to his dying day: *Don Bueno*.

She sat in the shade of the green and white awning on the wide terrace of the penthouse with a view of the Caribbean, a magazine held across her bare stomach, watching from her reclining chair the little boy stumbling among a heap of plastic toys. Unconsciously, she pulled at the strap of her blue bikini top and, shifting in the chair, turned the page of the magazine. She picked up the glass of gin and tonic from the tiled floor and sipped from it, glancing again at the boy who had snatched up a little red plastic car from among the toys and was pushing it along the lip of a large pot in which a double-flowering yellow hibiscus grew. The boy's pursed mouth made a continuous buzzing sound, changing to 'Brrr, brrr' when he stopped the car. Two more pots beside the large one obstructed his progress around the hibiscus. He had it in mind to complete the circle, and looked annoyed that his passage was blocked. He stared at the problem for a moment. Then he rested the car sideways, suspending it from the rear tires with its nose in the pot, and stretched his pudgy little arms to push away the first of the smaller pots. It was too heavy for him and, in his annoyance, he eyed the red geranium that grew in it. When another attempt to push the pot had failed, he yelled in frustration and began to flail his arms wildly. In a moment the leaves and the flowers of the geranium were on the floor.

'Simón, no!' the woman called, but he was already stamping his bare feet on the torn plant, his face tight with rage. She put the glass down and stood up quickly, the magazine falling to the ground. Seeing her coming, the boy ran to the opposite end of the terrace where, retained by a stone wall about a metre high, a strip of garden had been laid out. A profusion of flowering bushes grew there – a striking array of yellow, pink and red blossoms – broken up by horsetail palms, and at the top of the strip, where its branches hung over the railing along the front of the terrace, was a studiously pruned pomegranate made to grow like a slender tree. Simón ran toward the strip and, stepping over a low patio chair that happened to be next to the retaining wall, jumped into the vegetation.

By now the woman was shouting at him, 'Simón, stop it! You're being a bad, bad boy again. Now, don't go in there! All right, come out, I'm not going to take you to the beach today if you don't come out *at once*! Simón, did you *hear* me? Why do you have to be so de*struct*ive? Simón, stop that, you hear?'

He had begun to tear up branches and was throwing them out, rushing from one plant to another. She stood still, watching him and trying to control her anger. 'Simón, you were playing so nicely,' she said in a pleading voice, 'why do you suddenly have to turn into a monster?' He ran through the bushes toward the pomegranate. 'Simón, *no!*' she cried, rushing to the top of the terrace. He was holding the slender trunk with both hands and attempting to shake it. She stopped and watched with astonishment the little boy vent his inexplicable rage, as though his tiny arms could uproot the tree; she was relieved that he was too young to be climbing a tree and she resolved, in that moment, to have the pomegranate cut down, thinking to herself that it would not be long before her precocious and energetic boy attempted to climb it without thinking that its delicate branches, hanging eleven storeys above ground, would tear away under a lesser weight. But for the present, the rage with which he

152

fixed his hatred upon the tree distracted him from her presence, giving her a chance to creep up behind him and to snatch him away.

Holding him under his arms, she carried him in front of her and walked quickly toward the door. He beat his legs in the air and yelled. She put him down and, clutching his arm, dragged him along the ground. She did not notice the glass of gin and tonic on the way; he managed to kick it while being dragged, so that the glass fell on its side and broke, spilling its contents on the floor. She tugged at him harder. He screamed.

Finally, she had him inside the apartment and closed the door to the terrace. Picking him up strongly by both arms, she carried him to a bedroom and put him down forcibly.

'Now you calm down,' she said to him sternly. 'After a father who was a coward, we are not going to put up with a son who is a terror. And you can stop *that*!' He had begun to flail his arms. She held him strongly and turned him over and slapped him several times on the bottom. He renewed his screaming. She beat him harder and shouted over his screams, 'Simón, I'm not going to put up with your nonsense. I'm going to shut you up in this room if you don't stop being a bad boy. You will not go to the beach. You will have nothing to eat. Certainly no ice cream today. You are going to learn to be a good boy, or you are going to get nothing at all. You understand?'

She closed him in the room, where he continued to moan for some time, and went to the kitchen. Throwing ice into a glass, she half filled it with gin; she was about to pour tonic into the glass, but instead picked up the bottle of gin again and raised the level of the liquor in the glass two or three centimetres before adding the tonic. She took a good swallow, walked with the drink to the sitting room, and collapsed into a sofa. The boy's moaning could still be heard. The ocean could be seen from where she sat – an expanse of blue and the shimmering horizon

153

invading her mind with an intense glare. She rose up and quickly drew a curtain across the view and slumped back into the sofa. Torn-up bits of a newspaper were strewn on the carpet; a lamp lay knocked to the floor from a table, the shade smashed and the bulb in fragments – she looked away from the debris of Simón's rage.

She took a long swallow from the glass, exhaled her breath loudly, and picked up the telephone that lay on a table next to the sofa. When her call went through, she said, 'Give me Hector Santillana, please.'

'Leticia, you're back already?' Santillana said.

'No, Hector, I'm calling from the beach. It's no use. I'm coming back. The evening flight if I can get it, otherwise tomorrow morning.'

'But Leticia, you haven't even been away a week, you need a longer vacation than that! You've been killing yourself with work.'

'Hector, I've had it up to *here*!' Santillana imagined her hand raised to just below her chin. Leticia went on, 'Simón's driving me bananas.'

'Oh, Simón,' Santillana said. 'He needs a lot of attention.'

'A *lot*! That's an understatement. Hector, he's driving me insane. He plays quietly for five minutes and then for no reason at all he starts to smash everything around him. I don't know what I'm going to do with him. He's such a destructive boy, and he's getting worse each day.'

'He needs a . . .' Santillana stopped himself, and Leticia completed the sentence for him: 'Yes, yes, I know. A father.'

'If there is anything I can do,' Santillana offered.

She gulped some gin and said, 'Just *talk* to me, Hector.'

When Calderón had gone away, she had not been hurt so much by the fact of being abandoned by the man she had lived with for five years and whose child she bore as by the manner in which he left her: without saying a word to her but having a lawyer write to her, conveying information of what money had been transferred to her. She had been angered, too, by the lawyer's implication, when he stated that Calderón had left her the business, that as a woman she would naturally not have any interest in running it: he offered her his services in negotiating a sale. Determined to show her strength, she had found herself another lawyer, got him to establish the legality of the transfer and to make certain that Calderón could never claim a penny of the business, and set about directing it herself. Even her confinement was not an occasion for slackening, for she kept in touch by phone from the nursing home and then from her apartment until, a fortnight after Simón's birth, she was back at the office, if only for a brief daily visit during the first two months. She who had so delighted in conversation, especially when the discussion involved the interpretation of human behaviour, found a new passion: organization. From six in the morning until midnight, her day was precisely organized, devoted almost entirely to the advancement of the business. Simón was given fifteen minutes of her attention in the morning and then left to the care of the maid; in the evening, when she worked over some papers or talked on the phone in the bedroom of the apartment that she had converted to an office, she let the boy crawl about the room and sometimes had him in her lap, but asked the maid to take him away the moment he demanded real attention. She, who had prided herself so much in knowing the reasons for certain behaviour patterns, paid no attention at all to what she was doing to her child; and while she could glibly cite the received ideas of psychology and take pleasure in confidently identifying the source of others' problems, she saw no contradiction at all in the fact that when Simón did something wrong she simply pulled him by an arm and smacked his bottom. The lives of others were case histories; her own life, however, was perfectly normal.

She had bought the penthouse on the coast, in a fashionable resort town a two-hour flight from the city, as a tax write-off: each month the sales executive who generated the most business was awarded a weekend at the penthouse; six other weekends were reserved for other staff who showed exceptional merit. The penthouse also served the useful function of a discreet bribe for prospective clients – senior officials in government offices could, without too much subtlety, be persuaded to take a 'business trip' to the coast with a mistress in exchange for signing an order.

Within three years, Leticia had transformed Calderón's modestly successful business into a vast enterprise. Government ministries, law courts, museums, libraries, schools, many of them huge buildings that had never seen a cockroach or an ant, used her exterminating services. When she read in *Time* magazine that a certain chemical had been banned in the United States, she got on the phone to the corporation in California and bought up the surplus stock at a cheap price, and then used a government connection to have an import licence issued. It began to be joked about her in the city that with such a powerful exterminator at the nation's disposal, the country no longer needed jails. And once a cartoon appeared in a paper which showed the door of an unpopular government minister's office with two uniformed men about to enter it, the symbol of Leticia's exterminating business conspicuously visible on their breast pockets.

On the morning flight to the city, Simón sat by the window absorbed by the cloud formations outside. Whenever the plane went through clouds, he closed his eyes and, turning his head, pressed his face to his mother's shoulders. But a moment later, he would turn his face again to the window and half open his eyes, and if he saw that the plane was out of the clouds, he would throw a quick smile at his mother and then stare out at the immense blue. Leticia sat looking at a magazine and thinking what she should do with her difficult son.

She phoned Hector Santillana from the airport, and said, 'I'm back. Can you come for lunch?'

He could, and arrived at her apartment forty minutes after she did. Simón had given a yell of triumph on entering, running with one arm in the air to the maid's room behind the kitchen, shouting, "Nanda, 'Nanda!' Fernanda, a large black woman, stubbed out the cigarette she had been smoking and received him with a huge smile. She picked him up and kissed him, saying, 'How's my baby?'

Simón pulled at her ear and said, 'I went into a cloud.'

She gently held his hand and took it away from her ear, and walked with him to the kitchen. 'You had fun on the beach?' she asked.

Simón spread out a hand and loudly imitated the sound of a plane. Leticia had just come into the kitchen and, seeing the maid enter from the other side with Simón, said, 'Fernanda, you can put that big brat down and see about lunch. I'm expecting a guest.'

Fernanda lowered Simón to the ground. He gave a yell and ran off. Leticia looked into the refrigerator, saying, 'What do you have in the house?'

There was very little, Fernanda explained. She had bought only for herself, not expecting the mistress to return for another week. 'Yes, yes,' Leticia said, and quickly rattled off a list of groceries for Fernanda to go and buy. She walked back to the sitting room to get money from her purse and just as she entered it her ears were assailed by a deafening roar followed by loud static. Simón had punched a button on the stereo system and was turning the tuning knob left and right. Leticia rushed at him and slapped his hand away, and turned off the system. 'You can take this monster with you,' she said to Fernanda, giving her the money. 'And do something to your hair,' she added, staring sternly at the maid, 'you look as though you've done nothing for five days but lie in bed.'

When Fernanda and Simón had gone, she poured herself a drink and sat down. She was about to sip from the glass when she put it down and stared at it, recalling how much she had drunk the day before. No, she decided, she was not going to give in under pressure and lose her discipline. She was not going to look for an escape from her problems but confront them head on and smash them.

157

She took the glass to the kitchen and emptied the drink into the sink. She drank a glass of cold water and went to her room to change. By the time she was ready, having taken a shower and put on a light green dress of heavy cotton with tiny brown and red flowers on it, Fernanda had returned and begun to prepare lunch. Leticia glanced into the kitchen and saw Simón contentedly playing with long strips of potato peel at the kitchen table and Fernanda, moving between the sink and the stove, talking some nonsense to him. It must be the baby nonsense that Fernanda talked; she herself had never had the patience for such talk, and was simply not interested in inventing silly things to amuse a child. She was not jealous of Fernanda's capacity to hold Simón's attention; there was a natural affection between the two, she recognized, for Fernanda had looked after him since he was a week old while Leticia was busy with her work. But as far as Leticia was concerned, it was part of the service that Fernanda had to perform – it was merely a delivery of goods for which regular payment was made. And in this respect, too, her sharply analytical mind had a grey area where her perception was imprecise.

Santillana arrived in a light blue suit of a lustrous material that was neither silk nor polyester but a mixture of natural and synthetic fibres. He was shortish, with a slight paunch and thinning black hair. His lower lip protruded in a permanent pout, a defect of nature that he tried to disguise by growing a heavy mustache.

'Hector,' Leticia said when they were having lunch, 'I had a terrible thought last night. I had drunk too much gin and my mind was reeling. But I had a moment's clarity. And I wished I'd never had Simón.'

'Oh, nonsense,' Santillana said, wiping his lip with the napkin. 'He's an ordinary boy at the age when boys are bursting with energy.'

'But he's such a monster!'

'Where is he now? I don't hear him.'

'With the maid,' Leticia said. 'She has a way of amusing him.'

'And you do not,' Santillana said, 'which is what you resent.'

'I certainly do not! What an idea!'

'The problem is very simple. It is not just that Simón does not have a father; he does not have a mother either. Now, stop and listen,' Santillana added, holding up his hand and anticipating her objection. 'You wear a suit first thing in the morning and go off to your office and when you return you're looking at papers or are on the phone. In other words, you act exactly as a father normally would. You are, if I may put it so crudely, a sexless parent.'

'What do you want me to do, give up the business?' she asked, ringing the bell for the maid to take away the plates and serve the next course.

While Fernanda was in the room, Santillana said, 'The minister returns tomorrow from a visit to Africa. It's a joke, the Minister of Health going to Kenya and Uganda on an official visit. Everyone knows he's on a safari, but daily we send out a press release about his visits to hospitals and talks with researchers into tropical diseases. I'm seriously thinking of moving back to the private sector. Corporations don't lie at the taxpayer's expense.'

'I've told you before,' Leticia said, helping herself from the bowl of potatoes that Fernanda held near her, 'you're wasting your talents in the bureaucracy. Government is for plodders.'

'Yes, I do miss the excitement of business. At least one doesn't get bogged down in meaningless paperwork.'

When Fernanda had left, Santillana returned to the earlier subject. 'As for the boy, you do need to give him more of your time.'

'Hector, I just spent five whole days with him! He gave me hell all that time. And I'd intended to spend a full fortnight at the coast.'

'Well, I don't know,' Santillana remarked. 'I mean I don't know if you're cut out for motherhood and a professional career at the same time.'

'It's not *me*, Hector, it's the boy. He didn't have to be born with a destructive streak in him. I've got to do something about him.'

'He's too young to send away to a boarding school. The thought would be absurd even if he were five or six years older.'

'I was thinking,' Leticia said with a slight hesitation in her voice, 'that perhaps someone else could bring him up.'

Santillana looked at her in astonishment. Her capacity for being coldly ruthless seemed unbounded, and he was glad that he had suppressed the inclination he had had during the previous year to propose to her; they were intimate friends and he had been flattered enough by her companionship to harbour, for a few months, the belief that he was in love with her. Marriage with her would certainly have been socially and materially advantageous, but his observation of her had shown him her cold and opportunistic side, and he had withdrawn from making any declarations to her. He enjoyed his close friendship with her, as he would with a man, the kind one eagerly looks forward to meeting for a game of chess.

'Who can that someone be?' he asked, 'your mother?'

'I have thought of her,' Leticia said, 'but she might not accept him. You see, she did not approve of my living with César, and though she's reconciled to my ways now and is good with the child when she visits, I think deep down she still can't accept a bastard for a grandson.'

Santillana smiled at the directness of her speech, and said, 'Who, then? Not a bachelor like me!'

Leticia did not care to be humorous about the subject, and said, 'Someone I can pay for the service. That is the only way to get anything done properly. And with a clear conscience.'

'Well . . .?'

'Supposing I got myself a new maid . . .'

'What's wrong with . . .?' Santillana pointed a finger to the kitchen door.

'And suppose I bought *her* a little apartment . . .'

'Leticia, you're crazy!'

'No, Hector, I'm trying to find a way of stopping from going crazy with that boy around my neck.'

Santillana realized that she had already made up her

mind. Her inflexible will quickly stamped authority upon decisions that suited her. She had called him not so much to discuss her problem, which she had appeared to do, as to tell him of the decision she had already made, but doing so in such a way that she could have the conviction that the decision had been arrived at rationally after a careful discussion with a close friend.

He looked at his watch and said, 'Goodness, the time! I have to be at a conference in ten minutes. A completely boring subject,' he added with a slight laugh, 'a research report on hepatitis, but –' he shrugged his shoulders '– it's work.'

When he left, he wondered what demon possessed Leticia that she was completely drained of all feelings of motherhood. The solution she had suggested to her son's aggressive behaviour – which Santillana thought to be not at all abnormal – seemed to him a piece of monstrosity. It occurred to him that it was her treatment of the boy that had caused the behaviour that made her want to reject him – almost as though she had deliberately created the circumstances in which she could cast him aside without the slightest qualm. It was the kind of thing wicked step-mothers in ancient fairy tales were supposed to do, not real mothers in real life. What was it in Leticia that made her so hard, so ruthless and so desperately selfish that she was prepared to give away her own child? It was unthinkable, unbelievable, what she was proposing; but he had heard it from her own lips only a moment ago. He shuddered. She could not have the blood of a Spanish woman; not even the blood of a Spanish South American with its indigenous dilutions, for no woman with a drop of Spanish blood in her would so callously reject her own child. He was profoundly shocked, almost as though he had seen in her the incarnation of evil. But he saw that she was determined to have her way and that any remonstrance would only make her more stubborn. He shuddered again, imagining the horror that awaited the boy's future. Santillana stopped and peered into the door-

161

way of the church that he happened to be passing. He decided to go in and light a candle.

Dressed in a dark blue lightweight woollen suit over a white blouse with a ruffled front, she sat in the rear seat of the car, reading the morning papers, while the uniformed chauffeur drove her to work. She flipped through the pages quickly, scanning the headlines and glancing over scattered paragraphs, and quickly reading that which interested her.

The chauffeur drove through the parking lot which, during the five years that had now passed since Calderón transferred the business to her, had been widened to accommodate the additional fleet of twenty pickup trucks and the cars of the team of managers that Leticia had added to her staff. The chauffeur drove past the warehouse and turned on a wide circular drive in front of a new building, completed the year before, and brought the car gently to a halt in front of some steps that led up to the glass doors, each door stamped with the company's symbol of a brown insect in a green circle with a red diagonal line across it. The doorkeeper had run down the steps and opened the rear door the moment the car came to a stop. Leticia walked out briskly, and the man ran back to hold the door of the building open for her. A minute later, the chauffeur went into the building with her briefcase and newspapers.

She walked down the hall past the open doors of the offices of three of her managers and saw one punching the buttons of a computer, another busy with a calculator, and a third staring at some papers. The doorkeeper had quietly shuffled ahead of her and held the elevator open for her at the end of the hall, so that she entered it without having needed to stop from the moment she stepped out of the car. There was a potted palm near the door of the elevator and she noticed that a cigarette butt had been thrown into the pot. As she raised her hand to press the button for the next floor, she said to the doorkeeper, 'Take that cigarette butt out of there and if you see

162

any one throw one in there again, tell Señor Pérez to fire him.'

Coming out of the elevator on the next floor, she walked through a large room where eight secretaries were typing away. Once, a secretary had stood up when she walked past, and Leticia had said curtly to her, 'Your time working is more important to me than the respect you wish to show me. If I wish to be noticed by you, I shall send for you.'

She entered her own office, a well-lit, thickly carpeted room with a view of some of the skyscrapers in the downtown area. On a shelf behind her desk, there was a picture of her parents and herself, taken when she was ten years old, and also a picture of Simón when he was two. When she had moved into this office in the new building, she had thought of discarding Simón's picture, for by then he had already been living in the care of Fernanda in a small apartment that Leticia had purchased for the purpose, and she rarely went to see him. At the start, she had gone to spend half an hour with him twice a week and taken him to a park on Sunday afternoons, but on each occasion something in his behaviour had irritated her and she let longer and longer periods pass between visits. But she had kept his picture – she told herself, with cold rationalization – to remind herself of the mistake she must never make again.

Her secretary had placed a memorandum on her desk, next to the correspondence that had arrived, detailing the meetings scheduled for the day. Conferences with her managers and sales executives. Phone calls to return from certain special clients. It looked like a routine day, except for a luncheon with an executive from a corporation in Los Angeles with which she was negotiating a deal that would make her company the US corporation's subsidiary in the whole of South America. The thought excited her and in her projections for the future she dreamed of the South American corporate structure becoming so large that it devoured its US parent and took its place.

Her secretary had slit the envelopes open and Leticia

quickly snatched out the contents of each, pencilled notes in the margins of some, and placed the letters in several different piles. One letter, however, was out of the ordinary and made her sit back, deep in thought. It was from a lawyer in another country and was addressed to César Calderón at the company's address. It was a long, detailed letter, and she was amazed by what she read and was reminded of the talks she used to have with Calderón about his missing father.

The lawyer began by stating that his firm had been appointed by a court to dispose of the estate of the late Napoleon Calderón, and that, not having anything but the first name of one son, which the firm had found in some letters belonging to the deceased, it had taken all these years to establish the identity and whereabouts of the said César Calderón.

The letter then described the unfortunate circumstances of the father's death. Apparently, he was murdered in a bar in a town called Santa Rosa. It was one of those bizarre events in the interior that went unexplained. The police had found a quantity of money in different currencies and some gold at his house.

Leticia pondered a number of thoughts that suddenly invaded her mind. For what he had done to her, César, more than any man alive, deserved to suffer the worst horror that could be inflicted on a human being, and if only she could find out where he was. . . . She could send Simón to him and get the two of them forever out of her mind. . . . She could file a lawsuit against him for causing her mental damage. . . . She leaned back and thought, wondering which one of the possibilities would give him the most pain if she could find a way of inflicting it on him. She buzzed her secretary and, reading out the phone number in the letter, asked her to put in a person-to-person call to the lawyer in the foreign country. While she waited for the call to come through, she resolved that she would offer to pay for the hiring of detectives to find César Calderón.

\*　　　\*　　　\*

Nearly six years after he had left her, at a time when he was himself aimlessly going from place to place along the Pacific coast, Leticia took a plane to Valparaíso where the detectives had finally succeeded in tracing Calderón. By way of proof, they had taken a photograph of him leaving an apartment building. Looking severe in a black dress, she checked into a hotel in the city and decided to rest until the next day when, early in the morning, she would pay her once-beloved César a visit. She could not have said what she expected to achieve or what she was going to propose to him. What she relished was a piece of theatre in her imagination. She was going to wear a black hat with a veil, and when he opened the door and stared, wondering who stood before him, she was slowly going to raise the veil and say, 'Your widow has come to visit you in your underworld.' The rest of the drama would develop from that opening line.

And so the next morning, at seven o'clock, she took a taxi to the apartment building. It was not a particularly attractive street. Narrow strips of grass in front of the buildings and a few scraggly trees offered little relief from the succession of concrete and glass façades. Cars usually owned by people with middle incomes were parked everywhere.

Leaving her taxi, she walked to the entrance of the building. The plate-glass door was locked. She could see the hall through the door. It was carpeted in dark grey, had oak veneer walls with an oval mirror in a gilt frame on one wall; a potted philodendron, its leaves drooping, stood in a corner; in the middle of the hall was a small desk and a chair on which the night porter sat, his head slumped upon the desk next to the house telephone with its dozens of switches. She knocked on the glass door. The porter remained asleep. She took out a coin from her purse and knocked with that against the glass. The porter shook his head and stood up, seeing her. Picking up the bunch of keys that lay on the desk, he walked wearily to the door, and unlocked it.

'I'm sorry,' he apologized, seeing the elegantly dressed

lady, all in black, a veil thrown above her hat. 'No one visits at this hour.'

'I've come from a long way away,' she said, entering the hall.

'Whom do you wish to see?' he asked, shuffling back to the desk, sitting down and raising his hand to the telephone.

'I don't want you to call him,' she said. 'It is a surprise.'

It was irregular, but staring at her he could not believe that she could be a burglar in disguise and he let her go. She took the elevator to the sixth floor and walked with firm steps to the apartment door. She stood before it and took two or three deep breaths, staring at the door as though she saw Calderón already before her. She raised her hands to arrange the veil across her face, smiling to herself, and rang the bell. The door remained closed. Not a sound from the other side. 'Your widow has come to visit . . .' she rehearsed the opening line while pressing the bell button again several times. Then she pulled off one of her shoes and knocked upon the door loudly with its heel.

Ten minutes after he had let her into the building, the porter saw her come out of the elevator. She walked up to him and said, 'He must be dead asleep, and I'm afraid I'll have to try giving him a buzz on the phone.'

The porter picked up the receiver and handed it to her, asking, 'What's the number of the apartment?'

'Six 0 one.'

The porter threw a switch and then dialled the 6 and was about to dial 0 when he stopped and said, 'That apartment's empty.'

'What do you mean, empty?' she asked, a slight irritation in her voice. 'Perhaps I have the wrong number. Doesn't Señor Calderón live in this building?'

The porter grinned and said, 'Oh yes, Señor Calderón, he gave me a good tip. He was a good man, always said hello. He left three days ago.'

'Left?'

'Well, yes. I carried his luggage to the taxi. That's when he gave me a good tip.'

'Where did he go? Do you have any idea?'

166

'I heard him say "Plaza Sotomayor" to the driver. Everyone goes there. To catch a bus or a train or a ship. Or just to take a walk.'

Leticia clenched her teeth. This was too much. To miss him by three days. It was ridiculous. All that time and money wasted. It was stupid.

'Isn't there some way of finding out where he might have gone?' she asked the porter.

He looked at her for a moment and, shrugging his shoulders, said, 'You could go to the police, I suppose.'

He saw her make a face, and added, 'But if you're serious and in a hurry, you need my brother, Alfredo.'

'What can he do?'

'Anything. He's connected to the underground. He can do anything if the price is right.'

'All right. Where can I find him? Your brother Alfredo.'

He took a small piece of paper and a pencil from a drawer in the desk, saying, 'No one finds Alfredo. You will need to go and see my mother, Doña Bustamante.' He wrote down her name and address. 'You tell her what it is you want. She will arrange everything.'

The taxi driver looked dubiously at Leticia when she gave him Doña Bustamante's address and, since he could read nothing in her face, asked, 'You sure that's where you want to go?'

'Yes,' she said peremptorily.

He rolled his eyes and twisted his lips, throwing his head to the side as he shrugged his shoulders. Traffic had begun to build up, but most of it was going toward the business district and Doña Bustamante's address happened to be in the opposite direction. The road began to zigzag in a series of sharp bends as they climbed to the upper part of the city; now Leticia could see the ocean, which was then beginning to reflect the light of the risen sun, and now, as the car swung around, she saw a funicular going down to the lower city. The road became a winding street with dilapidated bungalows and chalets being crowded out by ramshackle little houses made of

167

corrugated iron. They drove across a flat area where a morose bowlegged man led a string of mules, and entered another winding street where houses, seemingly nailed together with any old material that happened to be available – from flattened tin cans to sheets of iron – were packed together. Women were emptying pails of dirty water from their front doors into the street, half-naked children were running around, and men, many with bloodshot eyes, stood around, smoking cigarettes and glaring at the passing taxi.

The driver eased the taxi to a halt in front of a house made of bricks, slabs of rock and sheets of tin with a corrugated iron roof. He remained speechless, keeping his grip on the wheel, and raised his eyes to the rearview mirror in which he could see his mysterious passenger.

'Well, is this the place?' she asked, catching his eye in the mirror.

He nodded his head.

'All right,' she said, opening the door. 'Wait here for a few minutes. My business won't take long.'

'Oh, no,' he said, suddenly turning back. She was just about to step out and stopped. 'I can't wait here,' he added.

'Why not?'

He looked exasperated and said, 'Lady, do you know where you are? The Pope wouldn't come here even if all the angels in heaven escorted him.'

'Oh, don't talk nonsense!'

'Nonsense, she calls it!' he exclaimed incredulously. 'Lady, this is the street that sends out its children to rob and kill. From this street, young girls go out to seduce old men, and they don't leave them until they've sucked their blood. You don't know where you have asked me to bring you. You've heard priests in church talk of hell. You're in it!'

He became suddenly frozen and stared open-mouthed at her. Some children had gathered outside the car and were gawking at Leticia. Two men were slowly walking toward them from a few houses down. The door of the house that they had come to opened and a short, stout woman, her dark brown face all wrinkles, stood there. A black shawl covered her head and shoulders, and a heavy charcoal-grey skirt fell to her feet.

Leticia stepped out of the car and said to her, 'Are you Doña Bustamante?'

The woman peered into Leticia's face and nodded cautiously. Leticia explained: 'Your son said his brother Alfredo could help me, he said I should come and see you.'

Doña Bustamante stepped back and held the door open in a gesture of inviting her in. The two men had come up to the taxi but were watching the lady in black with some awe, as were the children, to whom she appeared a fantastic figure in some dark mystery. Leticia plucked some notes out of her purse and threw them into the window of the taxi and, lowering her head, said to the driver, 'You may go.' She looked boldly up at the two men, sensing the power her appearance gave her, and announced, 'I'm sure these good people will help me to return.' Holding up her head and thrusting out her breast, she threw a dazzling smile at the men before turning to enter Doña Bustamante's house.

It was then, in the moment when she crossed the threshold, that the thought possessed her that she did not so much want to find César Calderón as she wished to send him to eternal damnation.

Doña Bustamante led her through the dark room to one at the rear where there was a view of the bay from an open window. Two small steamers were heading for the port and several lesser vessels were bobbing up and down. Doña Bustamante offered Leticia a wooden chair with a cane seat and herself sat down on a floppy cushion, crossing her legs and drawing the skirt over them. Light from the window fell across her face and created an effect of minute shadows, making the wrinkles appear like deep crevices in the loose, soft skin. A lizard popped out of a crack in the floorboards near where she sat and darted across the floor. Thin plywood from packing chests formed the walls, on one of which hung an old calendar with a faded picture of a dark blue, nearly black butterfly on a geranium flower whose pink had faded to a ghostly white. In one corner by the ceiling, the light from the window caught the fine, taut lines of a spiderweb.

But Doña Bustamante was staring at her and Leticia, conscious that she had been avoiding her little black eyes by looking around the room, determinedly met her gaze and said, 'I came to Valparaíso looking for a man whom I once knew.'

Doña Bustamante did not blink, her face remained immobile.

'About five years ago, I conceived a child by him,' Leticia went on. 'But he did not want the child and ran away. It is a long story, but recently I traced him to Valparaíso. He lived in the apartment building where your son works. The one who told me to come here. He knew the man I'm talking about and said he left the building three days ago. He said Alfredo can do anything. That you could arrange everything.'

Doña Bustamante nodded her head slightly but remained silent, keeping her eyes fixed on Leticia.

'How much money will you want?' Leticia asked.

'You want him back? Is that what you want?'

Leticia saw that Doña Bustamante had no front teeth and that when she spoke a little black hole opened and closed.

'You want him to pay for the child? You want his money?'

Leticia hesitated, and then said, 'No, that is not what I want. Not at all.'

'What then? You came expecting to find him in his apartment. What were you going to say to him?'

'I was going to say, "Your widow has come to visit you in your underworld."'

'Only that?'

Leticia did not answer, apprehensive that Doña Bustamante could divine motives in her that she herself did not know.

'You wish to kill him, then?'

'No, not kill,' Leticia said, looking away from the dark wrinkled face and the black hole that opened and closed. Her gaze fell on the old calendar and then on the spiderweb. Doña Bustamante stared at her, and saw fine wrinkles appear on her forehead. Suddenly, she turned her head back to meet Doña Bustamante's stare; her eyes seemed to be lit up by some awful power as she spoke in a louder voice than before. 'No, not kill. Give him pain. A terrible unending pain.'

Doña Bustamante closed her eyes.

'Can you do that?' Leticia asked, her voice almost shrill, an eagerness taking possession of her. 'Send him the curse of hell?'

Doña Bustamante opened her eyes and saw that a bright intensity flashed from Leticia's face. 'He did not want your child?'

'That is why he ran away.'

'There are many unwanted babies born in this street,' Doña Bustamante said. 'The girls go and sell themselves to the sailors. They don't know what they do. Sailors from foreign countries. Back by the warehouses, in alleys near bars. Wanderers who spill their semen in the darkness, in narrow passages.'

'Pain, pain!' Leticia cried excitedly.

'Lord, the unwanted babies!'

Leticia stood up and walked to the window. The buildings of the lower city reflected fragments of the sun. The ocean was glittering. A long black oil tanker was coming to port, preceded by two pilot boats. The ramshackle buildings of the upper city swept away around her on the wide curve of the hills, patches of brilliant colour bursting out of a mass of drabness. The air smelt of putrefying trash. She turned round and saw Doña Bustamante's face lifted, watching her keenly.

'Pain,' she said again, but now in a whisper, as if a sudden infusion of violent energy within herself had been exhausted. 'A beautiful, beautiful pain.'

'An unwanted baby.' Doña Bustamante, too, spoke in a whisper.

171

She had seen men trying to leave the oppressive circle of time and observed how, when the dream of their being drugged them into the belief that they had escaped the terror of a life closed within time, they suddenly awoke to find that their flight into timelessness had been only a seduction of the dream, distracting them from the circle that had continued to narrow and now clung to their necks like a noose.

'Yes, yes!' Leticia said with renewed eagerness as if she read the frowning woman's obscure thoughts, and stared wildly at her, for she saw that behind Doña Bustamante's concentrated look was a mind perceiving the inevitability of events and resolving the formula of the curse that must set those events in motion to transmit to César Calderón the deepest pain known to man.

# 7

Calderón cut the meat from the leg of lamb into cubes and added it to the onions just then turning golden in the pot on the wood-burning fire. He stirred the contents until the meat had browned and then added the mixture of dried herbs that he had pounded into a powder and when the meat had absorbed the herbs he sprinkled salt over it. Then he dropped the chopped-up tomatoes into the pot and let the lamb simmer in the juice thus created. While it cooked, he peeled potatoes and carrots and cut them into small pieces; he put them in a dish of cold water, ready to add to the meat later. The washerwoman Lucila had taught him how to make the lamb stew, bringing him the herbs, some years earlier, and he made it at least once every ten days: it was a favourite with Sofía.

He had discovered a great delight in cooking when he saw the pleasure some of the dishes he prepared gave Sofía. He spent two hours in the kitchen every day, working busily and thinking only of the moment when she would taste the first mouthful and look up at him with her wonderful blue eyes to express her approval. There were times, of course, and that frequently, when she gave no indication one way or another but swallowed the food indifferently. But the occasions when she looked up at him and opened her eyes wide, and then quickly turned to eat more, were for him moments of intense happiness. Having mastered three or four dishes taught him by Lucila, he had understood the basics of cooking sufficiently to become inventive, especially after he had found that no dish could really go wrong if it had a foundation of onions and garlic.

In his zeal, he had planted a herb and vegetable garden at the back of the cottage after a laconic hint from Lucila, and it had become a mania with him to have the choicest ingredients for the meal he was going to prepare for his darling Sofía.

Stirring the simmering lamb once more, he added a little water to it to keep it from burning, and turned his attention to making the dough for the sweet fritters he planned to fry for Sofía's dessert. She loved to snap up the golden crunchy rings scented with vanilla. He watched her eagerly whenever she ate, constantly revising in his mind that hypothetical menu which would give her the most perfect pleasure. It was only recently that she had begun to express decided preferences; and he, who had from her earliest days, when she was a baby clamouring for milk, sought to please her, looking for signs of what she preferred, encouraged her critical sense. At ten years old, most other children had no developed taste, but Sofía was a critic as well as an admirer of Calderón's cuisine. Sometimes, all she had to say was, 'You put too much salt in the cauliflower,' and he would be crushed. It mattered to him enormously that she took pleasure in what he had prepared, and sometimes even her criticism, revealing the subtlety of her taste, thrilled him – as when she once said, 'I think you used too much dill, it has ruined the flavour of the potatoes' – for it showed that he had succeeded in instructing her sense of taste so well that she had become remarkably precocious in discerning fine nuances in a particular flavour. No child of ten that he knew could even tell that the green sprigs smothered in butter and coating the potatoes were dill freshly harvested from the garden, let alone make a judgement on the effect the herb had on the dish. To have instilled such an education at so early an age was a fact to be proud of, he felt, and he loved his golden-haired Sofía for being such a wonderful pupil.

But he had not neglected her other education. He had begun to teach her the alphabet as soon as she could speak, and from the time she was four years old, the mornings were devoted to her schooling. He taught her to read and write, gave her instruction in arithmetic, and told her stories, some of which he remembered and some which he made up himself, in the absence of storybooks, searching in his mind for that fantastic imagery which would amaze her.

From the time that she could walk, Sofía took to water as if it were her natural element, dashing off on her little wobbly legs to the brook when he was playing with her in the front yard. He ran after her and, picking her up, waded into the water that, at its deepest, was no higher than his waist. She thrashed about with her arms as he held her in the water. The next day he let her float, supporting her with the palm of his hand on her stomach. She giggled and smiled up at him in pleasure. She screamed when he attempted to take her out of the water, and for several weeks it became part of his day to spend the afternoons in the brook. Before he knew it, she was swimming by herself, bobbing her head down and sending up bubbles and then surfacing with a smile and swimming toward him with perfect ease.

When she was five, he took her to the wide pool by the waterfall. He borrowed a horse, and with Sofía sitting in front of him, they rode out together early one morning, her straight blonde hair flying up in the wind into his face. The icy temperature of the water did not seem to bother her at all. While he could not endure the cold water for more than five minutes at a time, she stayed in it for as long as half an hour and came out with her skin glowing rather than having turned blue. He had taken a simple picnic of bread and hard-boiled eggs, some cut-up raw vegetables and fruit. She ate with a keen appetite and went off swimming again. They had returned to the pool many times, for she loved the place, and after she had turned eight she wanted a horse of her own. That, too, he enjoyed, watching her on the pony, her blue eyes sparkling in the light each time she turned round to look at him.

The fire under the lamb stew had burned itself low to the point where its diminishing heat would be sufficient to cook the vegetables that he now added to the pot and, the

175

burning wood slowly turning to ash, keep the dish warm until it was time to eat. He went into the bathroom and washed. His hair – most of the original black now turned grey – was cut short; and his body, though still generally lean, had added a little weight – the cheeks were fuller and the waist carried some slack flesh.

He put on a clean shirt over the beige cotton trousers that he was wearing, and walked out of the cottage. The warm late-afternoon air was just being touched by the cooler currents of the evening. The slanting light, at that hour, added a sharp radiance to the mountaintops and seemed to bounce down from there into the valley with a particular brilliance. The branches of the willow trees by the brook, with the light intense behind them, appeared like a green gauze stretched against the sky, penetrated by shimmering dots of brightness.

Calderón walked to the river where, in the calmer water of a wide bend, children swam, a swarm of black-haired heads, conspicuous among them the blonde Sofía. He derived an immense pleasure from seeing her in that crowd, the children all aged between six and twelve. She was invariably part of a group that swam races or dived from the highest rocks or invented games to play in the water. He stood by the bank, watching the screaming children churning up the water, and looking mostly where Sofía ran up some rocks in a line of children and then all of them tumbled down into the water like a school of fish leaping down a cascading river.

A number of older boys stood some distance from Calderón, watching the same spectacle. They were talking and grinning among themselves. It seemed to him that they were looking in the direction of Sofía, and a pang of jealousy suddenly quickened his heartbeat. She was only ten, and could it be, he wondered, that she was already attracting that kind of attention? At her age, she was taller than girls of twelve or thirteen who had been born in the valley. Although Sofía's chest was still flat, Lucila had quietly given her a home-made bikini top during the last year. Until now, when he saw the youths grinning and exchanging glances among themselves, Calderón had not thought of the obvious, that one day some young man would possess her. The image that came to his mind filled him with disgust. The community of San Clemente de los Andes traditionally encouraged early marriage. In such a remote village, where relations between the sexes were free and open, young people were bound to couple early, and it was to everyone's interest to institutionalize these attachments. Most of the males were married long before they were twenty and some of the younger brides were no more than fifteen. While Calderón had always accepted such a state of affairs to be perfectly natural, he was now appalled by the thought that in another five or six years he might lose Sofía.

He was distracted by some of the lumbermen walking back from their work, among them his friend Belisario who was now a foreman. Many of the men touched their hats as they walked by and said, 'Good evening, Don Bueno.' He greeted them in return, calling several of them by name.

Belisario came and stood with him for a few minutes. 'There are troubles in this world,' he said enigmatically, 'but it's good here. God's own peace, eh, Don Bueno?'

Calderón looked at him questioningly, and Belisario explained, 'There was an earthquake in Valparaíso and a volcano erupted in Mexico. There are wars in the other world, out there beyond Europe.'

'Where did you hear all this? In a dream?' Calderón was about to laugh, but Belisario said, 'No, not in a dream, Don Bueno. At the bungalow.'

The bungalow was the house the corporation that ran the timber business had built in San Clemente de los Andes to provide accommodation for the quarterly visits of its administrator.

'The *señor administrador* came yesterday, he was telling me,' Belisario went on. 'I think something's happening, Don Bueno.'

'What do you mean?'

'Maybe some change is coming. Two young men arrived

177

with the *señor administrador*. He had a name for them. Ex something . . . execute?'

'Executives?'

'That's it. I don't know what they're talking about and I don't know what they've come for. The *señor administrador* said they're just looking. But I don't know.'

The children were leaving the water and dispersing. 'Well, good night, Don Bueno,' Belisario said, going away.

Sofía still remained in the water when all the others had gone. Calderón stepped down some rocks to be nearer to her. She swam up toward him and, coming to the rock on which he stood, turned her face up at him and gave him a brilliant smile, and then, doing a quick somersault, she swam away from him, and he saw her slender white body floating just below the surface of the water. Her golden head came up first in the sunlight that gleamed on the water and then an arm, raised up to stroke the water, the tanned flesh also golden in that light. She turned round and floated on her back, gently stroking the water. Her blue eyes sparkled. He was going to call her to come out, but he stood there, speechless, overwhelmed with the happiness that came from the thought that he alone possessed this priceless vision.

The corporation's bungalow was a timber structure built on the side of a hill with a wide verandah overlooking a view of the river and the meadows that rolled away from its banks and a spectacular sight of a snowcapped peak. Two men in their thirties, wearing dark grey woollen trousers and tweed jackets over turtleneck sweaters, sat there having drinks and watching the rim of the mountains turning gold in the setting sun. The great peak still remained white, more vividly so as the twilight crept up from the valley. The two men had exhausted their vocabulary of praise for the beauty they beheld, and sat, staring at the spectacle with a profound sense of awe, until darkness finally fell.

It was the end of their third day in San Clemente de los

178

Andes. They had come out on a whim after a casual conversation with the administrator. The corporation's operations in San Clemente de los Andes were too small for its directors to pay any attention to them. The administrator reported to an obscure manager, and as far as the directors were concerned it was just one of their scattered properties that ran itself, gave no problems, and produced a regular profit. The two executives happened to meet the administrator in the lowly manager's office, fell into conversation with him and heard him say, 'Oh, it's the most beautiful place in the world.' Their curiosity was aroused and, vacation time at hand, they decided to go and see for themselves.

It was on the second day of their visit that the thought which now preoccupied them first occurred to one of them. The wife of a lumberman who worked as a housekeeper at the bungalow served them their lunch. The main dish was a beautiful steaming poached salmon. The two were of one opinion: it was the most exquisite salmon they had ever tasted. Where did it come from? they asked the housekeeper. Why, from here. Here? Why, yes. A lake nearby was full of salmon and rainbow trout.

A little later, smoking cigars on the verandah, one of them said, 'You know what I think, Claudio?'

'What, Ernesto?'

Ernesto pointed to the wide bulge of a hill. 'Imagine,' he said, 'a hotel on that hill. Imagine two hundred rooms at $120 a day. Imagine the profits.'

'You're crazy, Ernesto. Who can want to come so far out of the way for a vacation?'

'I'll tell you who, Claudio. Sportsmen from Scotland, Canada, the United States. For a start. That salmon was heavenly. There must be game, too, in the mountains.'

Claudio did not want to raise objections in case Ernesto's persuasive force carried with the directors. So, instead of saying that the idea was absurd, he said, 'We must discuss the problems.'

By the end of the third day they had discussed everything. They had seen more of the valley. Each segment of it seemed to offer additional potential for the proposal. The waterfall and the pool below it and the flat land near the pool suggested another site for a hotel. Some of the meadows could be transformed into a breathtaking golf course. And for future growth, Ernesto added, pointing to the snowcapped peaks, skiing could be developed. The more cautious Claudio became enthusiastic, too. The two already saw the waterfall on picture postcards.

A month after their visit, a team of workers arrived with mules laden with manual equipment. They worked for several months building huts for themselves and a temporary helicopter pad. The people of San Clemente de los Andes saw them from a distance, for their activity was contained in the farther end of the valley, in the area of the waterfall. A big change was coming. It was something to talk about. Some were curious, even excited by the prospect, and others indifferent to it. Calderón, enclosed within his obsession for Sofía, saw nothing, and heard the talk among the people as if it referred to some abstract subject, interesting, but of no vital concern to him.

The helicopters, taking a circuitous course through the mountain passes, began to fly in the heavier equipment and the building supplies. The valley trapped and amplified their noise as they flew in and out. Two years after Ernesto tasted the salmon, the skeleton of the hotel stood high on the hill to which he had pointed, black steel rods sticking out of the concrete.

Although she must have been five or six months old on the day Calderón found her on his doorstep, he counted Sofía's birthday from that particular day. He prepared a great feast when she turned fourteen. He had dug a pit at the back of his cottage and lined it with bricks which he had obtained from a man who worked on the construction then in progress, who also supplied him with steel rods with which he formed a grill to place over the pit. Over that he cooked a huge cut of beef to serve the twenty or so children, all teenagers now, who formed Sofía's circle of friends, and their parents. He had spent several days previous to the birthday making a variety of sweets with milk, flour and sugar.

At fourteen, Sofía was as tall as any adult in San Clemente de los Andes. Her fine, blonde hair, with a middle parting, hung straight down to the small of her back. The structure of her high cheekbones and square jaw together with a broad forehead and large blue eyes made her face appear to be that of a full-grown woman. Her breasts had begun to form soon after she was twelve and now already added a contour even to a loose dress. Calderón, who always marvelled at her beauty, sometimes wondered about her parentage. She looked distinctly Scandinavian. And sometimes, though much more rarely, he wondered what his feelings would have been had he accepted the child that Leticia was about to bear when he abandoned her. Had the child been a girl? Would he have loved her with the same intensity with which he loved Sofía? But supposing Leticia's child had been a boy? He would be lost in speculation for some time, but invariably concluded that no one could have possessed the magical loveliness of Sofía and given him so much happiness.

Sofía wore a green dress on which, following Lucila's instruction, she had herself embroidered little red flowers at the neck and the hemline. As though they had been waiting behind the trees all this time, the guests began to arrive one after the other, carrying presents, and soon there was a crowd of people milling about the front and the back of the house. The party extended from some of the older guests standing around Calderón's oven, praising its performance, to groups of children and adults in the front yard and on to a scattering of teenagers who had begun some boisterous game in the brook, next to the willows. Sofía darted from one group to another. Now she would be rushing into the house after receiving a present and now she would be hopping out carrying a tray of sweets to distribute to her guests. Calderón, leaning over the great roast, was cutting slices from it and passing them on pieces of bread to people drawn there by the aroma. From time to time, he came to the front of the house and called the people there to come and eat. 'Olmedo is threatening to eat all the beef if you don't come soon!' he shouted.

Every time he went to the front, he looked to see with whom Sofía was talking, and felt pleased by the fact that she was with a different group each time. He dreaded to discover her alone with a boy. Lucila observed him and understood his anxiety; and she, who spoke so little, went as far as to say, 'It has to happen, Don Bueno, it has to happen.'

A little later, he was carrying a heap of meat he had sliced and going from one cluster of friends to another, holding the dish up before the guests. Two women were talking when he came to them, one saying to the other, 'My Luisa is growing so fast, I don't know what I'll do if she doesn't get a husband in another year. And she's just turned fifteen.'

'Some more meat, Doña Soledad?' Calderón said to her, putting on a smile though the words he had heard had given him a shock.

'Oh, thank you, Don Bueno,' Doña Soledad said, accepting a slice. 'Your Sofía is growing into such a great beauty, who's going to be worthy of her hand?'

It was the politest thing she could think to say, but it had the effect of sending a current of pain through Calderón's body; he had the presence of mind to make the answer usually given in such situations by the people of San Clemente de los Andes. 'God will decide.'

'He will be a lucky man,' the other woman said, also accepting a slice of meat.

Much to his distaste, another group was discussing the same subject. It seemed to the people that the best compliment they could pay their charming host was to praise the beautiful Sofía, who, moreover, deserved the highest praise they could give, and that was to wish that some handsome young prince reigned over San Clemente de los Andes and made her his bride. Calderón smiled at their well-meaning fantasy and tried to present the appearance of being honoured by their words. But each word was to him as a scorpion's sting, sharp little jabs at his skin making minute passages through which a poison entered his body, accumulating in his veins and gradually invading his brain.

'Well, the hotel is completed at last,' Belisario said, apparently changing the subject. 'I hear that by next month the first party will arrive. Hunters and fishermen.' But he had not changed the subject at all, for he added, 'Who knows, Don Bueno, but the prince for your Sofía will be among them?'

Calderón again managed to smile and to say, 'God will decide.' Several women in the group nodded wisely at the expression of that sentiment.

Sofía was sitting on a chair on the verandah and several of her friends were crowded around her, all fourteen or fifteen years old, among them three boys. It was a small comfort to Calderón to see that her immediate companions were girls and he walked past them to go into the cottage, saying, 'I hope we haven't run out of sweets.'

As soon as he was inside the house, he made the noise of walking to the kitchen, and then softly crept back to stand just inside the door.

One of the girls was saying, 'All my mother worries about is who I'm going to marry. But I want to *do* things.'

'Do what?' another girl asked.

'Make babies!' said one of the boys, and the other males broke out in uncouth laughter.

'Ha, ha, ha!' the first girl mocked. 'You boys have only one thing on your brain.'

Calderón winced. Could they be talking so coarsely in front of Sofía? But he next heard her voice say, 'Pilar told me all about that. She made it sound beautiful.'

Who was Pilar? Calderón wondered. He could kill her.

'But it isn't *every*thing,' the first girl said.

'How do you know?' a male voice asked.

'Enough of that,' Sofía commanded. 'Let's go down to the brook.'

In a moment, they had all run down the front yard. Calderón stood behind the door, and found that he was trembling. He went to the kitchen and drank some water, telling himself to be calmer; it was, after all, natural for young people to talk about their expectations of life and for parents to speculate on their future. But when he came out of the cottage, he found himself walking toward the brook. He wanted to make sure that they were all playing together and had not dispersed among the trees in pairs.

When he was not halfway down the yard, Belisario came up to him and said, 'The hotel is going to change life here. They have good beer there, and other drinks. I saw the stocks that arrived for the bar. What do you say, we go there when they open next month, what eh, Don Bueno?'

'Yes,' he said weakly. His body felt cold even though he could see down to the brook and discern the golden head go in and out of the shadows, surrounded by a crowd of young people.

His skin itched and he lay in bed, unable to sleep, scratching his thighs. It was pitch dark outside. The only sound was the leaves on the trees surrounding the cottage being shaken by gusts of wind. If he listened hard, he imagined he could hear the sound of the waterfall across the valley. He tried to fix his mind on the waterfall in order to distract himself from the itching. There were particular details he ought to be able to remember. All those beautiful moments. Concise histories of happiness. He had gone there so often with Sofía. He ought to be able to concentrate his mind and relive that happiness. The little girl with her hair blowing in his face. Or the older girl on her own pony trotting ahead of him. But only a succession of images passed rapidly through his mind, vanishing within a minute; complete episodes eluded his mind in which random surges of impressions replaced the chronology of events. The past had become uncertain as though it were a landscape now fallen behind the horizon, and that radiance one had seen of a mountain rim lit by the declining sun remained in memory not as experience but as a transfiguration of time past. Sparkles flitted before him in the darkness, like fireflies.

The itch would not go away. He sought distraction by

planning the next day's meals. Sheep's kidneys fried in butter with parsley and very finely chopped onions. Sprinkled with coarsely ground black pepper. A small lemon sliced in wedges and arranged like a flower on the plate. The potatoes sautéd, golden. In his imagination, he looked at the colours on the dish, and added boiled carrots to it, cut in small round sections. The dark brown kidneys, the yellow lemon, the orange. . . . He played in his mind with other combinations. Broccoli instead of the carrots, to echo the green parsley. Or the startling circle of a section of a blood-red tomato. Then there was the question of aroma. Cloves and thyme. But in what proportion? Perhaps only thyme.

When he had finally resolved the preparation of the sheep's kidneys, he began to ponder a dish for the evening's meal, fixing his attention on poultry. Sofía was going to have a grand day, he thought, realizing that he had stopped itching. He took a long time deciding how to cook the chicken, and then examined the alternative of fish. He could not make up his mind whether Sofía would not prefer a simple baked fish to the chicken fried in an elaborate sauce.

But the culinary dilemma vanished from his mind, for he suddenly realized that he could not conjure up Sofía's face. The girl who had grown from a baby into adolescence before his very eyes, whose images had been coming to his mind while he lay itching, had suddenly become a blank. The more he tried to think what she looked like, the more the form of her face receded. It was absurd – they had been sitting together only a few hours earlier and he had, as usual, watched her closely. He tried to think of other people so that he could, without thinking about it, find himself looking at her. He saw Lucila so clearly, he imagined he could count the wrinkles on her face. He began to see people he had known many years ago. Zuazo appeared in all his carnival guises. He even saw clearly the characters he had observed in the streets of Santa Clara. But his mind refused to surprise him with an image of Sofía, the one person he had spent more years of his life looking at than any other. Again, he tried the game of recalling the faces of others. Leticia easily came to his mind. And then his mother at the time when she wore the spectacles that seemed to enlarge her eyes. He saw himself, too, a boy of two, holding on to the bars of an iron gate, watching a black tanker floating across the ocean. It was then that his mind was surprised. The image that suddenly invaded it was not that of Sofía but of the man in the bar in Santa Rosa, flinging himself at him while he stood there, frozen, with a knife in his hand.

He sat up in bed, finding himself sweating. Oh, Don Bueno, he said to himself, what are you thinking of?

He lit a candle and walked to a mirror. He stared at his own face. The eyes appeared round on the immobile face. He forced a grin, stretching out his cheeks, in order to change the appearance of his eyes – to remove from them the look of fear.

Holding the candle in its little saucer in front of him, he walked softly to Sofía's room. He had to see what she looked like.

She was asleep on her side, a blanket drawn up to under the armpit. He saw the golden hair first, fallen in a mass across the pillow and lying in a confused heap below it. The bare arm above the blanket caught the light and gleamed back at him. He stretched out a hand and moved it in a gesture of caressing the arm, but did not touch it. He saw the shadow of his hand move across her body. From where he stood, he could not see her face but only the curved outline of a cheek. He slowly walked round the bed to see her full face, noticing as he walked the arc of her hip under the blanket. He stood for a moment at the foot of the bed, and noticed that her head was thrown back a little on the pillow, making her chin and nose prominent in that position, leaving her mouth and eyes in shadow. Her breath came evenly. He walked to be in front of her face, wondering if she was having a dream. Just as he reached the top of the bed, a sound escaped her lips, and she turned her head while at the same time she pulled down the blanket, turned her body to the opposite side, and then lifted the blanket up to cover her shoulders. In that moment the candle lit up her face. The movement of the head, and the slight shaking of it as she settled it on the pillow seemed like a gesture of one expressing a refusal. Calderón took a step back, fearful of having awakened her, but saw her illumined face. It was a ghostly white in that light and, with the eyelids closed, like a mask of greyish-white plaster.

The next morning, before he could tell her of the lunch he planned to make for her, she announced gaily, 'I'm going on a picnic this afternoon with my friends.'

He tried not to look disappointed, and said, 'With whom?'

'Oh, there's just the four of us everyone calls the butterflies.'

'Four?'

'Well, yes. There's Lolita, Pilar, Teresa, and me.'

'I didn't know you were called the butterflies,' he said, wondering to himself if she were not dissembling.

'Oh, some silly boy gave us that name.'

'Is there anything I can make for you to take?' he asked. 'Some boiled eggs?'

'No, nothing,' she said. 'They're treating me.'

While talking to her, he saw her as a young woman and observed how charming were those features which any man might desire in his companion. He tried to think if there had been times in recent months when she had been away from him for an hour or two that he could not account for, but he could not immediately think of any. The offhand manner in which she talked seemed to him a kind of forced casualness, as though she were hiding from him her real motive for wanting to be away from him in the afternoon.

Finally, he made himself say, 'Aren't any boys going with you?' He smiled as if to suggest to her that, of course, he had nothing against such an idea.

'Boys?' she cried with what appeared to be genuine amazement. 'How can you think of such a thing?'

187

Her dismissal of the idea seemed so sincere that he felt his suspicion confirmed.

He watched her walk out to the verandah and it seemed that she entered the light that was flowing in at the door. Her body dissolved before him though the movement of her white frock into the light created a momentary transparency in which he caught the outline of her hips.

She was only walking out, as she sometimes did after breakfast, to go and sit on a rock under a willow and to dip her feet in the brook; but it seemed to him a rehearsal of her final departure that inevitably had to come. He looked at the light into which her figure had disappeared. There was only a brightness there that entered his brain as a form of nothingness, reminding him of the desert in Peru, when in a bus on his long journey from the interior he felt a profound sense of grievance that the bright sunlight revealed nothing but a painful glare, but suddenly there had been, like a sculpture made of curving strips of black iron, the skeleton of some large animal, the long ribs protruding out of the yellowish sand and casting bizarre shadows upon it.

# 8

After the trouble in Uruguay, Simón Bolívar Calderón was driven to cross the frontier and had no choice but to go and live in the apartment found for him in the Leblon district of Rio de Janeiro, a short walk away from the beach. His one comfort, as he waited out the time for the unfolding of events to which he had become blindly committed in the underground politics of South America, was that his girlfriend Mercedes had been able to come with him. It gave the waiting a holiday air – even that of a honeymoon.

He did not ask how long he would have to wait and what he would find himself doing next. For all of his twenty years, the crucial events of his life had occurred without his willing them; he had been involved in the obscure schemes of others, enacting whatever heroism or villainy was his lot merely by following directions whose ultimate source was to him a mystery.

Since he had been parted from Fernanda, who had been the only parent he knew, being taken away from her at the age of seven, he had been suspicious of all human beings, considering them potentially treacherous, until he met Mercedes whose honesty and simple approach to life first made him perceive that not everyone in the world was viciously selfish. She was large – wide at the hips with heavy legs – but sufficiently tall to make the largeness of her body appear well proportioned. She wore cotton shirts, behind which her heavy unsupported breasts knocked against each other when she walked, long denim skirts or jeans, and went barefooted except in very cold weather. She parted her black hair at the centre and let it hang behind her in a plait, and the glossy black hair together with the roundish features of her face gave her the appearance of being an Indian from Bolivia, an impression perhaps heightened by the several strings of large reddish brown beads that she wore at her neck and the half a dozen wooden bracelets on each of her arms. At twenty-four, she appeared to Simón to possess a maturity of mind and a serenity of spirit, giving him the sense of a smooth final approach to a safe landing after an excessively turbulent flight.

He had instinctively attached himself to her from their first meeting and although there had been no occasion, in the four months that they had known each other, for any intimacy, they already had a deep unexpressed commitment to each other. And when circumstances brought them to the apartment in Rio, it was as if they themselves had chosen to live together. Not knowing how long this existence would last and when the next summons would throw him into another world of violence and terror for which no explanations were given, he dared not allow a day to pass without clinging to her in the closest embrace.

He was amazed by her body. He had known only whores before. Thin young girls with pointed little breasts and bony arms. Or middle-aged women with loose flesh, stinking of some cheap perfume. Mercedes was his first real woman. He could sink into her soft roundnesses and yet be thrilled by the firmness of her body's response. When she had her thick arms around his back and drew up her wide thighs to drive her heels into his buttocks, he felt himself completely overwhelmed by her flesh as though he had entered it with his entire body. Sometimes he would lie curled up next to her, after falling to his side, his hand limp across her soft stomach and his head against her large, round breasts, as if his consciousness had never known a world apart from her body.

What his mind remembered as a knowledge of his past was fragmentary, dreamlike and absurd. Fernanda, the large black woman, was the only person from his earliest years whom he clearly remembered. She talked to him endlessly, telling him stories, or, cradling him in her arms, sang softly to him till he fell asleep. She sat next to him at the small table in the kitchen, patting his head as he ate the meal she had prepared. She took him to the market in the square where he ran around among the stalls heaped with vegetables and fruit, slipping on fruit fallen and crushed in the dust; and returning bruised and dirty to the little apartment, he would submit himself to a bath because he knew that she would give him an ice cream if he did so.

But there was another shadowy image in his mind, a slim woman whose features he could not recall, dressed always in navy blue or charcoal grey, who knocked at the door of the apartment from time to time. Fernanda would have had him dressed cleanly before she came. The slim woman said little; she took him in a car for a long drive. When he tried hard to think of her face, all he could see was a frown or the features of resentment and bitterness, and nothing of its living details, as if the woman herself were elsewhere and she had sent an unwilling body with a mask of her face to represent her. Then she ceased to come altogether for a long time, and it seemed that the weight of some grave responsibility had been lifted from Fernanda's shoulders; she became more lighthearted than before, sang to herself frequently, and let him do what he wanted.

He took to the street when he was hardly five years old, mixing with a horde of boys who swarmed the street, raising a great din, pestering shopkeepers and old women, offering to clean windshields of cars caught in a traffic jam, going off to the railway lines and sticking empty beer cans to the tracks with chewing gum, or going into a wooded area of the park and getting a thrill from showing one another their penises, screaming out in loud jeers at one whose member was the smallest. That boisterous time, with its illicit games and the callous bullying of innocents who did not belong to the group, seemed to go on for years, but in fact lasted only two; for when he was seven, the slim woman suddenly turned up one day in a charcoal-grey dress, a short, sombre-looking man with her.

Fernanda's eyes were red and she was speechless. The

191

woman's voice was speaking loudly and rapidly. He could tell the voice was scolding, but did not understand anything. She marched about the apartment, emitting the harsh flow of words. Fernanda stood near a wall, her head lowered and mouth open, her eyes staring wildly at the woman. The man stood by a window, his arms folded over his paunch. The woman saw a bottle in a corner and snatched it up. She plucked out its cork and bent her neck to put her nose to the bottle and made a shrieking sound, and then with two quick steps stood in front of the window, held the bottle out, turned it upside down. There was silence in the room. Everyone was watching the liquid pour out of the bottle and fall out of sight. Simón imagined the concrete courtyard three storeys below being splashed by the liquid. Then the woman put her head out, looked down and flung the bottle down. There was a moment's silence and then they heard the bottle crashing. The man said something in a low voice. The woman spoke, interrupting him, her voice pained and disturbed.

He was taken away. He spent three boring and frightened days at the woman's apartment. The place amazed him. There was a telephone in each room. The woman placed him in front of a huge television set. He had seen greying, snowy images on televisions in bars, watching from the doorway, but this one was clear, large, and in brilliant colour. The novelty of such privileged viewing died within ten minutes, however: it was only men and women talking endlessly, the men shouting, the women crying, then two of them suddenly embracing, and then a whole group of them standing in a cemetery where it was raining. It was too boring. He stood up and went to another room. There was a large desk there. The woman sat behind it and was speaking into a telephone. She saw him and, putting a hand across the telephone, said in a sharp voice, 'You go right back where I put you!'

He returned and saw the same man talking to the same woman. He went on and on. Suddenly, she screamed, walked rapidly up to him and slapped him across the face. It was too boring. Simón stared at all the buttons next to the television screen. He knew that there was a way of changing the picture. It must have something to do with those buttons. He rose and went and stood in front of the set. There were words below the buttons. But he could not read. There were numbers around a knob. He stood puzzled for a few minutes. The man and the woman who had earlier embraced were now lying on each other. But suddenly their place was taken by the umbrellas in the cemetery. Boring, boring, boring. He quickly put up a hand and pulled and pushed at a button. Nothing happened. He twisted it to the right and left. The picture began to shake and then go round and round. The umbrellas came in at the bottom and shot up at the top. And then everything went so fast the whole picture was a wild mixture of rapidly moving lines. He put his hand to the knob with the numbers around it and gave it a twist. The moving lines disappeared. Now the screen was filled with vivid green, red and yellow dots and the sound was a loud buzz. He was taken aback by the sudden blaring of the buzzing sound, and panicked. He twisted the knob again, and then again. Nothing but bouncing colorful dots. He turned another button and then two or three others in quick succession. The buzzing now turned to a high-pitched shrieking.

A hand fell on his neck and pulled him back and he saw the woman come round him, rage on her face, slap him across the face and push him back into the chair. She marched up to the set, flung up an arm and switched it off. She stood in front of him and glowered down at him. His panic, and then the stinging slap, had created fear and terror within him but he held his teeth firmly together, determined not to cry in front of this woman. 'Don't you *touch* anything in this house,' she screamed at him and walked stiffly away to the other room.

The man who had been with her when they took him away from Fernanda, came to dinner the first night. They sat down together at the table and when the maid had begun to serve the soup, the woman said to Simón to go and wash his hands. When he returned, she and the man were talking animatedly and paid no attention to him.

Their conversation meant nothing to him. All about priests and the Church. He had been into a church once. With a couple of kids. Stolen three candles. One of the boys had bet he could do something horrible with a candle. They had run to the wooded area of the park. He and the other fellow had lost the bet when they saw the third boy drop his pants and make the candle disappear.

'You can stop grinning like an idiot, and finish that cauliflower.'

Simón realized that the scolding voice was addressed at him. He quickly composed his face, speared a large piece of cauliflower with his fork and shoved it into his mouth. It was burning hot. He held it in his mouth but nearly choked, and found himself throwing his head forward, opening his mouth, letting the piece of cauliflower drop out, and beginning to cough, so that the unswallowed juice of what he had been chewing earlier, together with tiny fragments of food, flowed out in a stream. The piece of cauliflower fell to the plate's edge, bounded off, and shot across the white tablecloth, making a thick yellow smear across it.

'You are the most revolting child I have ever seen!' the woman screamed at him. She called the maid and said to her, 'Take this monster away. If he's going to eat like a pig, he can do it in the kitchen.'

Simón had lost his appetite and sat in the kitchen determined not to shed the tears that had come to his eyes. The maid, a young woman, paid him no attention, and when she had served the dessert, she picked up the phone in the kitchen that was connected to the one in the entrance hall of the apartment building, and said into it after punching a button, 'I'll be with you in thirty minutes, okay?' She listened for a moment and then said in a sharp, but lowered, voice, 'I don't want to hear about your miserable wife, it won't kill her if you're an hour late.' And she snapped the phone back on its hook on the wall.

He cried at last when he was alone in bed. He thought of Fernanda and how the woman had scolded her. And that bottle. Everyone heard the crash. It was like seeing a vulture just when it is rising from a dead animal's body, a long ribbon of its intestines in its beak. You felt terrible, seeing that. Hearing that crash. Something had died. It was strange, confusing.

The next day he was taken to a store and made to try on a lot of new clothes. Long pants! He looked ridiculous in the mirror. He suddenly had an idea. He would make a run for it when they left the store. He would escape. Run all the way back to Fernanda. But there was a policeman standing outside the store and he was scared. What if the policeman thought he was a thief who was running from the store after stealing something from it? At the same time, the woman was pulling at his arm, for she had hailed a taxi.

It was back to the colour television with the endless picture of men and women whispering or shouting at each other. Sometimes a man would pull out a gun and it would be interesting. Or a car would go chasing another round sharp bends on a mountain and one of the cars would go somersaulting over the edge. But the men and the women always came on again and talked and talked and talked. It was like water dripping on your head and you had no way of moving to the side.

The maid placed a suitcase near the front door. The woman had gone away early in the morning, wearing a dark grey suit. The bell rang. The maid opened the door after unlocking it from the inside. He should make a dash for it, Simón thought. But the short man who had come to dinner entered with two others, both equally short and fat. Priests, they were. Black cassocks; a circular tuft of black hair on each head; hands clasped across paunches; black beady eyes; purplish, dry lips.

They drove away in a dark blue Volkswagen that was nearly black with dust, he trapped alone in the rear seat and the two priests at the front. Their short bodies disappeared behind the back rests. Two circular heads on the top of the back rests. Two shining pates, the shaven skin bluish. Two wreaths of black hair. Occasionally, the heads wobbled. On the other side, invisible to Simón, the two mouths were speaking. Words; a story; laughter; dialogue; words. Once or twice, the one not driving turned to look at him, giving him a grin and a wink. A few times, the other leaned up to take a look at him in the rearview mirror.

They had left the city and were heading for a mountain road. The car went very fast along the straight stretch, swerving to overtake buses and trucks, the horn blowing. Once, a car coming in the opposite direction when the Volkswagen was passing a truck, which was itself going very fast, flashed its lights; the Volkswagen kept on gaining but not fully succeeding in overtaking the truck; the other car, not diminishing its speed, had come closer, and its loud horn could be heard while it continued to flash its lights. To his right, Simón could see the huge wheels of the truck, the mud flaps flying back. The other car seemed to snake on the road and smoke rose from its tyres. Now the very loud, piercing sound of the truck's horn filled the air. The other car held itself straight again and swerved to the right, so that it only had two wheels on the road, the other two in the narrow strip of banked dirt. The truck, too, swerved to its right, raising a huge cloud of dust. The Volkswagen shot forward at last. Simón saw his driver's arm fling out, the fist shake in the air, and just when they were passing the car that was teetering on the edge of the road, he heard the voice shout out, 'Drunk son of a whore!'

The engine made an ugly whining sound in third gear, forced to speed along the steep mountain road; and then it became louder still, being thrown into second gear when one tight bend succeeded another. Simón swayed in his seat and several times was flung from one side to the other. The loud noise of the engine, the rapid zigzag motion, and the buzz in his ears as the car gained height made him feel nauseous. The two round heads on the top of the seats in front of him wobbled, swung to the left and to the right, making him giddy. He was terrified to stare out of the windshield between the two heads as they blindly overtook a slow truck round a bend, and turned to look out of the window on his left. They had climbed high, the land below seemed to be swinging like a rotating disc, thin lines of rivers shone through the vegetation, the greyish mass of the city appeared in the far distance, and then, the car squealing round the bend, there was the side of the mountain outside the window, covered with ferns, rivulets flowing out of cracks in the granite.

After an hour's climb, the car left the mountain highway and entered a narrow dirt road with the limbs of tall trees arching above it. They went round a series of hairpin bends and came to a long, straight descent where fragments of broken bricks, tiles and small rocks had been thrown on the dirt road to prevent it from being slippery. Coming to the straight stretch at considerable speed, the driver switched off the engine and let the car hurl itself down in neutral. It went faster and faster and, in the comparative silence after the engine had been switched off, Simón had an eerie feeling of falling helplessly through empty space. Holding the two corners of the back rests on which the two heads reposed perfectly still, he stared out the windshield; far down in the distance there appeared to be a blackish wall: it seemed to be coming nearer and nearer each second and took on the appearance now of an iron bridge and now of the great side of an ocean-going vessel when seen at a dockside. Simón's terror increased as his eye fell on the speedometer: the silent car was travelling at 110 kilometres an hour and still gaining speed! The wall came nearer. No more than half a kilometre away. Less. Much less. Simón leaned over to look at the driver's hands. Surely, he was going to do something to prevent the crash? But he held on limply to the steering wheel, showing no concern.

They reached the bottom where between the end of the road and the wall was a clear area of dirt and gravel some fifty metres wide. The wheels bumped up when the steep road suddenly ended and the flat area began, and then made a crunching sound over the gravel, a good many of the pebbles knocking against the bottom of the car. Simón tightened his fists at the corners of the back rests. The wall was of granite blocks and was covered with a dark green

197

moss that made it appear nearly black in certain parts. Just then he was thrown back and to the side. The car had swung to the left where it shot along the gravel for some twenty metres, and then was swung again to the left where the gravel-covered clearing went back at an incline to the hillside. The upward slope had the effect of quickly slowing down the car, as if a parachute had opened behind it, and then of reducing its speed to zero as it came submissively to a halt in front of a door to a building. The driver raised his hands, palms facing the windshield, turned to look at his companion, beamed with great satisfaction, and said, 'Didn't touch the brakes once since leaving the highway!' The other raised a hand and they both jerked their arms to slap each other's palm with a smack before, laughing, they got out of the car.

Simón was left alone in a room which had nothing on its dusty brick floor but the small wooden bench on which he sat. The plaster of the bare walls was cracked and grey and marked in long black streaks by dampness. From a small window he could see the long granite wall that they had avoided crashing against a little earlier. His giddiness had increased and he tried to lie down on the bench, but it was too short. He sat, leaning forward and holding his head in his hands. He felt weak, hungry and terrified. Suddenly, a yell went up and he heard many voices begin to chatter simultaneously. No sound reached him as a particular word although the air was filled with voices talking boisterously. He longed to be with Fernanda, to be going to sleep in the warm shelter of her body. The voices were raucous and loud. He could not tell where they were coming from, but they seemed very close. He heard the iron handle of the thick wooden door being opened and the door creak when it was pushed back. A short fat priest in a black cassock entered, a cane under his arm. He came to the middle of the room and stared at Simón with black, expressionless eyes.

'Stand up, boy!' he commanded, plucking out the cane from under his arm with his right hand.

Simón stood up and looked at him, frightened by his

appearance, and found himself staring at the priest's nose which was shaped like a parrot's beak.

'What do you say, boy?' the priest demanded, taking a step toward him.

Simón's lips trembled.

'Well, what do you say, what do you say?'

'Sir?'

'Lord, I thank thee for bringing me to thy house. Come on now, say it, say it.' He walked round and flicked the cane at Simón's hip.

'Lord, I thank thee for bringing me to thy house.' Simón spoke the words in a rush.

'Good, good.' He walked round Simón, flicking the cane at him. 'What else do you say? Come on now, let me hear you clearly.'

He stood in front of Simón again.

'Lord, I thank thee for bringing me to thy house.'

'Yes, what else, what else?'

Simón watched the beak go up and down. The cane was flicking at his side. Tears were coming to his eyes. He held them back. 'Sir?'

'Lord, I am a worthless sinner,' the priest said loudly, hitting him on his left hip with the cane.

'Lord, I am a worthless sinner.'

'Giver of life, saviour of souls, I am at thy mercy.' The cane hit the right hip.

'Giver of life, saviour of souls, I am at thy mercy.'

'I shall learn to repent.' The cane on his left hip.

'I shall learn to repent.'

'I shall eat the bread of misery . . .'

'I shall eat the bread of misery . . .'

'. . . and I shall drink the water of sorrow.' The cane on the right hip.

'. . . and I shall drink the water of sorrow.'

On the left and on the right, the cane thrashed, striking harder. The priest spoke the phrases louder and louder. Simón repeated them breathlessly, staring wildly at the hand that flung at him from side to side. He did not know what he was saying. The priest's phrases entered his brain

199

and echoed back out of his mouth. The cane's blows stung him through his clothes. He stood at the centre of a storm of voices – the priest's loud roar, his own desperate echoes, the muffled chattering in the background, with an occasional yell – but could understand nothing. The sleeve of the arm swished, the fisted hand went to the right and to the left with increasing rapidity, the cane hit – *shuck*, *shuck*.

He fell to the ground, his voice breaking out in a scream. The priest leaned over him and shouted, 'Now you are learning!' And hit him hard on the behind three or four times. 'Now you know why you are here!' *Thwack*. 'Now you know why you were born!' *Thwack*. Simón rolled over, and fainted.

Seventy boys aged between five and sixteen sat on benches at four long tables, eating a watery stew with tin spoons, slurping the tepid liquid and sucking at the strands of meat. Hands tore at bread, dipped it into the tin bowl and stuffed it into the mouth, followed by quick successions of spoonfuls of the flavourless sauce to add to the bread being chewed. The spoons clinked against the bowls or were dropped on the table while the hands reached for the bread; some of the boys talked while their mouths were full of soggy bread, but the majority were engaged only in slurping, sucking and the smacking of lips. Simón sat some way down a bench, lost in the crowd of boys, eating slowly the stale bread and the salted water with the little strings of meat that passed for a stew. Far to his right, on a platform, a rectangular table was covered with cloth, and six priests sat there, raising their forks with cubes of meat and slices of potatoes to their mouths or holding the fork down a moment and lifting a glass of red wine to their lips.

As he ate, Simón watched the boys who had been his companions for four years. Poor souls, all of them, they knew nothing of the world outside the granite walls in which they were confined. Up in the morning at six, lesson succeeded lesson, each one a drill in learning by heart phrases, and then whole sentences, the class chanting back the words spoken by the priest. The population of Colombia is 25,000,000. *The population of Colombia is 25,000,000.* The largest city in Brazil is São Paulo. *The largest city in Brazil is São Paulo.* In the mornings the boys shouted back with gusto the sentences that taught them history, geography and Latin. In the afternoons, they laboured over problems in arithmetic, mumbled aloud haltingly over the words in a reader that contained stories of the saints, a finger pointed at the large print, and suffered the horror of dictation where each ten misspelled words equalled a stroke of the cane on the palm of the offending fingers. Meals and a game of soccer on a narrow dirt field in a walled-in compound were the only relief from the relentless schooling.

When in his first year Simón had displayed an unusual facility for learning his lessons and the priest had praised him in class for his exceptional memory, he discovered that his companions despised his superiority; they taunted him with sneers on the soccer field when his class went out for a game; players on his own side, pretending to pass the ball to him, kicked it hard at him from close range, laughing each time the ball bounced back from his body, and once, when a kick from five metres away sent the ball smashing into his face, drawing blood from his nose and knocking him to the ground, a great cheer went up. For a week after that, they called him 'Nosey-nosey, the scholar'. It was not until he had managed to get several lessons wrong and had received abuse from the priest before the entire class that he began to be accepted by the boys. He determined that he would remain an inconspicuous mediocrity, suppressing both his desire to show his real quality and his longing to commit some violent act. There were some weaklings who were an easy prey for the bullies, but Simón refrained from making their lives more miserable than they were – not because he felt pity for them but because he had realized that it was best to remain without a reputation of any sort. Some of the boys treated him as a friend and he behaved toward them as if he reciprocated their friendship, which, however, he did not feel in the slightest.

Malleable to all outward pressures and apparently an agreeable companion to many, inwardly he became hard, resentful and monumentally patient, waiting for the day when he would be freed from the torment of his present existence.

One day, when he had turned twelve, he was called out of his class and taken by a priest to the very room where he had fainted on the afternoon of his arrival five years earlier. He had long outgrown the clothes he had come with and wore what the priests had given him – a pair of baggy trousers, a size too large for him, with patches on the knees, a corduroy shirt with a frayed collar, and a sweater that had holes at the elbows.

He recognized the short man in the brown suit who was standing in the room. His hair had thinned and gone grey at the temples and his stomach was heavier, but Simón saw in him the man who had stood by the window in the little apartment where Fernanda had stared wild-eyed at the slim woman who threw the bottle out of the window. The priest and the man talked together in low voices, and finally the man said to Simón, 'Well, young man, it's time to take you from these kind fathers to the real world.'

The man asked him questions on the drive to the city. Simón answered politely. Yes, he had been treated well. Each of the priests was like a father to him. The capitals of the Andean countries? He recited them. The longest river in the world? He named it. The date of Columbus's arrival in the New World? He repeated it. The man threw an approving, almost a congratulatory, glance at him.

Simón was relieved not to be taken to the apartment of the woman who had made him sit in front of the television.

'You must be wondering,' the man said, giving him a glass of orangeade, 'where your mother is.'

Mother? Simón wondered as the man paused. Fernanda came to his mind but then was confusingly replaced by the other woman.

'She is away in the United States,' the man continued, 'on business. I undertook to see to your progress. It's the start of the school year next week, and you can't afford to be late.'

The next day the man took him to a store and had him fitted with new clothes. He had Simón's photograph taken in another shop. They went to a bank where he bought some foreign currency. They stopped at a restaurant where Simón ate a steak and had some ice cream. On the following four days, the man took Simón with him to his office – a large building on the doors of which was printed the picture of a large brown insect in a green circle with a red diagonal line across it. Simón walked around the corridors, looking timidly into rooms where men sat in front of machines, punching buttons and looking up at screens. Or he loitered in a large room where several secretaries were typing. The man took him out in his car and drove to a restaurant where Simón ate chicken and again enjoyed being treated to an ice cream. They bought more clothes and shoes.

On the evening of the fifth day, they drove out to the airport. The man had been explaining. This is your passport. Keep it in the breast pocket of your coat. There. This envelope is for the headmaster. Remember the name Paulo Abate. He will meet you at the airport. Keep this card with his name on it in your right pocket. In case he doesn't find you, go to the information desk. And this is your ticket. The first part is the flight to Buenos Aires, the other one for the internal flight.

Strapped to his window seat, Simón stared out at the lights racing by as the jumbo jet speeded down the runway and then lifted off to begin its steep climb. The lights of the city were spread out below but within a minute the plane penetrated the low ceiling of clouds and there was nothing but darkness outside.

He stood in front of the headmaster across the large mahogany desk on which papers and files were spread in neat groups. 'You have never seen a play,' the headmaster was repeating. 'How extraordinary!'

Simón stared at his pale blue eyes looking curiously at him over the half-moon lenses of his reading glasses and saw him look down again at the file before him on the desk. He had been questioning Simón for a quarter of an hour and was puzzled to find that though the boy appeared intelligent he knew practically nothing. Simón was struck by his large head that carried a great quantity of white hair – a mass of it at the top, two bushy eyebrows from which several individual hairs stuck out like antennae, and a mustache curled up to points in front of the broad ruddy cheeks that were marked with tiny purplish lines, like scratches. Behind him was a bay window through which boys in green blazers and grey flannel trousers were seen strolling in pairs or in groups.

The headmaster looked up. 'Simón Bolívar,' he said as though thinking aloud, 'curious name to give to a child. Simón Bolívar . . . hum . . . Do you realize,' he asked, raising his voice, 'what you have inherited with your name?'

'Yes, sir. I mean, no, sir.'

'Yes sir, no sir, what kind of answer is that, young man?'

Simón stood still, staring helplessly at the large face.

The headmaster leaned back and said, 'History.' He pulled off his glasses and fixed his eyes on Simón. 'Do you know what a liberation history is to us, and what a burden, too? An awful burden!' He shook his head sadly. 'Ah, if we really understood it! God left empty spaces in the human body – cavities behind the organs, little hollows in bones, minute interstices in the coilings of the brain – to leave room in our bodies for the history we must carry with us. Ah, if we really had a fraction of an idea of what is within us!'

He paused and put on his glasses and was about to look at the file when he again removed the glasses and asked, 'Do you have bad dreams, boy?'

Not having understood the earlier speech, Simón was confused by the surprising question that followed it. 'No, sir,' he said, and then quickly added, 'Yes, sir.'

The headmaster made a grunting kind of sound, quickly put on his glasses and looked at the file. 'This question of your father . . .' he began, his eyes on the file, but stopped himself abruptly, reading something else before him, and added in a louder voice, 'It seems we have a lot to teach you, you have a long way to go, a long way to go. Never been to a play, imagine!'

The headmaster raised the top page in the file without lifting it completely and glanced again at the cheque in US dollars that had been donated to the school. 'We'll make a man out of you,' he said, looking up and smiling at Simón for the first time. 'We will teach you the value of your name.'

Simón was entrusted to the special care of Paulo Abate, the young geography teacher who had met him at the airport, giving an outline of the school's history on the twenty-kilometre drive from the town across the hilly landscape of the interior with the tall eucalyptus trees swaying in the wind. It had been founded late in the nine-teenth century, taking as its model one of the great schools of England. The large brick building, he pointed out when they entered the school grounds, was one of the best examples in South America of English Victorian architecture. Simón listened quietly, having no idea what the man was talking about, but with a sense that he ought to look impressed. There was a crowd of boys in a distant playing field in green jerseys and white shorts. 'The school's game is rugby,' Abate said, 'we have nothing to do with vulgar soccer which is such a mania in this country.'

Simón grew to hate rugby; he was jeered at when he fumbled the ball and brutally brought down when he caught it. He hated, too, the school's sacred tradition of the annual play, which was a great obsession with the headmaster. But during his first year he passively tolerated the life forced upon him. Being practically illiterate, he was obliged to take extra hours of tuition, and the tedium they entailed was preferable to spending the time with boys who taunted and bullied him, for among them he appeared an insignificant foreign weakling with an absurd accent and uncultivated manners, fit only to be despised as someone unsuited to share the privileges of their cultured society. He patiently suffered the paper darts that struck his head in class and the mimicking of his accent that produced guffaws in a group of boys; but occasionally, on the edge of the playing field or in the dormitory, he could not repress his anger and fought back with his fists. Once, after a holiday during his second year, an older boy said to him, 'Didn't have a home to go to, eh?' And another curly-headed older boy, who had acted a main role in the previous year's school play and was a favourite with the headmaster, remarked, 'What do you expect when your mother's a whore?'

'You take that back!' Simón shouted, quickly removing his blazer and throwing it to the ground.

The boy looked at Simón with contempt and said, 'A rich whore who gives money to the school but has no home for her bastard son.'

'I said you take that back!' Simón's fists were shaking in front of his reddened face.

The boy, having his companion with him and convinced that his reputation as an actor was too awe-inspiring for the younger boy to carry out any threat, calmly added to his earlier remark, 'No one has heard of your father – some drunk gaucho with money in his hands and an erection in his pants?'

The two older boys laughed and the curly-headed one looked at the other to relish the approval visible on his face. It was then that Simón flung himself forward and landed his fist against the jaw, just then in profile, of the school's distinguished actor, following it quickly with a blow under the chin with the other fist. The boy staggered back and Simón threw himself at his throat and knocked him to the ground. The other boy fell upon Simón but the latter was too enraged to be overpowered by a larger adversary and struck more blows at his stomach and chest than he himself received.

Punishment followed. The older boys, suffering the indignity of defeat from one they considered an uncouth upstart, let it be known that, studiously preserving the school's unwritten code of honour, they had refrained from hitting a younger boy even during the extreme provocation of receiving blows from him, and thus they acquired an enhanced respect from the school. The actor went to the headmaster who listened to the case and pronounced judgement. Six strokes of the cane, an hour's detention each day for a week, and only soup and bread – no meat, fish or dessert – for a week. The event was much talked about among the boys and several expressed a secret admiration for the quiet young boy who had knocked out the vain actor.

Among them was one Guillermo Betancourt, who gradually became Simón's closest friend. His parents had died in an automobile accident and his uncle, managing his late brother's estate, saw to it that Guillermo received a good education and that the inheritance that would come to him on his majority was soundly invested; but he had no interest in his nephew and no desire to have him in his own house. Thus, Guillermo and Simón were two of a dozen or so boys who did not go home during the vacations. During the long summer holidays, one of the masters would be assigned to take them on a fortnight's excursion. Once, in the charge of the enthusiastic senior geography master, they trekked into the Andes, taking a slow laborious train and then hiking among the barren, rocky lower slopes and staying in dismal villages. A year later, the more indolent art teacher took them to Punta del Este where he left the boys to their own devices, having his own plans for himself. Most of the group spent the days swimming or playing volleyball on the beach, but Guillermo and Simón separated themselves and tried to flirt with the girls. A third excursion took them to Buenos Aires where the history teacher planned to show them the nation's culture.

Simón and Guillermo had both turned fifteen and to them the paintings of the war with Paraguay or the tomb of the Liberator, General José de San Martín, in the cathedral, were less interesting than the life in the streets where the glittering shops and throngs of people held their fascination. They took opportunities to escape from the group and made for the fashionable streets where they could enjoy looking at beautiful women, and at nights, when the teacher had retired to his room to let the march of history trample on his dreams, they slipped out of the hotel and sought out the areas alive with humanity. Guillermo had one fixed idea that he talked about ceaselessly: he was set on losing his virginity even if it meant finding a cheap whore. He had talked Simón into having the same idea, and as they walked the streets they looked with a desperate hunger at the attractive women passing by and kept up a coarse commentary expressive of their growing lust. On the fourth night, chance brought them to that part of the city where a man did not need to look twice at a woman to know what she was doing in the street, and it was a matter of choosing the one that appealed to one's fancy. The knowledge of their common experience made the two more attached to each other when, after experiencing the joys of debauchery for several more nights, they returned to the school.

A confusion of noise, as if a rabble were shouting insults and fighting, was coming from the hall when Simón came out of a class, sent by the teacher to convey the register to the school secretary. Rehearsals had begun for that year's play and it was being said with awe that the headmaster had taken on the most ambitious project of his life and had decided to put on a famous tragedy. The very word, tragedy, made one scared. Simón knew nothing about it and Guillermo had not enlightened him by saying that it was probably about sex and murder.

The hall was on the lower floor and was surrounded by a gallery on the floor above, from where the stage could be seen. The headmaster was stamping up and down in front of the stage, pushing back with a hand the locks of his white hair which kept falling across his forehead. A group of boys stood silently by a wall. One large boy stood at the centre of the stage, surrounded by several others. The noise had abruptly stopped with the headmaster shouting, 'No, no, no, we'll have to try that again!'

The boys all walked back to the stage, and the headmaster said, 'Before you enter, there will be trumpets and drums offstage. Remember who you are and where you

208

are. And Gerardo, please remember that you are a woman, a *queen*.'

Two boys standing next to Gerardo giggled. The headmaster gave them a stare. One of them went pale.

The activity seemed absurd to Simón and he went to the secretary's office. He was reminded of the previous year's play. The worst thing was to have to sit for three hours and watch. Comedy it was. The parents found it hilarious. Women with a lot of rouge on their cheeks, their funny hats shaking when they laughed. Men in dark suits going haw-haw-haw. The headmaster laughed the loudest and wiped his pink cheeks with a white handkerchief. It was boring, not funny at all. Guillermo had taken out a small penknife and quietly carved a dirty word on his seat. That was funny. Then the big reception in the refectory. The long tables all taken out. Small square ones with white tablecloths instead, and vases of flowers on them. The boys all in green blazers and grey flannels. Scrubbed faces, the hair neatly brushed. The mothers cooed, the fathers brayed. The prefects carried trays with glasses of wine. The boys obliged to stand with their parents while a teacher told them about their son's natural talent for algebra. He stood with Guillermo and the two succeeded in filling their empty Coca-cola glasses with red wine without anyone noticing. After the second glass, Guillermo whispered to him, 'I wouldn't mind screwing Gerardo's mother, look at her tits!'

Returning from the secretary's office, Simón heard the headmaster shouting in the hall. 'No, no, not *surfifor*, but *survivor* . . . the survivor bound . . . give that *bound* an emphasis, bound as in having no choice and as in tied up, both meanings must come through. And it's not *philial* but *filial* . . . get the stress and the pause right. . . . In filial obligation PAUSE for some term . . . start that speech again.'

There were several more weeks left of the vacation after the excursion to Buenos Aires and they were able to obtain permission to spend occasional days in the nearby town, travelling there on bicycles and, after Guillermo had extracted more money out of his uncle, on a scooter that he purchased and quickly learned to drive. They hung about in bars, drinking beer and smoking cigarettes, in dingy streets where bleary-eyed, pot-bellied barmen did not even look one in the eye while taking one's money for the beer. Children with bloated stomachs and hanging faces stood outside the bars, staring in with large expressionless eyes and putting out a hand every time someone walked by them. Guillermo had an easy facility for starting a conversation with strangers and in each bar that they went to he would greet some stranger who happened to be drinking a cup of coffee, and within five minutes they talked as if they were old friends. Guillermo had a simple aim in striking up the conversations; to discover if there were women available in the town.

After the school term started, they found it annoying to be deprived of their recent discovery, of which the fruits had been enjoyed for so short a time, that there were a number of discreet places in the town where pleasure could be purchased. But one night, Guillermo sat up in bed in the dormitory, and quietly went and awoke Simón. He said to him in a whisper, 'Come with me, and don't make a sound.'

The two quietly walked the length of the room. The door was closed and Guillermo slowly turned the handle and gave it a push. It opened. There was a night-light in the hall, above the staircase. Walking barefooted soundlessly over the carpeted hall and down the steps, they reached the outside door to the building. The front door, too, was open. They walked along the line of trees bordering the drive and Guillermo said, 'Well, that proves it. We can go back to sleep now.'

'Proves what?' Simón asked as they stood under a tree. 'My feet are cold.'

'I suddenly had an idea,' Guillermo said, 'lying in bed thinking of that lovely Francesca. And I wanted to test it out.'

'What idea?'

'We've just proved it. What do you think we've done?'

210

'Guillermo, what are you talking about?'

'Observe, my friend, the following. One, it is not yet midnight. Two, the entire school is asleep. Three, you and I have been able to walk out of the dorm and are free right now to go to the other end of the world. That is what we have proved.'

'But where can we go?'

'Oh, don't be so dumb, Simón, it was only an experiment. It occurred to me that the school remains open day and night. For two very simple reasons. One, there is nothing but deserted fields between here and the town and no one of the boys is going to contemplate walking that distance. Anyone starting a scooter or a car would be heard. At the same time there is no fear of foreign invasion, the whole country is too proud of the school to do it any harm. And two, the school believes that every one of its members is a man of honour who would not do so base a thing as walk out of it in the middle of the night.'

'What next, then?' Simón asked.

'Preparation, my friend. We will find in the next few days a spot a kilometre away where we can hide the scooter together with clothes and shoes. Then all we need to do when the desire for Francesca gives us no repose is to walk out, as we have done tonight.'

The scheme worked, and for the next few months Simón found himself plunged into a dissolute low life in dark, shabby streets inhabited by haggard and pathetically painted whores and unshaven pot-bellied pimps who hung around in doorways. He felt no distinct pleasure in what he did. It was as if he floated as a phantom in someone else's dream, a body driven to some awful and bestial coupling with a shadowy form, an existence in unreality in which no fantasy was inconceivable. Although a customer whose whims were sometimes cruel, he rather than the whore was the real victim, and he dimly understood that pleasure was not so thrilling as pain, that there was a terrible satisfaction in becoming a degenerate so debased that one despised the human body and was gratified to see it sink lower. He was indifferent to the

211

lovely Francesca, and a few others like her, but was attracted by the older women who, stripped of their gaudy costume, were miserable caricatures of the female shape. He was penetrating his own inner darkness to see if the horrid blackness did not contain one tiny glow-worm that by chance, for a fraction of a second, emitted the miracle of light and proved that the soul, indeed, had residence within him and only waited to be lit.

The daylight hours, when he was a studious and dutiful schoolboy, took on a new dimension, and seemed another form of unreality that had no connection with the unreality of his nightly experience. The majority of his companions were destined to be doctors, lawyers and corporation executives, and they had a complacent air of assurance, as if they already owned the world. He envied them the sense of certainty they possessed of their own origin and future, but their urbanity appeared to him no less a savagery than that openly exhibited by the creatures of his nightlife.

By the age of sixteen, the accumulation of his experiences had made him different from people outwardly of the same class. His companions did not need to seek pain to test the limits of the body's vulnerability, nor to enter the tiny little unlit room with its stink of vomit on the floor strewn with sawdust to take a drug that simultaneously drew flames from the blood and turned it to a sluggish, polluted stream. Their history did not demand violence from the body.

A boy feeling the need to go to the bathroom rose in bed one night and was startled to see two figures quietly walking past in the aisle below his bed. He saw them go to the end of the room and leave it. He got out of bed and walked to the door from where he could see them going down the stairs in the dim light. He recognized them, and softly walked to the top of the staircase from where he was amazed to see them leave the building. The next day he informed the house master. Three nights later, when Guillermo and Simón next ventured out, they found the front door locked. By now, leaving the school at night had become a routine with them, so that the actions and gestures of their bodies were instinctive: Guillermo's hand would automatically reach for the door handle, turn it, pull back the door, and the two would go out. And now, even as he was reaching for the handle, he was already in the process of moving toward the gap that was supposedly going to appear in a second. Instead, he banged himself against the door that remained closed and Simón, following him as usual, bumped into him. The noise was enough to wake the house master who slept in a room on the ground floor and who had left his door open.

Guillermo's story that he had been sleepwalking and that Simón had only followed him to make sure that he was safe was scornfully dismissed by the headmaster. He put the boys on probation – detention every evening, no games or gym, a restricted diet – and instituted an inquiry. He discovered from Guillermo's guardian that the boy had received excessive sums of money in recent months and was scandalized to see that one of the pretexts Guillermo had given was that this class was going on an expedition to Machu Picchu. The headmaster was outraged not by the extravagance of the lie but that one of his senior pupils, after five years of education and training in discipline at The School, should turn out to be such a scheming scoundrel. He was shrewd enough to guess in what quarters such amounts of money could have been spent and he soon collected the facts concerning whoring and drugs. He wrote letters to the guardians of the two boys, giving them a sketch of the circumstances and informing them that the boys were being given a week in which to leave the school from which they were, without recourse to an appeal or the hope of a pardon, dismissed.

What the headmaster's inquiry had not discovered was that on many occasions when Simón lay passed out or in a state in which he could not tell whether his sense of pain was not a hallucination, Guillermo spent his time talking with young men who, finding in him a companionable and sympathetic youth, had begun to exploit his naturally

213

rebellious nature in order to recruit him to their cause. On the walk back to school, after they had hidden the scooter, Guillermo sometimes talked about his conversations with them to Simón, but at that hour the latter was barely conscious and concentrated all his energy on reaching his bed, thus remaining quite ignorant of the scheme then germinating in his friend's mind.

The week in which they were dismissed coincided with the annual sports week when teams from other schools came to participate in field and track events. Tents were put up across from the playing field, each flying the colours of its school. There were crowds of boys everywhere and a great deal of shouting during the competitions. The masters were busy marshalling the crowd and running the competitions. The day of the finals was a gala event. The parents came to it, driving up in their expensive cars.

Ostracized, no longer allowed to wear the school's blazer, and confined to a room, Simón and Guillermo watched the cars arriving in front of the building where a master on duty received them with fawning gestures. Simón watched the look of patient benevolence on the fathers' faces and was filled with hatred; the elegantly dressed mothers left him cold. The parents walked away out of sight from where the boys stood at the window. By late morning, the area in front of the school was filled with neatly parked rows of cars, the last one of which must apparently have arrived, for the master on duty had gone to join the parties taking place next to the playing field.

'Why should we wait for our guardians to come and get us?' Guillermo suddenly said. 'There is nothing for us here.'

'What can we do?'

'You know, Simón, I was thinking. I don't know if you have a home to go to, but I know my guardian is not going to be thrilled to have me back. I think he will send me to another school. Some place worse. So, why should I wait for that pleasure?'

'I don't know what I'll do,' Simón said. 'I never liked this place. I hate everyone.'

After some thought, Guillermo asked, 'Do you know how to drive a car?'

'No.'

Guillermo looked down at the parked cars and said, 'There must be an automatic one there.'

'What about it?'

'My father had an automatic car and when I was twelve I pestered the chauffeur to let me take it back and forth on the drive in front of the house. He showed me how. I guess I could work it out.'

After walking with bent knees, so that they could not be seen above the roofs of the cars, and peering into some fifty or sixty of them, they found one that was automatic and also had the key left behind in the ignition. It was a dark grey Mercedes-Benz. They sat in it, and Guillermo spent some minutes studying its mechanics. Finally, he concluded, 'I guess all you do is put it in drive and go.' Shouts and clapping were heard from the playing field and Guillermo waited some more minutes. He switched on the engine the moment he heard a loud roar from the crowd, pulled the lever into drive, and pressed on the accelerator. The car shot forward much faster than he had expected and he threw his foot on the brake pedal. They were both thrown forward but were restrained by the seat belts.

'Don't worry, Simón,' Guillermo said, smiling at his friend who had begun to sweat. 'We'll make it.'

He let the car slide forward and steered it gingerly through the parked cars. 'It's easy,' he said, realizing there was nothing he had to do but steer, and becoming confident.

Three minutes later, they were speeding up the road. 'Do you know how much these cars cost?' Guillermo said. 'They're not even imported into this country. You have to bribe ten thousand generals to get one in. Imagine the blood of the workers that must have cost to buy this car.'

Simón wondered what he meant but his thoughts were focused on the distant curve in the road and he was more concerned about Guillermo's ability to keep the car from crashing into the trees.

\*       \*       \*

As in each previous phase of his life, Simón was again forced into an involuntary exile from the world in which he had earlier been placed without knowing why and then had become accustomed to as a sort of home. Now began a time when his home shifted from week to week and sometimes he was obliged to remain in flight for days and nights at a time, never fully understanding who his pursuers were and why he had found himself in a situation that demanded a desperate search for a safe refuge.

Guillermo drove the Mercedes-Benz to one of the shabby streets they had frequented at night in the town near the school. He talked to some young men he knew. Simón heard the conversation without grasping its meaning. Their voices were excited. One man took the car away. Guillermo talked with two others for a long time in a darkened room. Then they all stood up and shook hands and embraced. Simón, too, found himself being hugged by the two men who called him 'comrade'. They were driven away in an old van in which Guillermo carried on a mysterious dialogue with the driver. At last, Simón asked Guillermo, 'Where are we going?'

'Into the great future!' Guillermo said enthusiastically.

'We didn't take any of our things with us,' Simón reminded him.

'We don't need a thing,' Guillermo answered with abandon. 'We have everything.'

Simón was not at all enlightened, and said after some time, 'What about that car? Was it taken back to the school?'

Guillermo and the driver laughed, and the former said, 'That car was donated to the revolution.'

They drove for two days in a southwesterly direction until they reached a town on the edge of the flat grassland with mountains far to its west. They had spent the nights in the van, parked just off the highway, and stopped to eat at small roadside cafés. And thus Simón began his life training to become an urban guerrilla. He had never heard the term before and had no notion of the beliefs he was being made to champion, being taught the use of firearms

216

and explosives in a cause that he knew nothing about.

He learned to understand the nature of the abstract enemy and by the time he was nineteen years old he had very nearly acquired a conviction that what he did was right. He began to have a sense of political ideology and knowing of no other principles than those that motivated his peers he developed a complete faith in the ones handed down to him. He distinguished himself in the first real test when he was charged with five others to take part in the kidnapping of an industrialist in Córdoba. Lesser assignments followed – the dumping of chemicals into a river to create the evidence that a steel mill owned by foreign capitalists was poisoning the environment; the hijacking of trucks belonging to a national supermarket chain in order to create a food shortage in a small town that led to a short-lived workers' revolt. And then, when he had turned twenty, came the mission to Uruguay. Simón and three others were trained for it for four months; one of his comrades was Mercedes, a large girl from a well-known Buenos Aires family who had already proved herself in two bank robberies.

The details of the mission to Uruguay, which had as its objective the freeing of a number of guerrillas imprisoned in Montevideo, are irrelevant to the larger history of Simón's life. It was only one more bizarre accident in a succession of others equally essentially meaningless that took him to places where he had never intended to go. The mission failed because two of his companions proved to be traitors. The only important fact is that he and Mercedes were obliged to run and were not abandoned by their invisible superiors who succeeded in having them cross into Brazil.

They lay on the beach at Leblon in the shade of the parasol fixed in the sand, having come there in the morning after breakfast to enjoy the beach before it got too hot. Mercedes still wore a bikini though her stomach bulged out. Simón stood up and weaving his way through the crowd on the beach went for one more swim. After eight months in Rio, he still thought of his life in that city as that of a transit passenger at an airport whose long-delayed flight will be called at any moment. He nominally worked for a foreign newspaper so that he could secure a resident's visa, but that was only one more of the many frauds of life he had to accept wherever he found himself living. He enjoyed the idyllic life in Rio. One did nothing but go to the beach in the morning, sleep after lunch, take a walk in the evening and go to a restaurant. It was all paid for and all the details managed as if by magic. It was one more dream that he inhabited and sometimes he appeared to himself as a phantom, for he certainly had no existence in the common reality which constituted the life of others. Only Mercedes was real, and his child growing within her. But then, he had realized, she was his dream. Although he had said to her a million times that he loved her, he did not understand love, and obscurely felt that what he valued most in her was her wonderful capacity to absorb him into her body, to give him what no drug had ever given, the experience of nonbeing. Perhaps the child due to be born in seven or eight weeks would evoke in him a sense of reality he had never had.

Coming out of the water, he stood near her outside the shade for a few minutes, letting the sun dry his body. All the way down the beach to Ipanema, and beyond that to Arpoador, men and women lay on the sand or played games or went in and out of the water. Thousands of them. It occurred to him that he had nothing to do with them. Their lives, all together in one small place now, were all separate; and yet, when he thought of his past, chance had taken him out of his native crowds to far lands and for no logical sequence of cause and effect that he could see made him an instrument of someone else's fulfilling his destiny.

He collected the parasol and the towels and with Mercedes holding his arm, walked down Bartólomeu Mitre and turned right down Avenida Gen. San Martín where they lived. As had become usual in recent weeks, they had been discussing a possible name for their child and had exhausted a list of girls' names when they arrived at the apartment to find that the mail had been delivered in their absence.

The envelope bearing the address of the foreign newspaper for which he was supposed to be a special correspondent was not an occasion for surprise since he received a monthly cheque in just such an envelope. But when he opened it, he saw that the cheque was for a much larger sum than he had received before and that instead of an accompanying statement of the articles he was supposed to have written there was a long letter. He sat down and read it.

'What is it?' Mercedes asked.

He passed her the first of two sheets covered with single-spaced typewritten instructions, inscribed in a code that they both knew by heart, saying, 'They want me to go somewhere.' He passed her the second sheet when he had finished it and remained silent while she read it.

'It's an easy job,' Mercedes said, handing him back the page. 'It looks like a pleasant holiday, as far as I can see.'

'There doesn't seem any risk,' he said, smiling at her. 'Just look the place over and make a few contacts. I wish you were coming, too.'

'It would have been appropriate if we were a honeymoon couple,' she said, 'but in my condition . . .?'

She dismissed the thought.

'With this done, I suppose they'll let me alone for a good long time,' he said.

She went away to the kitchen to prepare the lunch and he reread the letter. The government of one of the Latin countries was hosting a summit meeting of several South American heads of state, each one of them a military dictator, to take place at a secluded resort in two months' time. Simón's job was to go and check out the place, make local contacts, and submit a detailed plan for wiring the hotel where the heads of state were to meet in order to blow it up when they were all assembled. Simón was instructed to fly to Valparaíso on the tenth of the month – in another three days – and take the helicopter service from there to the resort town known as San Clemente de los Andes.

219

Simón put the letter down on a small side table, and sat musing. The envelope was still in his lap and absent-mindedly he picked it up and was revolving it between his hands when Mercedes came in from the kitchen. She had put something in the oven that would take twenty minutes to warm up.

'So, you have to go in three days?'

'That's correct.'

'Well, that's not too inconvenient,' she said. 'Even if you're away for a month, you'll be back for the baby.'

'That's right,' he said, though not fully paying attention to her, his mind vaguely troubled, for he had no real desire to leave for even a short period the dreamlike existence in Rio that had made him so contented.

'But, Simón,' she said thoughtfully, 'we must always make an allowance for the worst. Suppose for some reason you are delayed and are not here when the baby is born?'

'There's nothing to suppose,' he said. 'I'll be back in a week or ten days. They've told me what to do, not how long I must take doing it.'

'But suppose.'

'Well, so what?' he asked.

'We were talking of names. Suppose the baby is born when you are still away.'

'I thought we had agreed on the name Alegría.'

'Yes,' Mercedes said, 'Alegría if it's a girl. But we haven't agreed on a boys name, and suppose it's a boy?'

Simón was just then staring at the envelope in his hands and his eyes fell on his own present address. Avenida Gen. San Martín. And without thinking of what he was saying, he said, 'José de San Martín.'

Mercedes laughed and said, 'You're joking! That is the name of the Liberator.'

'What can be more appropriate?'

220

# 9

He could hear the laughter of the girls from where he sat
on the verandah of his cottage, having waited there for
nearly two hours to see if Sofía would return for the lunch
he had prepared. The sun shone through the heavy
branches of the sycamore trees and, down across the front
of his cottage, past the flowering bushes that grew on the
sloping land, he could see the outer branches of the willows appear a lighter green than the branches partially in
the shade. The slope of the land gave him a view far to
the left that was obstructed by the lower branches of the
sycamores, but here and there, where the breeze made the
branches move in a fanning motion, or where there was a
narrow gap in the dense foliage, he could see the light
catch the moving figures and he almost imagined that
when he heard the laughter he could, the sycamore leaves
just then parting to give a glimpse of an animated face, see
the sun glinting from the white teeth in the brown face
thrown up in amusement. The group of three or four was
moving slowly, and there would be a moment's deadness
while the girls stood for some reason before there was a
burst of laughter followed by a rush of forward movement. Hearing tones that he assumed were indicative of an
innocent happiness, Calderón composed himself to be
amiable to Sofía when she finally left her friends and
returned to him, for during the time that he had waited for
her his increasing resentment at her disregard for his
reminder that she return in time for lunch had begun to
make him angry. For what, after all, was time to his dear
little girl who had known no other manifestation of it than

the casual flow of succeeding days, each one only continuing the enchantment of the day before? He was prepared to be reasonable and agreeable. She still had so much to understand! And he had been a poor teacher, he was prepared to confess to himself. He had been a jealous guardian of her growing beauty more than an instructor of worldly knowledge, and now that she had turned sixteen and had the appearance of a full-grown woman, he held on to his guardianship with greater vigilance than before.

Dawdling along the path, the group came nearer. The laughter reaching him was louder and possessed a greater warmth. But his ears now caught another sound that made him look hard where the group was concealed behind the sycamore branches and had apparently again stopped. It was a lugubrious, low-pitched sound, as though the voice were not uttering words but a moaning calculated to win pity, and with a sudden shock Calderón distinguished it as the voice of a young man.

A minute later, he saw the four of them on the path near the willow trees, having come out of the screen of the sycamore branches. Sofía, two girls, and a young man. They had again stopped; the young man appeared to be telling them some anecdote. Calderón could see how closely he held the attention of the girls, each one of whom had her eyes fixed on his face. The boy talked for three or four minutes, and not for a second did the girls look away from him. And then suddenly the girls were laughing loudly, shrieking almost in their mirth, while the youth grinned and looked greatly pleased with himself for the success of his story.

At last they parted. Sofía stood under a willow, watching her three companions go back on the path. A moment later, the two girls and the youth were obscured by a tree. But Calderón saw that instead of immediately returning to the house, Sofía lingered by the brook, going and sitting on a rock. He could only observe her face in profile and he watched her look at the water before her like one who sought an answer to the puzzle of her future. She raised her skirt to just above the knee and stretched out her leg to dip her foot into the water. She stroked the water with her foot, kicking it up gently. Then she pulled up both her legs, drew her skirt over the knees, and rested her cheek on the knees, clutching her legs in an embrace. Calderón wondered what was going through her mind. Was it happiness that she felt or a sadness? Why did she not return to him? He stood up and walked a little to his right to see if he could not get a fuller glimpse of her face. She seemed to be in a strange mood. What subtle thought possessed her mind that he could not know?

But from where he stood, the corner of his eye caught a movement far to the left where in a gap among the trees he could see that the other three had come to a stop. The boy was again saying something to the girls but from the way they looked at him it did not appear that he was telling another story to make them laugh. He made a gesture toward the willow trees and the girls shook their heads in assent. He shrugged his shoulders as though he regretted something and the girls smiled and threw up their hands, appearing to suggest that they understood and that whatever the matter was it was of no great importance. Then the girls turned round and began to walk quickly away while the boy, looking toward where Sofía sat, stared in that direction for a moment and then began to walk toward her slowly.

Calderón returned to his chair, sat down and firmly held the armrests with his hands that had begun to sweat. Sofía's head was turned away from the boy's direction and she did not hear him approach. The boy came to the edge of the brook, stopped, and looked at her for a minute before he softly called her name. Calderón saw her let go of her legs and turn her face. Surprise and pleasure were unmistakably visible on her face. She stood up and, leaping over the narrow channel of shallow water, came and stood in front of the boy. He spoke some words to which she listened very attentively, lowering her head as he spoke. His face had the expression of worry and doubt. Sofía looked up at him and spoke. He listened and shook his head as if in despair. She paused. He stared at her and she at him. She said something else. His face lit up and he bounced on his feet. She smiled and went and sat on the rock that served as a seat between the two willow trees. He went and sat next to her. They were both turned away from Calderón, so that their faces appeared to him in quarter profile. Occasionally, one would turn completely to look at the other, and Calderón read in the expression a tenderness, perhaps even a growing affection for the other. Calderón avoided thinking of the word *love*, but it was touching the corners of his brain and beginning to create little trepidations in his body. He wanted to rise and go away and not see the scene before him. He felt the blood move irregularly within his veins as though the word *love* had formed clots along its passage. But he could not take his eyes away and sat there like one unable to step back from a precipice, rooted by fear, terror, and the knowledge that whatever the next moment had in store for him, there was no escape from the pain that had begun.

For a few minutes, Calderón took comfort in his observation that the two did not touch each other. Sofía seemed to have her hands clutched together in her lap, and the boy leaned back, his two palms flat against the rock behind him. Things had not gone that far, at least. Calderón's relief was associated with the thought that he had time to tell her that she was still too young for any kind of attachment, that there was so much still for her to learn even before she could sit talking innocently with a boy. He had only her interest at heart, and he would tell her to be patient with him, for he was only going to do what was best for her.

But then suddenly, it was she who turned to face the boy fully and threw up her hands to his shoulders. Calderón was startled; his eyes burned. She was saying something, her hands still on his shoulders. Then the boy turned his face and rested his cheek against one of her hands, pressing it there in an affectionate gesture. She stood up, dropping her hands to her sides. He rose, too, and spoke some words. Then he put up a hand and held one of hers, bringing it up and appearing to squeeze it between both his own. In a moment, he turned round and walked away in the gait of one who had just discovered a wonderful new happiness. Sofía's steps seemed to be touched by the same discovery as she came up to the cottage.

She saw Calderón, and said with a smile, 'Did you see that poor boy? I've never seen anyone so unhappy before.'

Calderón did not say anything but looked at her questioningly. 'Poor thing, he has been so miserable.'

She noticed his stare and, teasing him by using his common name, said, 'Aren't you listening to me, Don Bueno? Don't you want to know why Jorge has been so miserable?'

'Why?' he managed to say.

'Because Pilar turned him down. He told me all about it just now. He is so much in love with her, and she has refused him.'

'Is that so?'

'Yes. And so when I saw how his heart was broken, I said I'd go and talk to Pilar. She always listens to me. I'll tell her to give him a chance. He's really a very nice boy.'

How pathetic were the little dramas of adolescents, he thought without realizing that from his perspective he was no judge of the younger generation, especially as he himself only a few minutes earlier had had emotions not unlike those that tormented the young. But he felt an enormous sense of relief. His Sofía was still not tainted by the attentions of young men not worthy of her. She was safe. If only he could preserve her thus, in the safety of his own bosom.

And when she suddenly said, 'You have not been waiting for me to have lunch, I hope!', he smiled and said, 'No, of course not.'

It did not hurt him when she remarked, 'We ate a salad at Cecilia's.' Indeed, he would not have been hurt had she gone on to say that she much preferred the titbits she ate at her friends' to the elaborate dishes that he prepared, not even if she had added some such coarse statement as, 'Don Bueno, your cooking stinks!' The patience required to bear such abuse was easy to summon, for it entailed little

225

emotional loss; a lost reputation as a cook could be regained with time, a lost love never.

Later in the day, it occurred to him that Sofía could have made up the story about the young man being desperately in love with Pilar to disguise from Calderón her own attachment to him. The relief he had experienced at her explanation of the tender scene by the brook vanished and was replaced by a subtler pain than he had felt before. Could his darling girl know to lie so cleverly that he could not distinguish her remarks from the truth? Perhaps young girls in love had an instinctive access to a charmingly deceptive tone that sparkled with the nuances of honesty and solicitous concern, the voice ringing like a true coin, when the true worth of their words was as grey and heavy as lead. There was a throbbing in his brain as if some nerves, suddenly receiving a rush of signals of pain breaking out in several parts of his body, had become knotted, and the entanglement caused a partial blindness in his perception that, in turn, generated more pain and tightened the knot with greater force.

In the evening, Sofía said, 'I'm going to Pilar to have a nice long chat with her.'

She did not interpret his silent stare as meaning anything other than a disinterested assent, and went away, after saying, 'I must persuade her to give Jorge a chance.'

He saw her walk lightly down the winding path at the front of the cottage, her golden hair hanging down behind her, her white frock making a clear outline of her body in the shadow that fell across the yard at that hour. The white form flickered through the screen of the dark branches, transforming her body in his vision into flashes of little white lines in a black void, and a little farther, where some slanting sunlight caught the white, he saw fragments of the form, like the dismembered petals of a marguerite being blown across a mossy wall. The pulsing white disappeared from his sight but remained in his mind where its pulsation intensified and became a throbbing. In the pain that overcame him, it seemed to him that his blood had ceased to flow and had collected as two stagnant pools in his eyes. 'Don Bueno,' he said, holding his head in his hands as he sat down on the steps of the verandah, 'you are the most wretched, wretched of men!'

Later that evening, Belisario came up and said, 'Don Bueno, you are too much alone. Come on, let's go and have a drink. A hunter gave me a good tip today for being his guide. Come on, what do you say to a drink?'

They went to the bar near the park by the river, the one that had existed long before the hotel was constructed. Belisario and Don Bueno had visited the bar in the hotel a few times, but no longer went there. It was too far to walk to and its atmosphere of catering to an international taste – the decor reminded Calderón of lounges at airports – together with the presence of the expensively dressed foreign tourists had been oppressive. The local bar was simply a hut with naked wooden floorboards, small square tables and stools, and a few oil lamps hanging from the low ceiling. Originally, it had only beer to offer, but with the opening of the hotel, the owner – a sixty-year-old man called Señor Jácome – had been able to acquire stocks of rum, whiskey and gin. In the past, when supplies of beer ran out and there was a delay in replacing them, Señor Jácome had begun to brew his own beer, and with time it became the preferred drink among the natives. Made from water that ran down the mountains, it had a body and strength not found in the bottled variety. When tourists began to come to San Clemente de los Andes, some of them, looking for local colour and quaint customs, wandered into the hamlet, photographing the cottages in their idyllic setting, and thus discovered the local bar. By now, a handful of them were invariably seen there.

Señor Jácome greeted Calderón and Belisario from behind the counter and served them the rum that they ordered. While he poured rum into glasses from a bottle, he said, 'Don Bueno, it could be the poor light here, but you look like you seen a ghost, you're so pale!'

'He doesn't have a young wife like you to keep him fit,' Belisario joked, handing him some money and picking up his glass.

227

Jácome laughed, counting out the change, and said, 'There are some thirsts the best beer in the world can't quench.'

Calderón was about to remark that sufficient rum could kill that kind of thirst, but another customer had come up to the counter and claimed Jácome's attention, and Calderón turned away with Belisario and the two went and sat at a table.

'You look the same as ever, Don Bueno,' Belisario said, raising his glass and smiling. 'Here's to your health.'

'To yours,' Calderón said, completing the formality that had existed between the two men since their first drink together.

'There's going to be a wedding,' Belisario said, 'the second in the family. Incredible, how quickly the children grow up. My son Carlos is getting married to Olmeda's daughter, Teresa.'

'Carlos? He's only a boy!'

'He's sixteen, Don Bueno, sixteen. He's shot up like a bamboo the last two years.'

A big foreigner with a red face laughed at another table, distracting Calderón for a moment. 'And Teresa,' he asked, 'how old is she?'

'You won't believe this,' Belisario said. 'She's a month away from her fifteenth birthday.'

'That's ridiculous!' Calderón exclaimed while Belisario laughed. 'How can you and Olmeda allow such a thing? Surely they can wait a few years?'

'But mother nature can't. You see, Carlos has gone and got her pregnant. What can we do but put the best face on it? Well, let me go and get another drink,' Belisario added, seeing that Calderón had drained his glass.

'Is this kind of thing common?' Calderón asked, accepting the second glass of rum from Belisario. 'I mean young boys and girls like that, you know, doing it, without, I mean with no one knowing what's going on?'

'Oh, it happens all the time.'

'With all of them?'

'I guess so,' Belisario said casually, as though the

228

question were not of grave significance. 'This is a small place. The men and women are busy working all day long, what can the children do but play with one another? It doesn't hurt anyone, it only makes them settle down more quickly.'

Calderón poured the rum down his throat and stood up to buy the next round. Belisario had not yet begun to drink from his second round, but Calderón went and brought back two more glasses of rum in any case.

It was the first time since the occasion twenty years earlier, when he had become comatose with whiskey following Leticia's announcement of her pregnancy, that he had drunk so much. He did not remember later how he got back home and fell into his own bed where, in the middle of the night, he woke up feeling an intense nausea welling up inside him. He rose out of bed to go to the bathroom. His head was throbbing. His mouth hung open, panting for air. He knew the way to the bathroom in the darkness, but found that his legs had lost their capacity to support his body and he collapsed after two or three staggering steps. As he fell forward, his forehead bumped against a wooden obstruction that, even in the desperate turbulence of the moment, he had the sense to know was the door. He reached for the handle, pulled himself up by holding it, opening the door at the same time, and rushed out. The bathroom was behind the kitchen to his left, and in his eagerness for release he instinctively made for the veran- dah that was nearer, knowing, too, that his legs, which were giving way again, could not be trusted to see him as far as the bathroom. He fell forward across the threshold, tripped over the steps, and rolled down the slope into the bushes in his front yard. Coming to a stop, he raised him- self on his hands and knees, his mouth hanging open in expectation of throwing up all that was contained in his body. But nothing happened for some time; he merely remained fixed in the posture of a dog with its tongue hanging out. Then, suddenly, as if some constriction had been removed, a burning sensation tore up from his bowels and exploded from his mouth. As the long stream of vomit poured out from his mouth, he was aware of the coldness of the night and that it was not pitch dark but a soft glow reached the earth from the heavenly bodies.

More than his normal breathing was restored when he had finished; his legs could stand, and even walk steadily. He could see his way to the brook. He went and sat on its bank, and rinsed his mouth several times with the cold water, washing his face and hands. Standing up, he breathed in the cold air and felt clearer in his head. He slowly walked back to the cottage.

She was standing at the top of the steps, a candle in her hand, in a white nightgown, her face lit up by the candle like a round moon. 'What happened? You gave me such a fright,' she said, seeing him approach. 'I heard some noise, someone falling on the floorboards. It startled me. I thought I was having a nightmare, but then I heard a loud grunting and a moaning. And I was really scared.'

Calderón had no memory of any sound escaping his lips but imagined that he could easily have been howling in pain, for he did have a memory of pain.

'I'm sorry,' he said, sitting down on the top step, near her feet.

'Then I lit a candle,' she went on, 'and came out to look. Your room was empty, the blanket was thrown to the floor. I thought that perhaps there had been an intruder and you had chased him out and were now gone after him. But then I thought there is nothing to steal from this house.'

'I'm sorry,' he said again, putting a hand to her ankle and stroking first one foot and then the other. 'You don't want to catch a cold.'

She sat down next to him and clutched his arm, holding herself tight against it. 'I heard the water,' she said. 'What were you doing? Washing yourself in the middle of the night?'

'Yes,' he said, turning slightly to enable his free hand to reach her head, and stroked her hair. She pressed her cheek against his shoulder. He was going to add that he had been sick, but his hand, stroking her hair, fell across

230

her ear and passed along the curve of her left cheek, and as she still held him tightly, her right breast against his arm, he continued to stroke her hair and cheek, and remained silent. She raised her face and kissed him on the cheek, and said close to his ear, 'There, I think you're better now.'

She stood up quickly and, taking her candle, walked away to her room. He did not wonder what her words meant and sat touching his fingers to his cheek, trying to relive the moment, so recent in time, and yet already a remote event, when he had felt the warm sensation of her breath just before her lips made their brief impression on his flesh. The moment seemed to have awakened him from a long sleep, and he identified the pain that had been tormenting him. It was the re-emergence within him, after an unnaturally protracted dormancy, of sexual desire.

He rose to return to his bed but saw a light coming from Sofía's room and softly walked to it. He looked in. She had placed the candle beside her bed and gone to sleep. He walked in gently, trying not to make a sound, and standing before the candle, bent down in order to blow it out. Just as he formed his lips for that purpose, he heard her say, 'Oh, it's you.'

Still in the bent position, he turned his head to see her eyes looking at him. He stood up straight, and said, 'You left the candle burning.'

'I forgot. But it doesn't matter. The light doesn't bother me.'

He sat down on the edge of the bed and pulling up her blanket, patted it around her shoulders, saying, 'You will be better without it.' He leaned over and kissed her on her cheek and then, rising, blew the candle out, and found his way to his room. He went to bed but was unable to sleep.

It took Simón three days to accomplish the task for which he had been sent to San Clemente de los Andes, and as he did so, his thoughts were on his recent happy life in Rio de Janeiro, his woman, who was a source of wonder to him, and his imminent fatherhood.

But he lingered on, discovering new delights in the place each day, excusing his postponement in his own mind by saying that he needed to double-check the plan he had formulated to blow up the hotel. His life in Rio, during the previous eight months, had been perfectly idyllic, and he expected to be able to continue to live in the same circumstances when he returned. But he was enjoying his present break and thought that his pleasure on returning would be all the greater the longer he was away. He took long walks in the region of the waterfall, or hired a horse and rode into the forest. There was amusing company in the hotel bar. Friendships among sportsmen were easily struck. There were several attractive women among the tourists and while he had no intention of taking advantage of his single position, especially when it was quite apparent from the glances of some of the women, and in the warmth of their voices, that his youthful and melancholy aspect aroused their interest, he was nevertheless flattered by the admiration he could sense. He told himself that Mercedes was everything that he desired in a woman.

He was curious to see the native inhabitants of the hamlet and walked there one day, looking about him with great curiosity. There were children swimming in a bend of the river. An old woman washing clothes, beating them against a rock. The charming little park. He loved the cottages, each a simple structure but possessing some touch that made it individual. Flowering bushes and tall trees surrounded them. One cottage particularly struck him as made for a perfect life and he imagined living there with Mercedes and their child. He hoped they would have a chance to come here together, so that she could see for herself the places that were giving him so much pleasure and which, he felt certain, were bound to delight her, too. He found the bar some tourists had told him about and stopped to drink a glass of its famous beer. He enjoyed it so much he stayed to drink two more. It was early in the evening. There were only three of the locals in the bar; a couple of others he recognized as tourists from the hotel, but he did not feel inclined to join them since he was enjoying making a succession of plans for his life with Mercedes, pleasant little reveries all, and so remained at his table near the entrance.

When he was having his third beer, two men walked in, and the taller of the two, a grey-haired man in late middle age, was heard to say, 'This time I'm not going to drink rum. Just a couple of beers.'

The other one made some joke about some recent occasion when presumably the two had got drunk together. They walked up to the counter for their drinks, and Simón, staring out of the door at the mountains, saw himself and Mercedes walking up a trail and pausing from time to time to look down at the beautiful view.

The two men sat at a table near him. Simón glanced at them when they were taking their seats but continued to look out, finding his daydream more appealing than the locals. A few minutes later, he heard the two men laugh loudly and he looked at them. The grey-haired one appeared different to him from the other natives he had observed; somehow, he seemed out of place, for he did not have the appearance of a working man. Simón's glance remained fixed on him for some time as he tried to think what role such a person could perform in that society.

Suddenly, the man stopped laughing and his eyes, catching Simón's curious glance, glared back at him. Simón felt uncomfortable and was about to look away when the man shouted, 'What are you staring at? Where do you think you are, at the circus?'

Simón quickly shook his head, saying, 'No, no, I'm sorry, I didn't mean to, no offence, no, no.' And even as he was speaking, he stood up and hastily walked out.

As he proceeded along the road back to the hotel, he thought that perhaps he ought not to have rushed out of the bar like that. He should have apologized more properly. He was a visitor, after all. It was vulgar to intrude into other people's lives. It was their world. He should have been more polite. Offered to shake hands. Stood a round of beer. It had been foolish to run away. But it was too late now. Perhaps he would go there the next evening. Offer his regrets. A round of beer. Get to know the real people.

The next afternoon he went riding up a trail on a mountain that took him as high as the snow line. The dry, cold air was exhilarating. How Mercedes would love coming here! And thinking of future pleasures, he let the mare follow its nose down the trail. He came out of his daydream when he heard voices. Four girls sat by a stream, having a picnic. Their laughter, their ringing voices filled the air, the enchanting sound of young females. The trail went within three metres of the stream. They heard the hooves pounding the ground and looked round. Passing them, he brought the mare nearly to a stop; he bowed his head, smiled at the girls and said, 'Please excuse my disturbing you. If I had known my way fell across other people's enjoyment, I would have chosen another.' He prodded the mare to move on. All the girls smiled, two of them laughed, one holding a hand in front of her mouth as she did so, and then, seeing him begin to trot, all of them waved at him when he looked back. One of the girls with blonde hair and blue eyes struck him as exceptionally beautiful and was so unlikely to have been a child of the darker natives that he wondered at the extraordinary genetic chance of her breeding. And for a few minutes, before his thoughts returned to Mercedes, his mind played with the idea of an altogether different life, one in which he lived here with the blue-eyed girl.

When he had gone, the girls rapidly exchanged remarks about him. Pilar immediately pronounced him handsome. Teresa went further and declared that she would abandon her wedding plans for such a prince – whereupon the girls teasingly chided her, for she was pregnant by the young man she was going to marry, a fact she had herself proudly revealed to her three friends.

'And you, what do you think of him?' Pilar asked Sofía.

'I don't know,' Sofía said, pouting her lower lip. 'I guess he's *nice*.'

'*Nice!*' the other three cried.

'Well, nice-looking.'

'But would you let him *have* you?' Pilar persisted – and this for her was the crucial criterion.

The following day, Simón packed his bag with the intention of catching that morning's helicopter service – one of the two weekly flights – to Valparaíso and, having done so, went and stood for a few minutes on the balcony. It was a wonderful day, the snow on the mountain peaks brilliantly white against the sharp clear blue of the sky. The waterfall roared down some distance to his right, a large cloud of mist swirling around the wide area where it fell. The natural pool of blue water sparkled, and the meadow beside it was lush with green grass and spotted with yellow flowers. From his tenth-floor hotel room, he could see where, beyond the pool, the water from the fall bounced and jostled among the rocks and burst out in three separate streams that then became one and flowed swiftly to join the river that wound its way down from the hamlet. He could see that one, too, and followed its meandering line toward the settlement of huts, observing the pastures where cattle and sheep grazed and the patches of cultivated land.

Returning to his room, he picked up the phone and called the reception desk in the lobby. He cancelled his reservation on that morning's flight, deferring his departure by three days.

Going back to the balcony, he stood taking deep breaths, filling his lungs with the exhilarating air that seemed to possess the very essence of freedom. And, indeed, he had never felt so free before; perhaps it came from a sense of attachment which no society or landscape had given him before until he came to San Clemente de los Andes. Of course, it could be only a sentimental indulgence, a passing intoxication with novelty; and he was aware, too, that he was enjoying being by himself although the pleasure of being again with Mercedes remained a keen anticipation in his mind. But the feeling that he could belong here was strong, and several fantasies simultaneously filled his imagination – a simple lumberman's

235

life, days spent fishing, an earthy existence, children, a woman who was a loving mother. He sighed, knowing that he could not prescribe the terms of his existence but must follow what was destined for him by his invisible masters with their grand scheme for ruling the world.

Late that morning, his walk took him to the park in the hamlet, near the bend of the river where children swam. There was a swarm of them in the water about two hundred metres from where he sat on a park bench, their screaming reaching him as a confusion of cries. Some older children were also in the river and his attention was caught by a blonde head, a girl. A moment later, he saw her come out of the water and recognized her as the blue-eyed girl he had encountered on the previous day. She wrapped a white towel around her, tucking it under her armpits so that it fell from her chest to the top of her thighs. A crowd of children scampered up the bank and jumped and screamed in a circle around her, apparently wanting her to return to direct their games in the water. She raised a hand and spoke to them. One or two still yelled. She shook her head vigorously and spoke some more. She seemed to control them like a stern schoolteacher, for the children soon dispersed, many of them back to the river. She walked away from them, and Simón saw that the path she took came in the direction of the park; it forked some distance from him, one branch following the bank of the river, the other coming in a straighter line to go past right in front of where he sat.

When she came to the fork, she hesitated for a moment, glanced down toward the river, and then took the straighter path. She saw him vaguely as she walked but his identity did not register on her mind until she was close to him and saw him rise and say, 'I hope you've forgiven me for yesterday's intrusion.'

She put a hand to the top of the towel under the left armpit to secure it there and saw him smile when he had spoken. Watching him, Pilar's question had come to her mind, making her stare become conditioned by a search for an answer to it, and she found herself blushing when

236

she replied, 'You didn't spoil anything, there's nothing to be sorry for.'

He noticed the colour come to her cheeks and felt an excited surge of blood within himself. 'You're lucky to live here,' he said, 'it's such a wonderful place.'

'Where do you come from?' she asked.

'Oh, from just about everywhere! But most recently from Brazil.'

'I don't know any other place but this, but sometimes I dream of the sea.'

She was about to walk on but she liked his voice and lingered a moment to see if he had anything else to say. He talked of the ocean near which he lived in Brazil, and after a few minutes it seemed natural that they should be sitting together, talking about trivial things or just looking across the park at the river during the pauses. Once, she looked back from the river and found that he had been gazing at her with a curious intensity, and she lowered her head. A little later, it was he who hung his head and she stared at him without knowing why she did and when their eyes met on his suddenly raising his face, they laughed, their heads falling forward toward each other's shoulder. His forehead briefly touched her bare shoulder. He asked her about her friends. She gave him simple answers. She found an inexplicable satisfaction in his company. He wondered at the twists of destiny that bound one to an attachment and then made one meet a person whose attractions measured perfectly to all the ideals one held.

He would come here again tomorrow, he said, when after an hour she rose to leave. She promised she would be there. Would she show him that walk she had just been talking about? Yes. He could bring a picnic from the hotel, what did she think? A good idea. Should he come earlier, say at noon? Yes.

Her assenting voice stayed with him after she had disappeared and he had begun to walk back to the hotel. He was in a daze of expectations. The figure of Mercedes came to his mind and appeared there in a grotesque, gross form, and was expelled by Sofía whose name he pronounced again and again. Why should he feel any guilt, he wondered, he had not done anything wrong. Not as yet. But the desire that possessed him entailed treachery to Mercedes. His eyes had sinned a thousand times already. If Mercedes thought it was all right for him to plan cold-bloodedly for the simultaneous assassination of several heads of state, then who was she to demand he observe a moral scruple toward herself? He was cheered by the thought, and was enormously pleased with himself for having decided to cancel his flight.

Calderón was happy that he had not had to wait unusually long for Sofía to come home for lunch. She had changed into a simple white frock and had combed her long hair. Calderón served her the lamb stew from which a steam rose, filling the air with an aroma of herbs. She ate slowly and had a dreamy expression on her face, as if her mind was elsewhere. He waited to see the look of pleasure in her eyes when she tasted the food, but it never appeared. Finally, he made a critical statement to see if it would not elicit praise from her: 'The lamb could have been a little more tender. I'm sorry about that.'

'It's fine,' she said with an absent air, as though it were entirely insignificant that he had prepared the dish to perfection. Perhaps it was no longer her favourite dish, he thought, and chided himself for believing that the preference of her childhood would last for ever. But it gave him some satisfaction that she ate with a good appetite even though her answers to his questions were only monosyllabic responses.

He was also pleased that after lunch she did not have any plans to go and be with her friends, but noticed that she preferred to be alone. He did not mind that, and was content to see, when he looked into her room in the early evening, that she was embroidering something on the hemline of a dress. He went to the kitchen, deciding to make a cake for her.

Since the night that he had been sick, he had been content to watch her come and go and had tried hard not to be over-curious about where she went. She invariably said she was going to see Pilar or Teresa. For much of the time, he believed her. Her tone and manner were the picture of honesty. But when the hours passed and she did not return, he went over her words and gestures again, repeatedly, to see if she had not been dissembling. He could have no proof unless he followed her one day – and that course he considered to be too despicably treacherous. She appeared so innocent whenever she returned that he inwardly scolded himself for having had thoughts that doubted her virtue.

The evening light fell through the sycamores in diagonal beams and made brilliant the red and magenta flowers of the bushes. The outer branches of the willows seemed illuminated from within and were a pale green, almost yellow. A flock of birds flew out of the trees, swooped low across the distant meadow, and ascended as a trailing arc, a thin black line that was suddenly pulled into the dazzle of the western light.

She sat on the rock between the willows where the light fell across her, making translucent her white frock and marking the lines where the shadow of her body ended. Her hair shone, falling loosely behind her. Her white skin glowed with a warm golden hue.

He saw her from the verandah, and stood there a moment gazing at the shadowy substance of her flesh. The heaped-up and folded material of her frock curved out confusedly below her waist, but above it, where the cloth was stretched by her posture of leaning forward, her back appeared in outline, creating in him a sense of her body almost as though it emanated a distinct odour. There was no Sofía there, but a female. His eyes shone as he walked toward her. There was a soft throbbing within his skull. A wild rush of messages seemed to be coursing between his heart and his brain. He had lived for so long now in extremes of happiness and despair. The pain surged within him and then went dormant and then, having gathered more force during its sleep, tore at him again, day after day, and he sensed its latest attack. But how soothing it was to see her sitting alone, so still, so tranquil! Light shivered down the willow branches as they swung in the breeze, and in the shifting of his perspective, a golden beam bounced off her head and then burst into white dots, giving her the appearance of emerging out of foam. He felt as if he were bathed in radiance though the throbbing within his skull persisted, the intense pain there no longer distinguishable from a manic anticipation of pleasure. A smile formed on his face and the thought passed his mind that his long suffering was almost at an end.

He came to her and held her shoulders. She looked up at him. Her eyes blazed. She seemed to slip into a trance and remained passive. He could not imagine what thoughts pre-occupied her and did not observe the sadness on her face, having himself become possessed by a blind desire and feeling only an elation that he had emerged as from a long sleep, released from the horror of desire and infused now with a lust for possession as if all the errors of his life and the inexplicable rejections of relationships and obligations of his past, driving him to venture into the dead ends of the self with its mysterious bifurcations, had led to this moment when he must deliver his body to the overwhelming release it sought.

She was in a confusion of longings, beginning to feel impulses in her blood, and wondered how fateful had been the meeting with the young man and what must happen tomorrow. The large mystery of the future made her melancholy; her sadness was an anxiety with time, for the morrow appeared to her to be desperately far away. What importunity must she submit to? she wondered, and was too much in a turmoil of expectations than to do anything but stare when his hands touched her shoulders. But suddenly her voice uttered, 'Oh, Don Bueno!' As if he could instruct her in the disguises that human passion took and show her how the dead eyes of a mask were really animated by an overflow of emotion, he whose own eyes looked now at her with solicitous concern and concealed from her the ferocious beam of lust.

So that when he took her hand and said, 'Come,' she

heard the voice of a concerned counselor, and rose and walked with him to the cottage, vaguely believing that he had an instinctive sense of her anxiety and was about to initiate her into adult knowledge. He held her gently by the shoulder and did not say anything and, remembering that he had earlier spent a long time in the kitchen, she wondered if he was going to do nothing more than offer her a new delicacy, but, sensing in him a different sort of concern and wanting to give him confidence, she flung her hand out to hold his waist and leaned her head against his shoulder. She was not surprised when he led her to her own room, and resolved, as he opened the door, not to let him feel embarrassed by what he needed to tell a young girl about what awaited her in the adult world.

The door closed and a beam of light hit it just above its centre, forming a bright circle there. The sycamore leaves made a sudden, distant commotion as a breeze shook them. There was no sound from the room. The breeze fell and not a leaf stirred. Far from across the river, a cow moaned. The light, low and falling horizontally across the valley, was brighter than at noon.

Suddenly, cries and screams came from the room. A shriek of horror tore from its wooden walls. Now the tall sycamores gathered the light of the setting sun and cast it in a greenish diffusion to the ground. Here and there, slanting beams still delayed the advancing darkness. There were the muffled sounds of some desperate struggle. Another shriek. And then a piercing scream. A silence then, broken by a low panting. High on the sycamores, a flock of birds descended with a flutter of wings.

The door opened and he came out and walked away to his own room, leaving the door open. A beam of light entered through it and fell on the lower corner of the bed that could be partly seen from the entrance. A blanket lay fallen in a heap below the bed. The light touched a section of the white sheet, creating a bright area. She lay turned on her side.

Her frock was torn and lay loosely about her across her back. Her legs were drawn up so that her buttocks stuck out prominently. Her right arm was raised with the hand, clenched in a fist, pressed against the ear. Her eyes were wide open and were fixed in the expression of not being able to turn away from the horror they witnessed. Her mouth was open. The very low moaning sound that passed through them was scarcely audible.

Calderón fell into his own bed, conscious only of an enormous sense of being relieved from some inner pain that had tormented him for a long time. A contentment came over him, putting him into a sound sleep. His dreams were vivid but possessed no menace. There was a beach on a wide stretch of a river, a narrow strip of sandy loam on which he walked. It was a balmy night. The stars were bright and he had the sensation of being among them, floating weightlessly and gradually becoming transparent as the light from the stars transformed itself to a universal dazzle. In another dream, he saw a white launch slowly swinging round to be docked; he saw himself looking at the name painted across it but in his dream he could not make out the name, seeing only the blur of black letters. He turned in bed, woke up during that brief moment, said to himself, 'What was the name of that launch?' and fell asleep again.

When he awoke again, the window was brightly lit. It was broad daylight outside. He had the sense of having slept for a very long time. His eyes caught the glint of a spider's web in the corner of the window. He sat up.

'Oh, my God, Don Bueno, what have you done!' he suddenly said aloud, the memory of the previous evening coming back to him with a terrifying force.

'Oh monster! What came over you, oh, my God!'

A new turbulence began to pound within him. He rushed to Sofía's room. The door was open. She was not there. Seized by a terror, he ran to the kitchen and then to the bathroom. She was not there and he cried aloud, 'O monster, what have you done!'

He went outside the house, calling her name, softly at first, as if in supplication, and then he cried her name out aloud, demanding the woods and the sky to release her form.

The sun was already quite high. On any other day he would have concluded that she had gone to her friends. But now he sat on the steps at the front of the cottage, his face in his hands, thinking only of what he had done.

The thought came to him: '*Don Bueno, you do not deserve to live.*' The pain that now possessed his body was not severe enough, he deserved worse. Where was the pit of splintered glass into which he must hurl himself, where the river of acid into which he must plunge? This stabbing at the heart was nothing, nor this roar in the brain. He deserved worse. Where was the virus that could eat his body one cell at a time?

When he looked up, Lucila was standing in front of him, her head wrapped in a black shawl that fell over her shoulders.

'Don Bueno, what have you done?' she said, startling him with the question that echoed his own earlier cry. He stared wildly at her.

'She tore two branches from the weeping willow,' Lucial said. 'So she must have done, for the branches were wound tightly round her body, like a serpentine embroidery on the heavy cotton of her dress.'

'What are you saying, Lucila?' he cried at her. 'You never talk. Why are you uttering so many words?'

'She wound another branch around her head, a vine with tiny pink flowers.'

'Lucila!'

'She played with the rocks and pebbles, choosing the larger ones to put into her pockets, greedily overstuffing her pockets as though she had found a treasure. So she must have done, for her pockets were like anchors. She did not need a river, an ocean, the shallow brook was deep enough.'

'LUCILA!'

'Do not shout, Don Bueno. You cannot awaken the dead.'

She stared at him, her wrinkled face showing no feeling.

243

She took a step back and was about to turn away. He stood up and cried at her, 'Where is she?'

'Are your eyes not blind already? Do you want to gouge them out, too, Don Bueno? No, you will never see her again.'

She began to walk away. After a few steps, she heard his loud howl, and stopped. She turned round and said, 'There was a time, Don Bueno, when you would not remove your mask and you kept your pain a secret. Howl now. Let the world hear you and let everyone see your eyes that can no longer give you the comfort of tears.'

She went away, her body soon vanishing behind the trees.

O the most wretched, wretched of men! Now he cried for the man he had been, a body that had hunted the self out of itself; but the self had never left the body, only taken on a new disguise, that of relinquishing desire, and stayed on as a worm in the flesh, a tiny pus of vanity, until it grew into a monster.

The trees echoed back his cries. The crime, the evil!

Don Bueno, Don Bueno, what, what have you done! If all the tortured prisoners of the world could transmit their combined pain, the sum of it would be as a pinprick on this vile flesh. Where is that place in the world where the rain that falls is vomit? Where is that landscape where the blades of grass are the tongues of vipers whose poison burns the flesh without ever consuming it? The desert under the noonday sun was too comfortable a habitation, Antarctica in its midwinter night was too kind to the body.

What have you done, what have you done, Don Bueno! Was there no corner of the earth where only vermin bred?

But there was no one to hear his lamentation.


Simón arrived in the park at noon. Since seeing Sofía there on the previous day, his mind had remained in a state of heightened excitement, filled with joyous expectancy. He had slept fitfully, awakening frequently to see again the lovely Sofía in his mind. Another wonderful day had dawned. How could he ever leave this beautiful valley?

244

Thoughts of Mercedes came to his mind with decreasing frequency. Now, as he strolled about the park, or sat on the spot where Sofía had the day before, only a succession of fascinating images entered his mind. Time passed, and she did not come. Perhaps people had a different sense of time in this valley, he thought, and waited. If he knew where she lived, he would go there. But he did not want to leave in case she happened to come from a direction that he had not taken. He continued to wait. Then he began to wonder whether he had really seen her the day before. What a silly idea, he thought, he was not that kind of a dreamer. It was nearly two o'clock, and still she did not come. He saw that the local bar was across from the park. He could go and sit there with a beer and keep an eye open for her.

There was a crowd of people in the bar, but he found a stool near a window and sat there with his beer, glancing out. Two of the locals sat at a table near him, and a third joined them. The newcomer looked very pleased with himself.

'I was out with a hunter early this morning,' he said to his friends. 'Guess what he gave me?'

He brought out a small knife from his pocket and placed it on the table. It had an ivory handle with silver trim on it, and a short, pointed blade. Each of the men took it up and examined it. One praised its weight and balance, the other the silverwork. Its new owner, who could not look at it frequently enough, placed it in front of him on the table.

Simón could see no one enter the park. More people came into the bar. Some stood by the counter, others took the remaining stools. Simón wondered whether he should not leave. He was beginning to be depressed by the frustration of his expectations. Just then he saw the grey-haired man enter whom he had seen in the bar a few days ago. The thought suddenly came to him that the man looked as different from the locals as Sofía did from her companions, and yet both were native inhabitants, and that perhaps the two were related. He thought he should ask the man if he knew her and could tell him where to find her.

'Hello, Don Bueno,' Jácome said to him from behind the counter. 'Just give me a moment, and I'll serve you,' he added, pouring beer into a glass for the customer he was already serving.

'Give me a double rum,' Calderón said to him a moment later.

'Take it easy now, Don Bueno,' Jácome said jokingly, measuring out the rum. 'You know how rum goes to your head.' He laughed, but stopped abruptly when he saw that not even a smile came to Calderón's lips at the reference to his recent overindulgence.

Calderón poured the rum down his throat, put the glass down on the counter with a thump, and said, 'Another double.'

Jácome's gaze expressed a mild amazement but he essayed another joke as he refilled the glass. 'Who's going to carry you out?'

Calderón picked up the glass, swallowed a good half of its contents, and turned round. He walked among the tables, but saw that there was not a seat to be had. He was standing near where the three men sat with the knife on the table, and he saw the young tourist staring at him, the same one whom he remembered scolding two or three days ago. His presence irritated him and he was about to turn away when the young man said, 'Excuse me, sir, but would you know of a young girl who lives in this village and who . . .'

Before he could begin to describe Sofía, Calderón roared at him with, 'What right do you have to talk to me of young girls?'

Simón stared at him incomprehensibly.

'Who knows this man?' Calderón shouted, looking wildly about him. A hush had fallen. 'Who is he to come and talk to an old man of young girls?'

'I'm sorry,' Simón said, shaken by the man's violent tone, but eager, after his previous experience, to remain polite. 'I only thought you might know a young girl. Blonde. Blue eyes.'

Calderón had drained his glass and put it down at a

nearby table. Incensed by the descriptive words, he shouted, 'Who are you to guess whom I might or might not know? Do I keep young girls in cages with labels on them? Does anyone know this miserable motherfucker?' He swung his head around as he shouted the question. The knife on the table glinted in his eyes. He stared at it for a moment, the silverwork gleaming from its handle.

Simón could not understand the source of the man's anger, and made another attempt to remain polite. 'I'm sorry,' he said, 'I did not mean to trouble you. There was a girl I met – it's nothing. I just thought she might be your daughter.'

A terrible howl from Calderón filled the room. Jácome stared from behind the counter, wondering what had come over Don Bueno – first he drank like a madman and now yelled like one. Some others in the bar took quick swallows from their drinks but stared silently at the raging man. Only the new owner of the hunter's knife looked away to trace his finger over the silverwork.

'Who knows this motherfucker's name?' Calderón shouted. 'We have them here from time to time. They come prowling to steal our daughters, the sons of pimps and whores. A rat is a happier sight than they, a snake is more beautiful.'

Simón did not know why he was being abused and his resolve to remain polite gave way to anger. His body became tense, blood rushed to his brain. The man was continuing to shout: 'I'll tell you what they came into this world for, these vermin in the shape of men! To nibble at the flesh of our daughters until they are driven senseless and cannot see the fat rat thrust itself into their wombs and fill them with a new generation of vermin!'

Simón decided that he should either step forward and fight the man or leave. The situation had become intolerably ugly. He did not know what he had done to deserve such terrible abuse. In spite of the anger that welled to his brain, he had a sufficient control over himself to do the more prudent thing, and he quickly made for the door.

'Ha, look at the rat run! Look at the coward scamper

toward its hole!' Calderón rushed at him with these words and reaching him by the door, flung himself at him. Simón fell across the threshold. Calderón stood just inside, his body positioned to spring at the young man again. Simón stood up. He had only to turn round and run, but the taunt of cowardice had stung him, and he found himself shouting, 'You take all that back! I've never done a thing to you, I've never known you!'

There were several murmurs behind Calderón, and someone said, 'Has Don Bueno gone crazy, or what?'

Calderón swung around. A lumberman sat near him, at a table next to the door, and Calderón noticed that he had placed his machete on the ground beside him. He pounced upon it and brandishing it in the air, shouted, 'Who is crazy? Did someone lose his daughter? Did someone spend the night in fornication? Breed more vermin?'

He turned to face Simón again and noticed that he stood tensed, in a crouching position. A hush again fell in the room as Calderón stood confronting the young man, the machete raised in his hand.

'What should I take back?' he shouted at him. 'That a monster bred you? That toads spat at the cunt through which your rat-body fell on this earth?'

'God damn it, you take all that back!' Simón cried aloud, his body trembling, his fists shaking.

Calderón took a short, sudden step forward. Simón instinctively shifted sideways, his eyes on the hand that held the machete. Calderón threw the machete down and sprang at Simón. The latter tried to disengage himself, but Calderón, possessed by a terrible power, held him by the neck and pushed him to the ground where the machete lay. 'Pick it up, coward!' he yelled at him.

Simón stood up, holding the machete near his waist, its curving blade pointing up. Calderón stared at him with wide open blood-shot eyes. 'Come on, then, what should I take back?' he said, stepping to his rear and watching the effect his words had on the young man – making him come in from the doorway, his fist tight on the machete but uncontrollable tremors shaking his body. 'What, what?'

Calderón cried at him. 'That rattlesnakes donated their venom to fill your father's balls? Come on now, what should I take back? That your embryo grew in a pool of vomit? Ha! Come on, what else? That the rat who fucked your mother had pus for blood?'

With each phrase, Calderón took a step back; and each insult drew Simón to him. The two now stood in the middle of the bar in a narrow passage between tables.

'You take all that back!' Simón shouted at him again.

Jácome had come out from behind the counter and walking toward Calderón, was saying, 'Come on, put an end to this stupidity. A joke's a joke, but this is getting insane, Don Bueno.'

At that moment, Calderón's eyes caught the glittering hunter's knife on a nearby table. With a loud cry, he snatched up the knife and swung round in a circle, and once again facing the young man, said, 'They should invent a new circumcision, chop off the whole fucking thing then let it lie there bloated with poison!'

'You've gone mad, Don Bueno,' Jácome cried at him, 'What nonsense are you talking?'

Simón, on seeing the man now armed, holding the knife up in the air, found his own body stiffen, his hand holding the machete seemed to be stuck to his waist, the blade with its upward curve sticking out. He could not move, could not utter a word.

Jácome moved behind Calderón, gesturing to the men near him to rise and overpower the crazed Don Bueno. But before he could effect his purpose, a louder howl than before filled the room and Calderón flung himself with a leap at the young man.

For a moment, it appeared as though he had embraced him, clutching him tightly to his bosom. During his leap, he dropped the knife from his hand, and when his body hit the young man's, his arms seemed to fling themselves over his shoulders and his hands to grasp his neck as if his only wish was to be pressed close to him. Then he fell back and dropped to the ground, the blood pouring from him where, just under the ribs, the wide blade of the machete had entered his body.

Simón leaned down near him, held his shoulders and, looking desperately at his face, said, 'Why . . . why? I never did a thing to you, I never knew you. Why . . . why?'

A fierce look, or one that witnessed horror, was fixed on Calderón's eyes. His lips moved. Chairs were being shuffled back, the men in the bar were shouting, 'What a crazy thing to have happened . . . had he gone mad or what? . . . The poor boy had done nothing.' Simón put his ear close to the man's lips to hear what he had to say.

In this dying moment, Calderón had two unconnected thoughts. The pain he felt was not severe enough to punish him for his crime. And the dream he had had last night in which he saw the white launch and the name of it that had remained indistinguishable – he remembered the name now and found himself saying it aloud in a whisper: 'Simón Bolívar.'

Some weeks later, Mercedes gave birth to a male child in a hospital in Rio de Janeiro. Simón had not returned, and she gave the child the name he had wished to call it if it were a boy.

THE END

# A New History of Torments
## Zulfikar Ghose

'A splendid tale of the South American unknown, with
haunting and compulsive narrative drive'
JOHN FOWLES

Erotic, fantastic, sardonic, *A New History of Torments* is a
work of extraordinary imaginative scope by a writer at the
height of his powers – a novel which blends allegory and
thrilling action, illusion and disillusion, passion and suspense
into a rich adventure set in the South American jungle.

'Tremendous power and pace'
THE SUNDAY TIMES

'Constantly surprising . . . A charming, sustained performance
with a shocking but dramatically satisfying ending'
PUBLISHERS WEEKLY

'An exceptional novel'
TIMES LITERARY SUPPLEMENT

'An uncanny mixture of poetry and suspense. A fine novel'
EDNA O'BRIEN

'Marvellously exotic, wonderful adventures – a rare piece of
fiction indeed'
MICHAEL MOORCOCK

0 552 99046 9                                              £2.50

BLACK SWAN

# A Canticle for Leibowitz
## Walter M. Miller Jr.

'An extraordinary novel, terrifyingly grim, prodigiously
imaginative, richly comic'
CHICAGO TRIBUNE

First there was the Fallout, the plagues and the madness. Then
began the bloodletting of the Simplification, when the people –
those who were left – turned against the rulers, the teachers
and the scientists who had turned the world into a barren
desert where great clouds of wrath had destroyed the forests
and the fields. All knowledge was destroyed, all the learned
killed – only Leibowitz managed to save some of his books.

And the monks of the Order of Leibowitz inherited the sacred
relics. They spent their lives copying, illuminating and
interpreting the holy fragments, slowly fashioning a new
Renaissance in a barbarous and fallen world.

*A Canticle for Leibowitz* is the brilliant and provocative classic
of the post-nuclear age, ranking with *1984* and *Brave New
World* in its visionary power.

'Angry, eloquent . . . a terrific story'
THE NEW YORK TIMES

0 552 99107 4                                        £2.95

**BLACK SWAN**

# The Complete Knowledge of Sally Fry
## Sylvia Murphy

'You should have absolutely no difficulty in laughing aloud
. . . a new, original comic writer . . . tremendous fun'
SUSAN HILL

Sally Fry has gone to Cornwall on holiday with her mother for
some good home cooking and enough peace to write her thesis.
Not only is her thesis not progressing, however, her life is also
falling apart at the seams. Her teenage son Sebastian –
accident-prone since conception – has disappeared; her sister
Kate has been rushed into hospital, leaving Sally and her
mother to look after the children; and soon Julia, her other
sister, arrives cold-hearted and Sven-less from Sweden.

Over the long, hot summer, chaos threatens to take over. Sally
Fry's solution is to impose order in an unproariously funny
world by writing it all down in her Complete Knowledge, where
family, friends and lovers all find their true place.

*The Complete Knowledge of Sally Fry* is a first novel of
genuine comic originality.

'The true A to Z of the matter is, of course, that it's the quality
of the narrative and the shape of the characters that count. A
coolly amusing book, promising well'
NORMAN SHRAPNELL, THE GUARDIAN

'Acidly observant and bitchy'
THE OBSERVER

'Fun to read . . . fresh and unpretentious, a clever and
immensely likeable first novel'
ALANNAH HOPKINS, THE STANDARD

'Most accomplished . . . very funny, very human'
HOMES & GARDENS

0 552 99094 9 £2.50

**BLACK SWAN**

# The Textures of Silence
## Gordon Vorster

'Strong, sensual and vivid, almost tactile . . . a rich and
readable novel'
RAND DAILY MAIL

*The Textures of Silence* is a remarkable literary achievement, a
powerful affirmation of the potential of life and of man.

At the age of three weeks, Daan Cilliers is critically injured in
an accident that leaves him blind, deaf, dumb and spastic.
Unthinking and unfeeling, he lives in his own world until the
age of fifty, when Maria van der Kolff enters his life. *The
Textures of Silence* is the story of Daan's miraculous rebirth to
awareness and life, but it is also the story of the people around
him and of the forces of love, guilt, passion, endurance, and
knowledge that bring this amazing novel to its triumphant close.

An artist whose paintings are internationally known, an actor
who appeared opposite Athol Fugard in *The Guest*, a producer
and director of both feature and documentary films, Gordon
Vorster is arguably the most versatile creative personality in
South Africa today. With *The Textures of Silence*, he emerges
as a major new novelist to rank alongside Nadine Gordimer,
J.M. Coetzee and Andre Brink.

*The Textures of Silence* won South Africa's Golden Cape
Award for Fiction.

0 552 99101 5                                       £3.50

**BLACK SWAN**

# A Coin in Nine Hands
## Marguerite Yourcenar

'Among her best work'
THE SPECTATOR

The main story of *A Coin in Nine Hands* is the half-realistic, half-symbolic account of an attempt to assassinate Mussolini in the eleventh year of the Fascist dictatorship in Italy. Around this core, Yourcenar groups a series of secondary stories – portraits of Roman life out of *commedia* or rather *tragedia* dell'arte. The coin of the title is a link between the characters as it passes from one to the other.

Yourcenar's Rome, brilliantly evoked, is both the Rome of Fascism and the great city of life and of the imagination. *A Coin in Nine Hands* was the first literary work from France and one of the first from anywhere to confront the reality of Fascism. Written originally in 1934 and revised completely in 1959, the book is one of Yourcenar's major works. It is a novel of heroism; it is, as always with Yourcenar, a meditation of love; it is a profound examination of political evil – a question perhaps even more relevant to our own time than to the period portrayed in *A Coin in Nine Hands*.

'Fifty years on, it is as psychologically profound, as contemporary, and as moving as any novel published in the last year'
PHILIP HOWARD, THE TIMES

'Delicate intricately structured yet powerful . . . A minor masterpiece'
ANDREW HISLOP, SUNDAY TIMES

0 552 99120 1 £2.50

**BLACK SWAN**

# Coup de Grâce
## Marguerite Yourcenar

'One of the most imaginatively challenging novelists of the century'
PAUL BINDING, THE LITERARY REVIEW

Set in the Baltic provinces in the aftermath of World War I, *Coup de Grace* tells the story of a strange and unhappy threesome: Erick, a young Prussian engaged with the White Russians in fighting the Bolsheviks; Conrad, the beloved friend of his youth; and Conrad's sister Sophie, whose unrequited love for Erick becomes an unbearable burden. An anguished intimacy grows up among the three young people, hemmed in by the civil war, fearful of the future and their own confused emotions.

'By grip and style and form, she is a major illuminator who is always a pleasure to read'
GEOFFREY GRIGSON, COUNTRY LIFE

'The book is one of those performances which, in its persistent artistry, its high concentration on sense impression and reflection, makes the strongest argument for the short novel form'
NEWSWEEK

'Told with great economy and restraint. It also has the sense of inevitability that so often marks works of exceptional quality'
MARTYN GOFF, DAILY TELEGRAPH

'Extraordinarily profound . . . The title is dreadfully precise'
GAY FIRTH, THE TIMES

0 552 99121 X                                    £2.50

## BLACK SWAN